Reflected

TOR BOOKS BY RHIANNON HELD

Silver
Tarnished
Reflected

Reflected

Rhiannon Held

TOR®

A TOM DOHERTY ASSOCIATES BOOK
NEW YORK

This is a work of fiction. All of the characters, organizations, and events portrayed in this novel are either products of the author's imagination or are used fictitiously.

REFLECTED

Copyright © 2014 by Rhiannon Held

A Tor Book
Published by Tom Doherty Associates, LLC
175 Fifth Avenue
New York, NY 10010

www.tor-forge.com

Tor® is a registered trademark of Tom Doherty Associates, LLC.

Library of Congress Cataloging-in-Publication Data

Held, Rhiannon.
    Reflected / Rhiannon Held.—1st. ed.
        p. cm.
    "A Tom Doherty Associates Book."
    ISBN 978-0-7653-3039-0 (trade paperback)
    ISBN 978-1-4299-9114-8 (e-book)
    1. Werewolves—Fiction. I. Title.
PS3608.E3853H45 2014
813'.6—dc23

                                        2013025946

Tor books may be purchased for educational, business, or promotional use. For information on bulk purchases, please contact Macmillan Corporate and Premium Sales Department at 1-800-221-7945, extension 5442, or write specialmarkets@macmillan.com.

First Edition: February 2014

Printed in the United States of America

0 9 8 7 6 5 4 3 2 1

To Rowena
The sister, brainstormer extraordinaire
Not least because she thinks her "the" is as funny as I do

ACKNOWLEDGMENTS

This book extended my research into new areas, so I have several new people to thank this round. Commander John Suessman and everyone at the Washington State Criminal Justice Training Commission Basic Law Enforcement Academy in Burien were friendly, welcoming, and very patient with all my hypothetical questions. You know you're doing your police research right when you have to use a multipoint turn to escape the one-way lane in the parking lot because there's a traffic stop exercise blocking the other end. Elizabeth Tereno (Esquire!) answered my legal questions, and Olwen Sanderson, my therapist ones. All mistakes are the fault of gremlins.

On the writing side, this book owes its quality to the usual, faithful suspects. Corry Lee, Kate Marshall, Mae Empson, Renee Stern, Harold Gross, Erin Tidwell, David Silas, and Kim Ritchie read early drafts, among others who I am sure I am forgetting. Rowena Held heroically helped me brainstorm, and it's for her that I made the sympathetic sister the younger one. Not that *either* of us is *ever* unsympathetic, annoying, or frustrating.

This book was shaped by my wonderful and patient editor,

Beth Meacham, and agent, Cameron McClure. I'd also like to thank Melissa Frain, Amy Saxon, Alexis Nixon, Aisha Cloud, and the whole team at Tor.

The director and members of the Market Street Singers community choir have kept me sane along the way, and this time they can look for a loved one of one of their own tuckerized within, in gratitude for their donation to the choir. My life is also enriched and bolstered by the archaeologists, gamers, writers, singers, and now fans who surround me. Thank you all!

Reflected

1

Felicia ran full tilt, tongue lolling out as she panted. She'd let Tom catch her soon, but not quite yet. She skidded in a U-turn, showering a bush with dirt and needles kicked up by her paws. Up ahead, near where they'd left their clothes, erosion had carved the descending path into a bare, hardened slide. Exposed roots provided improvised steps only here and there. It was much harder to navigate on four feet, without hands to grab at branches, but Felicia cleared most of it in one soaring jump and skidded down the rest.

At the bottom, she turned back in time to see the sandy-colored werewolf trip and slide down nose-first. Tom rolled into it, ending on his back with his legs in the air. He gave Felicia an upside-down canine grin. Felicia snorted. Dignity? What was that? His fur tended to stand up every which way anyway, so the additional disarranging hardly made a difference.

Even without dignity, he was good-looking as a man and had an intriguing scent in both forms. Felicia twitched her tail as he righted himself and crouched low over his fore-paws in an invitation to wrestle. Felicia waited to make sure he was watching her, then shifted back to human. No one cared about nudity, but watching the exact moment of shifting was very intimate. She knew he'd look away if he had warning. She wanted him to see her shift.

The Lady was near full, so the shift was as easy as diving into water from the bank above. When she finished and straightened, fully in human, his face showed he realized what she'd done. He turned his head belatedly.

Felicia crossed her arms under her breasts and waited. Even though it was June, it was late enough in the day that only slices of direct sunlight peeked through the trees, leaving much of her body in cool shadow. Seattle hadn't managed to muster much of a real summer the three years she'd lived here. She supposed at least they were better than the summers near Washington, D.C., where her father's home pack had been based before he'd expanded their territory to the rest of the country.

Tom shifted after an awkward moment. Felicia watched un-apologetically. The twist of muscles from wolf to human had a real grace this close to the full.

"Felicia . . ." Tom pushed himself to human feet, his cheeks flushed with embarrassment. He held his ground, but only barely, as she walked up to him, rolling her hips. "What are you doing? We were just playing."

Felicia placed her hand on his shoulder and went to her tiptoes to breathe his scent from the curve of his neck. His light hair was too shaggy in human to stick up, but it tried anyway, making him look perpetually rumpled. His attraction was clear to smell, and it fed Felicia's own. She was tired of all this waiting. "You don't smell like just playing." She nipped at his ear and he shivered.

"That's not fair." Tom pushed her to the length of his arm. "I can't help that. But your father would kill me—"

Felicia caressed his wrist until he had to release the pressure holding her back if he wanted to avoid the touch. "What, I have to be celibate forever because I'm the alpha's daughter? How is *that* fair?"

Tom huffed. "It's not just that—" This time, when Felicia touched him, palm against his chest, he didn't push her away. He was still lankier than she thought of as her type, but he'd definitely filled out some muscles since she'd first met him. She wanted to caress them, sternum to navel and lower, trace the delicious curve of his hip bone, but she stopped herself.

He didn't push her away, but he didn't pull her closer, either. Felicia's stomach wobbled. Was he making excuses because he wasn't actually interested? She'd smelled attraction, but every Were knew that was sometimes physically unavoidable. Just because you smelled it didn't mean the other person wanted to act on it.

Felicia shook out her hair, wishing the black waves would curve smoothly together rather than always curling against each in an unruly mass. She looked down at her side, checking the smooth curve to her hip. There were other young men she could invite to a game of chase—*had* played that game with. They thought she was pretty enough. But Tom had never thrown himself at her. If she was honest with herself, she'd have to admit she could never really tell what he was thinking under the silly exterior.

Well, fine. If she was going to get herself rejected, she might as well get herself rejected for really trying. "I'm eighteen. Even the humans think that's legal. I can make my own decisions." Felicia balanced against his chest to whisper in his ear. "But if you're so scared of my father you can't get it up, I'd totally understand—"

Tom jerked back, but only to give himself room to claim her lips in a fierce kiss. His hands came up to her back and ass, yanking her tight against him. Felicia arched her body within the hold and gripped those glorious hips. Thank the Lady. She hadn't misread him. He did want her.

When they came up for air, he glanced at the lowering sun. "You know this close to the full the rest of the pack will probably be coming out here to hunt once they get off work," he said, resigned laughter in his voice.

"We have plenty of time. That just makes it more exciting." Felicia braced herself for another round of objections—why did Tom care so much what other people thought?—but he just grinned mischievously. He freed one hand and ghosted fingertips down her spine. The sensation was surprising, not quite ticklish, but something that made her back muscles arch without thinking. She gasped and shivered all over.

Tom rocked back a step, grinned wider, then danced out of her reach. "Better capture me quick, then." He dropped to rest fingertips on the ground as he shifted back to wolf.

Felicia shifted as quickly as she could to follow. Wouldn't want to give him *too* much of a head start, though she didn't want to capture him immediately either. That was the best part of sex, catching someone who was delighted to be caught.

Tom raced off through the thickest part of the underbrush, and Felicia dashed after, jumping branches and crashing through ferns. Rather than going for distance and speed as they had in their earlier running, he captured the intensity of this chase by using the obstacles to keep them tangled close. When he darted one way, she darted the other, trying to cut him off, but he countered her every move until she panted with canine laughter.

Time for a new strategy, Felicia decided. She sprinted in a straight line away from him and hunkered down behind a downed tree's upturned roots. She pressed herself flat to the ground and watched between hanging clods of dirt as he followed her trail, slowly and suspiciously.

She surged out of her hiding place and bowled him over, both of them nipping at each other's fur as they rolled around in the dirt and pine needles. She knew perfectly well he'd been expecting that, but she didn't mind. She got on top of him and he surrendered with a flop of his head to lie stretched out flat on his side. She scrabbled back just enough to give herself room to shift to human to smirk at him. She'd captured him fair and square.

Tom shifted back and pushed to his feet, head bowed. Too late, Felicia caught the grin he was hiding. He lunged away, but she was fast enough to get a tight grip on his ankle. "Dirty cheat!" She was breathing almost too hard to get the laughing words out.

"You didn't think I'd make it easy on you—" Tom lost the rest of his words in the wheeze as she yanked his foot out from under him and he fell on his ass. She grabbed his calf and then the opposite thigh as she climbed up his body, knees on either side. No way was she taking her hands off him now.

"Gotcha." Teasingly, Felicia stopped short, straddling his

thighs rather than his hips, and slipped her fingers along his length. She began by mimicking the ghosting pressure he'd used on her, growing more and more insistent. He moaned, whatever smart answer he'd been planning lost for good. She used her free hand on herself, rocking her hips as she tapped into the familiar delicious rhythm.

Tom touched her upper arms and drew her up until she was leaning over him and he could draw her nipple into his mouth. Felicia was about to prompt him, but his own experimental graze of teeth against it made her gasp and he increased the pressure until she almost couldn't stand it.

When she moved down his body again, she stopped at his hips and guided him into her. His hands settled on her hips as she wriggled, finding the perfect angle. Then the rhythm, slowly increasing. Felicia abandoned herself to it.

Tom might have seemed silly, but he was really good with his hands. And tongue. Like any first time together, it took some experimenting to find just the right pressure, just the right rhythm, but when they collapsed to tuck against each other, Felicia had no complaints. That had been *nice*.

Languid contentment pooled in her limbs. Even when the sweat drying on her skin started to chill her, Felicia didn't want to move.

Tom slid his arm over her waist, probably feeling the same chill. "Wow," he commented, tone warm rather than teasing.

"What, you thought I was as innocent as Father wishes I was? My first was back in Madrid, before I even met Father properly." Felicia tried to burrow against him for more warmth, but it was a losing battle. She finally surrendered and sat up. Tom stood first to help her up and then draped his arm over her shoulders as they wandered back up to the trail in search of their clothes.

They'd stashed their bags with their clothes in a tree a couple yards off the trail. Even if Felicia hadn't remembered where, the werewolf scents layered on that of human-made fabric stood out sharply among the growing things. Tom knocked their packs down, and they both rummaged. Felicia wished she'd thought to bring a brush. Her hair was probably a sight.

Cars had been coming intermittently up the winding road that bordered the Roanoke pack's hunting land, heading for the houses buried in the trees farther up the hill. Now one engine rumble slowed, changed direction, and stopped. A slammed door from close by made it clear someone had turned in.

"Lady!" Tom hurriedly dumped all his clothes into a pile rather than pulling out each piece in order. "Roanoke Dare is going to kill me."

Rather than jump to conclusions, Felicia waited it out until a few moments later a breeze came at the right angle to bring the newcomers' scents. "Father's not with them. It's just Silver and the beta."

Tom frowned. "Roanoke Silver, you mean." He threw her an apologetic grimace. "Sorry, Felicia, but your stepmother's just as scary."

"She's not my stepmother." Felicia immediately regretted the snap to her tone, but it was true, wasn't it? Fine, her father could have anyone he wanted as a mate, but that didn't give her any connection to Felicia. "They're not married. She's not my anything."

"She's still one of your alphas." Tom froze, underwear in his hands, as voices reached them.

"Go ahead. I'll be up by the stream," Silver said, presumably to John, the beta. Her white hair showed in flashes here and there through the trees farther down the trail. Felicia suppressed an instinctive urge to look back over her shoulder. The stream beyond them wouldn't have moved in the last few minutes.

Sudden laughter bubbled up in her. What were they worrying so much for, anyway? She was an adult; she could make her own choices. What did it matter if Silver found out? She'd had enough rest to regather her energy since the last shift, so she shifted to wolf and snatched Tom's jeans out of his hands. She stopped a few yards away, her turn to bend over her forelegs, and growled an invitation for him to try to get them.

Tom frowned without the humor she'd hoped for and grabbed for one pant leg. She took off, as fast as she could go on four legs. A beat later she heard Tom's growl, from a wolf throat this time. No surprise. No way he could keep up with her on two legs.

Since she was trying to avoid the beta and Silver as well as evade Tom, Felicia headed off the trail quickly, straight to the edge of the property. She ducked under the pathetic barbed-wire fence that marked the property line but couldn't really keep anyone out. It snagged a fluff of fur in retaliation.

Across a shallow ditch, pavement sliced through the trees. She hadn't realized she'd been heading for the road, but it had probably been inevitable. The pack's hunting lands weren't that big. Tom crashed through the underbrush behind her, and she danced onto the road to keep out of his reach, grinning as she dragged his jeans along the ground. She backed onto the grassy rise on the other side until her tail brushed the fence, and she waggled the pants back and forth.

Tom tumbled under the fence and into the ditch, righted himself, and glared at her. After a moment and with a visible sigh, he bounded after her.

Then everything went wrong all at once.

Felicia registered the purr of a sports car barreling down the hill barely a heartbeat before the car itself flashed past. Tom gave a sickening canine shriek, the car thumped, skidded, swerved, and the engine growled away at even greater speed.

Felicia hurled herself back down onto the pavement. Tom. What had happened to Tom? Was he all right? Lady, please let him be all right.

Silver looked at Death when she heard Tom's scream, even as she pounded into as much of a run as she could get from her human legs. He seemed amused, no more, as he effortlessly matched his pace to hers, the advantage of four wolf legs. The low growl of some great beast, perhaps the cause of Tom's misfortune, disappeared down the mountain.

Something Silver couldn't see caught at her legs, tried to scratch and trip her. Thorns, her eyes told her, reaching malevolently for her skin, but she knew better than to trust her eyes. They suffered from the shadows that poisoning had brought to her mind. The deeper the shadows, the more unexpected the truth beneath. To help Tom, she needed to find that truth.

Two hands would have helped, but Silver did the best she could with one after tucking her scarred and useless arm more securely, hand in pocket. If the thorns caught that, she would bleed before she was done. She tore the plants up at the roots with her good hand and half slid down a hillside to reach Tom.

More shadows there—rushing water, tumbled to white over rocks, foaming up around the flat place where Tom lay. Water that Silver knew wasn't water. In her worry for Tom, the harder she tried to see something else, the more the rushing sound filled her ears. Felicia waded out into the current from the other side, red-tinted black fur remaining pristine and dry as she reached Tom and whined over him in shock.

"I'd hurry," Death said, using her brother's voice. Good advice, like her brother would have given, even though it wasn't him speaking.

Silver nodded and darted out to Tom. Water that violent meant danger. The sooner she dragged Tom out of it, the better. Felicia looked up from trying to nose Tom out of his protective curl around his injuries, so they could see the damage. Silver stroked his tame self's hair, sandy like the wild self's fur, and eased it to lie more comfortably, trapped beneath the wild self. Blood from both mixed on her hand and Felicia's ruff and in the water.

Felicia kept whining and Silver wished she could make the

sound properly with her human throat. Finally, Tom's wild self relaxed enough for her to roll him over to see the wounds. The torn and abraded skin wasn't knitting, which meant his healing had more important things to do, like repairing smashed organs. They needed to get him out of the river to help.

Not river. *Path.* Having a plan focused her, and Silver found that understanding with a bubble-pop of relief. They needed to get him off the path. Felicia must have been thinking along similar lines, because she crouched and began to switch her wild self for tame with hands useful for carrying.

"No," Death snapped.

"No!" Silver held out her hand to stop Felicia before she even quite understood what Death was reacting to. Another growl approached from up the mountain, more uneven in tone than the beast that had hurt Tom. Felicia, surprised by Silver's order, settled back onto four feet as a human arrived and stepped out of her vehicle. A vehicle, not a beast.

"Oh, my God! Your poor dog!" The human woman smelled of children, though she had none with her at the moment. She jogged up and leaned over Tom, slippery black hair fanning down to hang over her shoulders.

Silver smoothed Tom's ears, trying to imagine he was a pet, not a Were she was desperate to get away from human eyes so further healing at werewolf speed would not raise alarms. "If we can just move him out of the way, my friend's around, we'll—"

The woman gasped in objection. "That'll take too long. I'll give you a ride down the hill, the—" She said a word Silver didn't understand but could guess at. One who healed pets, not humans. The last thing Tom needed, though he could have used a Were doctor. "—we use, she's really great. I'm sure she can do something for him."

Silver looked again at Tom's wounds. Which was the greater risk? Going along to the pet doctor, hoping that Tom's healing, without additional sleep or food, would stop short of the torn skin, leaving something to at least explain the blood? Or would it be better to knock the woman down, run for it?

And how would they take Tom with them if they did run? Felicia couldn't help carry him as her wild self, couldn't switch to her tame in front of the human. Silver couldn't drag him one-armed without showing strength greater than a human woman should have. She seemed to have no choice but to pray to the Lady the doctor would see nothing more than a pet with wolf ancestry.

"Thank you," she told the woman, accepting. She helped the human lift Tom into her vehicle and glanced back to see Felicia standing in the path, stock-still and smelling of anger at Silver's choice. Silver squashed exasperation she had no time for. Even if Felicia had a better idea, circumstances didn't allow her to share it, so better she put her effort into making this one succeed.

"Run, girl," Death said in a woman's accented voice that belonged to Felicia's and her father's past, not Silver's. Silver saw what he meant immediately. If Felicia ran off, Silver could justify coming back to find her later, after treating Tom. Meanwhile, Felicia could warn John what was going on.

But of course Felicia couldn't see Death. She stayed where she was, and the human woman turned back to her. "C'mon, boy," she crooned in a voice for a pet or a baby. "There's room in the back for you too." She got a grip in Felicia's ruff.

Too late. Silver would have to bring her other "pet" too. She almost called Felicia by her real name, but of course that wasn't a pet name. Silver wanted to snarl a curse. Names were hard enough for her to remember as it was. Glaring at Felicia's wild self, she remembered a thought she'd had on first meeting the girl: so much of her childhood had been shaped by flames.

"Smoke," Silver snapped, using an alpha's command in her tone before Felicia could decide to fight free of the human. "Come." She took over the woman's grip on Felicia's ruff, pushed her into the vehicle, and climbed up after. She smoothed Tom's fur along his head, one of the few places free of blood, and wondered what in the Lady's name she was going to do once they reached their destination and the only one who could speak was the one whose sight was obscured by shadows.

The human woman chattered in a bright tone as they traveled down the hill, but Silver could smell the stink of her worry. She seemed to think Silver would fall apart if she wasn't distracted. Silver would have preferred silence, though if the woman could have gotten Felicia to stop staring at Silver with wide, frightened eyes, Silver would have hugged her. She needed to *think*.

"I'd do it now, if I were you," Death said. He used what Silver thought of as "his" voice, though of course he had none of his own since the Lady had taken his from him. This voice must have belonged to someone long dead.

Silver pressed the heel of her hand between her eyes. Even if she could have said "do what?" out loud to Death with the human listening, he would have just laughed. She knew what he meant. She could see past the shadows, but the pain that caused had been worth it only once before.

She checked Tom again first, to stall. He was still unconscious, and the tears across his side seeped slowly and did not heal. Silver had no food for him, to give him more energy to heal, so perhaps the doctor would find something to explain all the blood after all.

But there would still be questions. Her name, the location of her home, payment. Silver knew she couldn't give the kind of answers the humans would want without one of her pack members with her. Unless she did what Death had already decided she must do. Lady, wasn't there any other choice?

She supposed not.

2

When their path flattened at the bottom of the hill, Silver could put it off no longer. Lady help her. Or more rightly—Death help her. Silver tried to catch Death's eyes, though they were perfect darkness within the greater darkness of his fur, and were not for someone to ever meet straight on. She couldn't ask him, but he knew what she needed anyway.

A name.

"Selene," he said, in her brother's voice once more. That voice had a name too: Ares. Those names had childhood teasing: Why were they named after human gods? Why didn't they have normal names? That childhood had a home: Seattle, then Bellingham. And Bellingham had a massacre.

Selene doubled over, digging mental fingers into the name, to hold it to her even as the memories tried to hurt her so much she let it go. Yes, her brother, her niece and nephew, her whole pack was dead, bleeding out slowly from torture, but there was a young man here and now who was not yet dead. If she wanted "cell phone" and "credit card" and "veterinarian," she had to reach into the very heart of the fire of memories and pluck them out. Out from among the feeling of liquid silver injected into her arm, burning away parts of her mind; the bright joy of the one who had done it; the children's dying screams.

Things snapped into crystalline clarity, every surface ready to scrape her skin away until nothing was left, but Selene had what she needed. When the SUV stopped, she opened the back door before the human woman reached it, and jumped down. Tom sprawled, blood staining the carpeting on top of a row of folded-down seats, while Felicia had to crawl out from where she'd pressed herself under the next upright row.

"I bet Dr. Sarrento has a burly vet tech. Let me go get him," the human woman said after frowning at Tom. She probably remembered how heavy he had been when they loaded him.

Selene pressed a palm flat to a taillight and swallowed nausea along with the feeling of a phantom burning stealing up her arm. The silver nitrate was gone, leaving only scars and an arm she couldn't use. "I left my cell phone and wallet in my car," she told the tech when he arrived, more weedy college intern than burly anything. "Can I use your phone to get my boyfriend to come out here? It's not far, he should be back by the time you're done stitching him up." Belatedly, she remembered she was a worried pet owner, and she gave tech a wan smile, implying her hope stitches would be the only thing needed.

"Sure." The tech gestured inside without looking, too deep in calculating angles that would allow him to lift Tom without jarring the injuries.

A bell tinkled as the human woman pushed back out through

the glass-paneled front door and held it open for Selene. "Calling my boyfriend," Selene said and nodded inside. "Thank you so much for your help . . ."

The woman chattered more reassurances—Selene was very welcome, she was sure her dog would be fine—until Selene slipped past with a worried grimace. The woman seemed to read that Selene's attention was on her pet, not conversation, and left for her car with a final wave.

The vet's waiting area was shiny and clean, with a linoleum floor, plastic couches, and acrid odors of sickness and cleaners. The scent made Selene's eyes water and she wavered until Felicia arrived and pressed herself against her leg. It didn't give her quite the feeling of security Death's presence did, but Selene couldn't see Death—if he was even real. That question was far, far more than her mind had room for at the moment.

The counter had no entrance from the waiting room, only from a hallway that led somewhere back behind the exam rooms, but Selene could see the phone. She stood on tiptoe, snagged it, and set the whole thing where she could punch the buttons.

She smacked into a mental obstacle with a force that felt almost physical. She didn't know Andrew's cell phone number. Or the numbers of any of her pack, because she'd met many of them after her memory could no longer grasp such things. Selene stifled a sob at the promise of being able to speak to her mate coming so close and then being yanked away.

But she could do this. John. Her beta and her cousin. She'd known his number before, when she'd been Selene. She didn't think he would have changed it. He'd be closer than Andrew, even, because he was at the hunting grounds just up the hill rather than at the pack house a twenty-minute drive away.

John picked up on the second ring, voice flat and distracted. "Hello?" He didn't recognize the number, Selene realized.

"John." She was anxious to get her words out and hang up before he asked questions about her mental state, or other things she couldn't properly answer with humans around. But a name for Tom escaped her. What *did* humans name their dogs? She accepted the first name her memory threw at her, from television or something. "Lassie got hit by a car. Someone stopped, so we were able to get him to the vet right away, but I left my wallet in the car—can you drive down here and pick us up? We'll probably be done before Andrew—" Selene caught herself. As Silver, she always called her mate by his last name. "Dare could get here, so if you do call him, tell him to meet us at home, okay?"

John's silence was resounding for a breath, before he apparently set aside everything that was wrong with what she'd just said and ran with the part that did make sense. "Which vet?"

Selene's head swam for a moment. She hadn't looked at the name above the door. Fortunately the business cards in a holder next to her elbow had it in large font: Squak Mountain Animal Hospital. She read it out to him, then hung up and offered the whole phone back to the gray-haired, white-coated woman who had arrived from the back. The vet, she presumed.

"We let our dogs off-leash on our land, up—" Selene pointed in the vague direction of the hunting grounds. "There must have been a hole in the fence, he got out onto the road, and the car came out of nowhere . . ." She scrubbed at her face. "I'm sorry, I'm pretty shaken."

"We'll take good care of him," the vet assured her with a brisk smile.

"Thank you." Selene made it to one of the plastic couches before her legs collapsed. Felicia watched Tom being carried in and whined as the door to the back shut behind the staggering tech. It took her two trips from the door to Selene and back before Selene got it: the vet wouldn't let another dog in to watch her work, but she would allow the owner back.

Selene leaned over her knees and pressed her palm to her face to hold herself together. Her prayers to the Lady would be no more fervent for being made from Tom's side rather than in another room. The blood scent twisted into her nostrils even from here, though that might be the lingering scent of his passing through the entryway. Blood had been in every breath when her pack had been killed, blood and silver metal. Each breath now brought her one step closer to reliving those moments in full sight and smell.

"Hold down the den for me, would you, girl?" Selene buried her hand in Felicia's ruff and surfaced gasping from the bloody memories into Silver again.

Silver folded over, forehead to her knees, and held herself together. John would be here soon. Death said nothing, but his silence had an approving quality as he sat straight upright beside her.

Felicia tried going back to the door to the exam rooms one more time, even though she knew Silver had understood her. Apparently Silver preferred to go off into her own crazy land rather than check on Tom. Felicia paced back and forth from the counter to the couch on the opposite wall. Lady, how could she have been so stupid? It was her fault Tom was hurt, and now she couldn't even help because she was trapped as either a dog or an inexplicably naked woman in front of the humans.

Silver had handled everything better than Felicia had feared, she had to admit. She'd thought the woman couldn't use phones unless someone dialed for her. She smelled upset enough about it, though. Some of her pure white hair had slipped from the long braid she kept it in, hiding her face from Felicia's angle. She looked frail, sharp angles under pale skin, hard to match with the intensity of her normal body language as alpha.

Felicia's nails scritched on the polished floor. Wasn't this all sort of Silver's fault in the first place? If she hadn't showed up, they never would have run toward the road. The moment she thought it, Felicia knew that wasn't fair, but she indulged the tight satisfaction of imagining things that way for several paces anyway. In the end, it was Felicia's fault. Her fault for getting Tom hurt.

A vehicle turned into the clinic's parking lot, and Felicia pricked up her ears as she recognized the engine's sound. Tom's pickup. John must have found Tom's jeans and keys and brought down the vehicle that would be better for transporting Tom home.

Felicia darted to the front doors and accidentally forced John to shove her aside with the glass because she forgot they opened inward. He looked reassuring at least, the solid muscle of him in the doorway, brown hair disordered as usual. Felicia skidded on the way to the door to the exam rooms, but the infuriating man stopped at Silver first.

"Selene?" John set a hand on her back and she slowly sat up. The rank mixture of her fear and worry wafted to Felicia. "Are they working on him right now?"

"Silver," Silver said, almost too soft to hear. "He's—" She gestured vaguely in the direction of the back of clinic, then scrubbed at her temple and frowned at Felicia. "Take her in, would you?"

Felicia waited, ears pricked high for sounds of what was going on in the back of the clinic, but John opened the front door instead. He waited pointedly, smelling of exasperation.

Oh, of course. John meant to take her inside in human. Felicia sprinted for Tom's pickup and John followed to undo the canopy and tailgate. Felicia nosed around in Tom's detritus, including his toolbox and extra pair of hiking boots. No clothes unless you counted a raincoat. John returned from the cab and tossed her backpack onto the bed. The very blankness of his expression was a louder comment than a snicker would have been. How had he figured it out? As soon as Felicia got her nose close to the backpack, she realized. It reeked of sex, transferred from her hands where she'd touched the zipper and pulled it open.

No time to worry about that now. The moment the tinted canopy door closed, Felicia shifted back and started pulling on her jeans before the soreness in her muscles from all the back and forth faded. She was lucky it was near the full, not the new, or she'd have collapsed by now. She dispensed with underwear and knocked on the window for John to let her out so she could sit on the tailgate and jam on her shoes.

She jumped down and would have sprinted right back to the clinic, but John caught her shoulder in a tight grip. Not so tight she couldn't have escaped, but tight enough to remind her who outranked whom. "You look like you squeezed through the middle of a blackberry mound," he said, and smoothed down her hair with rough efficiency. "Now." He released her shoulder. "Go."

Felicia let herself into the exam room now that she had hands. The vet looked up suspiciously from where she was stripping off her gloves, apparently done with Tom. John entered a moment later with smooth explanations about how this was his friend's dog, and Felicia his friend's daughter. Felicia left him to it and hurried to the metal table that held Tom, still unconscious. His side looked strange, shaved in a wide patch, with lines of stitches here and there where the road rash had been especially bad.

She petted his ears. Intellectually, she knew that if werewolves didn't die of their injuries immediately, they wouldn't die at all, given food and rest. But that didn't convince her emotions as she stood here, smelling the blood and sheer wrongness hanging around him as a miasma.

John nodded as the vet told him how lucky they were that the internal damage had been so minimal, and he made the right noises of embarrassment as she chided him about the lack of collar and license. Then the vet disappeared back into the clinic and the tech took John up to the front counter to talk payment. Given the illusion of being alone with Tom, even though she knew the humans could hear from the other rooms, Felicia leaned in to rest her cheek against the soft fur on top of his head. "I'm sorry," she murmured. She hadn't meant any of this to happen.

John returned and tossed Felicia a brightly colored zippered foil bag. She barely caught it after hesitating too long figuring out what it could possibly be. She turned it over to stare at the foolishly grinning German shepherd puppy on the front. Dog treats? Was John trying to insult her, or Tom, or both? She sniffed and brought the bag closer to her nose. Well. It didn't smell bad. Smelled pretty good, actually.

"He should get his calories as soon as possible." John made a show of grunting and settling the weight carefully when he picked up Tom to hide how easy it was for him.

Felicia assumed John's emphasis meant *before he shifts back.* She nodded. He did have a point about that. She jogged a few steps ahead to open the doors for John, but when she started to follow him across the parking lot to the truck, he jerked his chin in a clear order. "Get Silver," he said.

Felicia turned back to eye the woman huddled on the couch. What if she didn't want to be the crazy-person guide? She went to grab Silver's wrist to pull her up, but Silver reversed the grip at the last minute, catching Felicia's wrist tightly instead.

"You were on the other side. He was chasing you," she said as they stepped outside, voice steady. Felicia avoided her eyes, not just to be polite and avoid the measuring of dominance but because that slightly scary intensity her father's mate usually displayed had returned.

"I know it was my fault," Felicia hissed under her breath. "I'm sorry." She'd make her apologies properly to Tom once he was awake, but beyond that, what else was she supposed to do? Promise not to do it again? Of course she wasn't going to run out on the road again. She hadn't even meant to do it then, she'd just got so caught up in the game of it all, running before Silver arrived and figured out what they'd been doing—

Felicia stuttered a step. She'd forgotten about that in her worry about Tom. Did Silver know? John knew, definitely. Would they tell her father? Surely he wouldn't come down on Tom, not injured as he was. As long as Tom didn't get in trouble, Felicia would be happy to take whatever consequences her father dished out.

Felicia tried to lead Silver around to the passenger side of the truck, but Silver dropped her wrist at the back and climbed up beside Tom. After a moment of hesitation, Felicia threw Silver the treats and closed the tailgate and canopy. She'd wanted to ride with Tom, but better the cab than awkward silence in the back.

The passenger side door never shut properly on Tom's truck unless you slammed it, which usually amused Felicia, because the driver's side was the junkyard replacement of the wrong color. Felicia had to open and slam it again before it caught, but John waited patiently, not starting the engine.

The silence was pretty damn awkward up here too, she realized. She turned and faced straight ahead out the windshield into an overenthusiastic bush at the edge of the parking lot, but John still didn't turn the key.

"Playing chasing games as well as literally chasing, were we?" he said. Felicia stayed stubbornly silent and stared at the bush.

He knew the answer already. Was she supposed to apologize for that too? That wasn't the part she'd done wrong.

He snorted. "And a bonus game of 'piss off your father.'" He turned the key and the truck cranked into reluctant life. "Tom doesn't deserve to be part of *that* game, especially now. I didn't smell anything—this time. You two start playing chase regularly, someone's going to tell Roanoke Dare."

"Someone like you?" Felicia muttered in Spanish. It was childish, but her father liked to nag her about the rudeness of speaking in a language others couldn't understand. Even though he wasn't here, flicking her tail at him that way still made her feel better.

John didn't seem terribly insulted by her Spanish. "Lady preserve us from roamers who haven't left yet," he commented generally to the air and turned his attention to driving in silence.

Felicia twisted to look back into the bed through glass dimmed by grime too ingrained to wipe away. She had no idea what that was supposed to mean. She wasn't some kind of lone, wandering around without a pack. Maybe in North America that was an insult.

John drove over a set of railroad tracks and growled in frustration along with Felicia. Silver kept Tom braced, but he was still jarred enough that his head came up groggily. Silver murmured reassurances and dumped some treats onto her palm for him. He accepted them delicately.

Felicia let a breath of relief trickle out, hopefully slow enough John wouldn't notice. At least Tom was all right. Maybe the talk her father would undoubtedly want to have would go well too. Felicia doubted it.

3

Silver could see the concern in her mate's face when they arrived, but John must have warned him, because he didn't look surprised at Tom's condition. Tom insisted on walking inside on his own four feet, the food having done his healing some good already. Dare walked beside him into the den but didn't support him, all confidence-inspiring alpha in his manner.

If Silver watched very carefully, she could see the slight hesitation in Dare's step from old injuries of his own. It added to the gravity created by the white locks at his temples, stark against his otherwise dark hair. His wild self, pacing beside Tom's, showed his scars plain to see in its fur—though of course Silver was the only one who saw the selves not currently dominant.

John came to walk on Tom's other side. Though both the other men's tame selves were taller, Tom was lanky and Dare lean, giving John the advantage in mass in both forms. That added to the feeling of strong support he projected as the beta.

Felicia brought up the rear, practically slinking in. If she didn't want her father to know she'd had a part in causing the incident, she wasn't doing a very good job of hiding it. Silver caught Dare's attention and tipped her head to the young woman, an offer to stop her slipping away to her own room, but Dare answered with a subtle shake of his head.

"But discipline is so much more fun in front of an audience," Death said, entering behind Felicia like the chill of twilight. He let his tongue loll in a canine laugh as he followed Felicia away. He must think the kind of excitement and trouble he liked would center around her, not Tom. Silver had to agree.

"What happened?" Dare asked, as they got to the room Tom shared with one of the pack's other single men. Before Tom could attempt the jump, Dare scooped him up and set him on his bed. Tom whuffed in annoyance but didn't otherwise struggle. Dare sat down beside him.

"The cubs chased each other onto the road, apparently," John said, neutral but for the diminutive. "I was pretty far behind and didn't know where they'd gone until Silver called me in."

Dare looked away from Tom and raised his eyebrows at Silver. "Called?"

Silver looked away, suddenly doubting herself. Maybe she shouldn't have put herself through that, maybe she should have let Felicia deal with her own mess, like an adult. Wasn't that what you were supposed to do with children? Teach them how, and then let them stand on their own four feet? Silver didn't want to be a cruel parent to her mate's child, but she didn't want to be too lenient, either. It was easier when she could let Dare handle Felicia's discipline.

But that excuse was wearing thin, three years on. Maybe this was a sign from the Lady it was time for her to take on some of the responsibility for Felicia herself. Silver didn't regret having helped Felicia, but she didn't want the young woman to take that for granted, either. She should be the one to make sure Felicia understood that. "I called him to come help deal with the things I couldn't see," she said. Let Dare make of that what he would.

"Mm," Dare said after eyeing her. Silver could smell that he knew there was more to it, but he didn't push. "Tom? You up to talking? No rush."

Tom shook his head in denial of the offer of more time. All three of the adults looked away as he shifted back with panting grunts of effort. The process of shifting always brought more healing with it, so it was good to push him to it quickly anyway.

"Who decided to go for the road? Was it on purpose?" Dare put a calming hand on the back of Tom's neck, making the gentle concern in his words clear. Not an accusation, or a challenge.

Tom bristled anyway. "On purpose? Why in the Lady's name would we do that?"

"Boredom. A hankering for excitement and danger?" Dare looked into the intermediate distance. In Felicia's approximate direction, perhaps. Silver certainly wouldn't have suspected Tom of any of that, and she doubted her mate did either.

Tom carefully touched the stitches along his human side, head down to watch his fingers. "I was running and lost track of where I was going, that's all." Even when he let his hand drop, he didn't look up.

"Before or after playing chase with my daughter?" Dare's voice sharpened and Silver started forward. She wasn't going to make him look weak by interrupting, but she wasn't going to let him take out his anger on Tom either. Young people played chase, usually with all the wrong people. That's what they did.

Dare waved her away and only sighed when Tom clenched his jaw and didn't say anything. "I know it doesn't seem that way to you two, but you're both still young. As her father, I'm telling you to stay away from her for a couple years. Then I won't stop you two from doing whatever you want, if you still want to. Understand?" He sharpened the last word with an alpha's command.

Tom nodded with a jerk, head still down. "Yes, sir."

"Good." Dare gave the back of Tom's neck a last squeeze and stood. John preceded them out, and Silver waited for Dare to come even with her so they could lace their fingers together. The touch felt like the warmth of summer sunlight on water-chilled skin. She reveled in the simple security of being with her mate until they were out of Tom's hearing, alone as they could ever be in a den always filled with pack and guests.

"We were all pretending we didn't know," she told Dare, letting humor give an edge to her tone. Pretending to no purpose, apparently.

"I don't think they would have believed me if I'd pretended too," Dare said, bringing their hands up to kiss the back of hers. "I've smelled them for the last few weeks, and there's no way to hide the fact that they were out there on the hunting lands alone before you and John arrived."

Silver searched Dare's face and scent, finding resignation

rather than anger. Understanding dawned all in a rush. "You did that to protect him."

"Yes, but don't ever tell him that. Leave the poor boy some pride." Dare laughed, low, then pinched the bridge of his nose. "I'm well aware my daughter tends to—as the humans would say—take no prisoners. He seems the more likely to get hurt."

Silver nodded. She couldn't argue with that. "I don't think she was courting the danger either. When I spoke to her after she seemed . . . more shocked that such an outcome even existed than disappointed she'd failed to cheat it."

Dare's lips thinned, but he nodded after a moment. "Either way, I still need to do something about her."

Silver squeezed his hand. Disciplining her couldn't be easy for Dare either, when she'd been kept away from him by his in-laws for so much of her childhood. The least she could do would be to come along and support him as they went looking for Felicia. And Death, of course.

Felicia had relaxed enough to at least stretch out on her bed with her computer, checking the status updates of her friends in Madrid without really reading them, when the knock came. She took a moment to compose herself, shoved her computer under her pillow, and sat up straight. "Come in."

"Felicia?" Her father's voice, of course. He didn't come in, and Felicia swallowed. That meant he wanted to say what was coming in front of the others. She had really fucked up, then, if her punishment was going to be in front of the whole pack.

"Coming." Felicia started for the door, changed her mind, and shucked off her shirt. She added a bra from the pile of clean-enough-to-wear-again clothes on the floor before pulling the shirt back on. She wanted to look calm and collected for this, and looking like she had dressed in the back of a truck was the opposite of collected.

Her father and Silver stepped back down the hall toward the head of the stairs when she came to the door. No one was so crass as to gawk out of doorways, but she caught one of the kids peeking around the gnawed banister at the bottom, which probably meant people were listening out of sight on the ground floor.

"You're not in trouble," her father said, surprising Felicia into an exhaled laugh. Uh-huh. Sure she wasn't. But at least he didn't seem angry? She drew in a breath to see if she could distinguish him from the background noise of a house full of Were, and he seemed more frustrated than anything. A parental kind of frustration she recognized immediately, like she was failing at some grand quiz show when he thought the answers should have been blindingly obvious.

"I warned you several times you had to plan for what you were going to do after high school. I let it slide while you still had classes, when you missed the college application deadlines and didn't put out any résumés, but now you've graduated, this is it. You have three choices." Her father dropped Silver's hand to tap a finger for each option. "You can go to college—you missed the deadlines for fall, but you can start the next semester. You can get a job. Or you can go out roaming. It's up to you. But what you can't do is sit around home, doing nothing. If you don't choose, there will be consequences."

Felicia stared at her father. She probably looked like an absolute idiot, her mouth hanging open. She'd opened it to say something, anything, but she couldn't find the words at first. Consequences? Sure, her father had nagged her about applications, but that was what this summer was for. She'd planned to get around to them eventually. *"You'd kick me out?"* She slipped into Spanish without meaning to.

"Language, Felicia." Now her father did start to sound annoyed. "I'm not kicking you out. Go to school, find a job, or go roaming. Same choice every young Were gets. Be as much a part of the human world or not as you choose, though you'll have to get used to interacting with it eventually."

Felicia pressed her fingertips to her lips, focusing on keeping her emotions even, so they wouldn't show up in her scent. She could run off and scream at trees later, when no one could hear or smell her. She hadn't been delaying on purpose, she just hadn't thought it was that important. "What's that supposed mean, anyway, roaming?"

Her father was silent for a moment, surprised. "Madrid didn't have anyone come through when I was there, now I think about it. Fits the European mind-set, I suppose, to close their borders, even to kids. That's what teens do, in North America. Get a car, or even just a backpack, and start traveling. See the sights in human and wolf. Meet other Were, other packs, see who you get along with, where you like living. Everyone's pretty relaxed about crossing territory, especially now they're all sub-packs of Roanoke. You've met roamers visiting here."

Felicia tried not to flush. She'd played chase with a few, which her father had undoubtedly guessed. She'd assumed they were on vacation. She hadn't realized North Americans had full-time wanderers like that.

She chewed on her lower lip as she chewed over the idea. Her father wasn't kidding, that was different from home— from Madrid. Home was in North America now. Being young and alone in Spain, even at the edge of your own territory, was asking to get your ass kicked from here to the Lady's realm by a gang from the next pack over.

"So what if I roam back to Madrid?" she shot back, more to give herself time to think than anything. Where was he expecting her to go? She was sure the other North Americans would be suspicious of her as some kind of evil European. She didn't want to go run around in the wilderness, either. She liked this pack, and Tom, and even her father when he wasn't being stupid and high-handed.

"I'd recommend getting a job somewhere for a while to earn the money for the plane ticket," her father said, face and tone neutral, though he took Silver's hand again. Silver grimaced. Felicia couldn't tell if it was because she was imagining his internal reaction, or because he'd squeezed her hand too hard and hurt her.

Great. Just the way to convince her father not to kick her out: threaten to run back to the relatives who had kept her away from him for most of her childhood. Felicia liked it here. Even if she'd wanted to go back to Madrid, she doubted they'd let her after she'd chosen North America over them once.

"Fine, whatever," Felicia said, suddenly wanting out of this conversation. She needed time to think, to kick things, where no one was watching. This close to the full, the pressure of emotion and judgment brought a shift near the surface, yawning under her like a chasm under a thin bridge. She'd rather die than fall into wolf right in front of everyone.

She strode into her room and shut the door on them all. She didn't slam it, though. She wasn't thirteen or something.

4

Felicia went running that night and slept in the next morning, purposely avoiding the time when the pack usually ate breakfast. They allowed her to avoid them, which did sort of drive home that she didn't have enough to do, when she stopped to think about it. No one was nagging her about getting to school on time, or asking her pointedly if she needed help with her homework. Since it was the weekend, most of the adults weren't at work, but everyone ignored her and went about their business.

Around two o'clock, she slapped together a sandwich from what was lying around in the fridge and went in search of Tom. His room was empty, door open. Felicia peeked inside. It smelled vaguely of pain, but that was overpowered by the layered masculine scents of the two Were who shared the room. Tom's side of the room was fairly tidy, considering: bed rumpled, but all his clothes in the closet, and his collection of Westerns on DVD stacked neatly on the shelf opposite his bed. His roommate Pierce's side was scrupulously neat in a way that highlighted the decade he had on Tom. They shared because they were both single at the moment, and they seemed to get along well enough.

John's son, Edmond, a sturdy four-year-old, trundled past her at great speed from the direction of the bedroom used as the nursery. He was shrieking with laughter and clutching his stuffed puppy.

"Edmond!" His mother, Susan, followed with his shirt in her hands. Felicia started to step out of the way, but Edmond paused and then darted for Tom's room, so she scooped him up. Tom—and Pierce—wouldn't thank her if she let the kid rampage around in their stuff.

That left her face-to-face with Susan and her human scent. Even though Susan had been there all the time Felicia lived in the Roanoke pack house, it still sometimes came as a little jolt to find a human acting as if she was a Were. Felicia understood it was because she'd earned it, defending the pack, besides the fact that her son and husband were Were, but she never knew quite how to treat the woman. In Madrid, they killed any human who found out about them.

"Thanks," Susan said and took Edmond from Felicia. Susan always looked so put together, like an executive of some corporation on TV, brown hair kept professionally short. Edmond squirmed around to mock-growl at Felicia playfully, and she mock-growled back. "Tom's at work, if you're looking for him."

"Seriously?" Felicia frowned at Susan as if that would convey the expression to Tom. Werewolf healing was all very well, but today was the full. She wouldn't want to be out dealing with annoying humans with a shift so close, so easy to lose control, even when she was completely healthy, never mind exhausted from healing. Back in Madrid, it was perfectly acceptable to stay home and not interact with any humans if you thought you weren't up to it.

"It's hardly manual labor," Susan said with a shrug.

"Down!" Edmond was apparently bored with their conversation, so he pushed his arms out straight against Susan's chest. She sighed and set him down but didn't release him until she'd pulled on his shirt.

"But he has to deal with so many—" Felicia caught herself at the last second. "People."

"Humans," Susan corrected, expression unbothered, though Felicia caught a whiff of exasperation. "Movie theaters are generally full of them, you'll find." Edmond glanced one last time at Tom's room, but when Felicia moved to stand more firmly in the way, he and his puppy headed for the stairs and whatever entertainment might wait below.

Susan watched him go and then turned her attention back to Felicia. "By the way, do you want any help on your résumé? I've probably had the most experience with them, though I think John's helped with interviewing where he works so he might have some insight from the other side."

Felicia dropped her head to hide a flush of frustration. That was another thing she'd let slide until summer. And now it was summer, and she didn't have an excuse anymore. "I don't . . . have one yet. To help with. I was waiting until classes ended to work on it."

Susan's exasperation grew more marked in her scent. She started downstairs after her son, slow enough to encourage

Felicia to follow along and continue the conversation. "What did you think you were going to do about a job? You know everyone in the pack besides the alphas has one, unless they're watching the kids. They have Were money trees in Spain that we North Americans aren't aware of?"

The "we" sounded weird too, but Felicia didn't comment. Being the beta's mate didn't automatically give Susan a similar status, but she read as plenty dominant on her own. Felicia didn't know how she did it, as a human. "Well, I'd work for the pack company. That's different."

They reached the ground floor and Susan raised her eyebrows in silence, so Felicia expanded after a moment. "Every pack has one. Madrid's makes—" The names came first to her in Spanish, so she had to sort through to find one with the English equivalent handy. "Tractors. Farm equipment and stuff. I probably would have worked in the office, but there's something for everyone. Actually making them, or selling them, or running the computers with the budget software, or . . . whatever."

Susan stooped to pick up a wooden toy car that had been abandoned in the middle of the hall by one of the other kids and made a thoughtful noise. "Andrew talks about starting something like that here. I can see how it would allow you guys to bring more Were culture into the workplace as well." She stepped into the living room to drop the car in the nearest toy box. "But since that's not up and running, my bank does have an opening for a teller right now. I'll be happy to give your résumé to HR once you have one. You would have to be polite, though."

Felicia bristled. "Are you saying I can't be polite?"

Susan just raised her eyebrows. Felicia tried to stay strong, but she dropped her head after a moment. She'd just proved she'd probably be complete shit at talking to humans all day, and they both knew it.

Susan took pity on her after a moment. "There are plenty of jobs that don't need a lot of interaction. Brush up your computer and filing skills. I find data entry soul sucking personally, but—" She shrugged. "Think about it, anyway. Like your father said, everyone has to go through it sometime."

Somehow, the sympathy made Felicia feel even worse. She recognized how stupid that was, given that she'd been moping so recently that she didn't know what to do. But now someone else was implying she didn't, she wanted to show Susan how wrong she was. "I'll think about it," she mumbled. "I'm going to go see Tom."

Susan nodded without comment and let her go. Felicia rummaged through the bowl on top of the gigantic shoe cubby by the front door. Most of the vehicles that nominally belonged to various members of the pack were in the driveway or along the street since it was the weekend, but she knew better than to borrow some of those without asking. Her father's, for example. She dug around until she found the keys for the old Honda beater and headed out.

Felicia hesitated when she reached the lobby of the multiplex, multicolored neon lines from the lights above mixing with the sunlight at her feet. Two red-vested employees manned the gaps in the velvet ropes on either side of the concession stand, so she couldn't get back to talk to Tom without buying a ticket, and he wasn't answering her texts. Lady, why was she so stupid? He probably wasn't allowed to be on his phone at work. She should have thought of that.

Well, she could at least ask someone, and then hang around in case Tom walked by within hailing distance on the other side of the rope. Felicia selected the employee on the right, a bleached blond woman only a few years older than her. She looked like she might be sympathetic to Felicia searching for a friend.

The woman proved indifferent rather than sympathetic, but she did get on her walkie-talkie and ask for Tom. Felicia edged off to the side when the woman gestured, so a loud family with tickets could get past.

Tom appeared from an employees-only door down the hallway and stopped abruptly when he saw her. With a sinking feeling in her stomach, Felicia wondered if he had been actively ignoring her texts. Was he still angry? She clenched her hands into tight fists in her jeans pockets. If he was, what could she do to make it up to him?

After that hesitation, he did come over, though. He stepped over the velvet rope and brushed his hair out of his eyes. "Felicia, I'm at work."

"I know, I—" Felicia bit her lip. The feeling of doing something that smacked of groveling made her grit her teeth, but she did deserve his anger. "I'm sorry—"

Tom waved away the apology with a half smile that made him look much more like his usual self, too mellow to maintain anger for very long. He sobered quickly, however. "It's not that. Your father wants me to stay away from you for a few years."

A flash of anger tightened Felicia's chest all at once. She knew her father would interfere. "He can't—"

"No, he's right, we're young. A year isn't forever. And we can still be friends, okay?" Tom looked away, body language drooping. "Just not right now. It's too easy to fall into other stuff again. So we should keep some space for a while."

Felicia stepped back and crossed her arms. Fine. If he didn't care enough about her to defy her father, she didn't want him anyway. Coward. "I didn't come about *that*. I wanted to get your advice on what kind of job to look for." Her accent was getting worse and she couldn't do a thing about it. She hated the way it underlined the scent of her mood, so she pressed her lips together and didn't say anything more.

Tom hesitated, then waved to the blonde taking tickets. "I'll take my break." She nodded absently. Tom put his hand just behind Felicia's shoulder, refusing to quite touch it as he directed her toward the large glass panels of the front wall and doors. Once she figured out what he was doing, Felicia lengthened her stride to get ahead so he couldn't have touched her if he'd wanted to. She shoved the door open with more force than necessary.

"So you've decided not to go roaming?" Tom stuffed his hands into the pockets of his black work slacks as they followed the sidewalk along the building to an empty wing of the parking lot.

"If Dad wants me gone, he'll have to kick me out. I'm not going to go roaming when everyone will be suspicious because I'm a European." Felicia crossed her arms again until she realized it probably made her look sulky. That wasn't sulking; that was the truth. Better to admit it and deal with it.

"It's not like that." Tom looked at his feet and his bangs flopped forward into his eyes. "You've been here three years, and anyway, roamers are roamers. Everyone expects you to be a little bit of a dumbass. People are used to it. Just don't go around killing people's pets or getting photographed. And there's plenty of land all over the West to run around in, without encountering a pack's patrols for days."

"I'm not a lone, though." Felicia kicked a piece of ornamental gravel that had escaped from the base of a tree along the sidewalk. "That's what I don't get about all this. You talk like nearly everyone goes roaming, but most Were aren't lones. Am I supposed to have some lone/pack switch that's tripped when I get older?"

"So find a nice boy—or girl—to have a roamer's chase with." Tom grinned. "That's when half the Were here figure out the kind of person they'd like as a mate eventually, anyway." His tone turned more factual, but the grin lingered. "Packs expect you to stop by. You kind of should anyway, to get official permission to cross territory from each alpha. So it's kind of more like a tour than anything. Run across country for a few days, stay a couple nights with a pack, go sightseeing with some of them, then head off to the next territory. Don't your paternal grandparents live back East somewhere? You could visit them."

Felicia searched his face and scent to find any reaction to the idea that she might go out and play chase with other Were not him, but he seemed thoroughly interested in the hypothetical possibilities of touring around the country. She grimaced. "They live in North Carolina. I did visit them once with Dad, but it was unbearably awkward. I don't think they ever liked my mother much." Time to nudge the subject in

another direction, because she definitely didn't need him trying to talk her into *that*. "You went roaming, I take it?"

"For about a year. I left when I was nineteen, after I'd tried
some semesters of community college. Came out West, fell in
love, she fell out of love first. That's when I joined your father,
just before he and Silver challenged to be Roanoke." Tom
bounced up on his toes and Felicia had to smile despite herself. He always did that when he was talking about something
he was really into.

"I saw the Grand Canyon, and I visited Yellowstone, but the
true wolves there were getting pissed, so I had to leave early. I
stopped by Vegas—that one's really not worth it, it's just bright
and noisy—and Fort Mandan." Tom waited, like Felicia was
supposed to have some reaction to that. "You know. Where
Lewis and Clark picked up the Were living as a trapper who
joined their expedition."

"I'll admit I'm historically ignorant when you can name me
one famous Spanish Were," Felicia countered and snorted at
his hopeful expression. They'd had this discussion before. She
held up one finger, forestalling. "Who's not famous for being
killed in the Inquisition."

Tom laughed. "Tell me you at least know Virginia Dare,
even if you don't know any other North Americans."

Felicia pulled a face at him. Of course she knew about her
own ancestor, and that ancestor's part in the colony that had
given her own pack its name. Honestly.

Tom grinned at her annoyance, but then his humor trailed
off. "Anyway. I think you *especially* should try roaming. Get to
know more of North America. Reassure yourself that people
don't actually much care where you came from."

"Mm." Felicia resettled a lock of hair behind her ear. However much you dressed it up nice with all the places you got to visit, roaming still sounded to her like a big excuse to get annoying teens out of the pack. "Well, I'm going to get a job right now, but I'll keep that in mind for later."

"You have all your documents and stuff in order? They're paranoid about checking those when you get hired lately." Though he was still offering advice, Tom glanced none too subtly toward the glass doors back into the multiplex.

"Father got our ID guy to make me what I need as a citizen when I first moved here. They're worn in by now." Felicia blew out a breath. "Lady. Go ahead and go. I'm sure your break's nearly over or whatever."

Tom hesitated a moment, then impulsively grabbed her hand and squeezed it. "It'll all work out. Being eighteen, nineteen, totally sucks, until you settle into yourself and into a pack. A couple years, and things'll be clearer."

"Because you're so ancient at twenty-three," Felicia countered with a snort. Tom's only response was to lift his fingertips in a wave as he headed back inside. Now he was no longer watching, Felicia let herself cross her arms tightly again. She didn't have to roam, because she was perfectly capable of getting a job.

Just watch her.

5

Silver pretended not to notice everyone getting ready for the evening hunt and focused on Edmond playing beside her on the floor. Though the residual poison in her blood trapped her forever in human form, she was their alpha, and they would hold themselves to the pace she set on two legs. But tonight she didn't feel like much running. Yesterday had brought what she used to be too close to the surface. She didn't want to chase the faint shadow of it. She'd go with the pack, but she'd wait, let them circle back to her when they'd made a kill.

She could use the time waiting to plan what she was going to say to Felicia. The young woman would be too busy with the hunt tonight, but perhaps tomorrow Silver could pull her aside.

Silver reached for one of Edmond's toys, a black-and-white spotted cow, but he growled at her and grabbed it first. He put it in his mouth so he could push himself up with both hands and run away. Silver caught the back of his shirt before he got more than a few steps. "Manners, Edmond!" She turned him around and spread one of his hands open. "When we're in human, we use our hands, not our mouths."

Edmond whined, apologetic, and spat the cow into his hand. He offered it out. He was far too young to have a wild self yet, but she could see hints of it behind his eyes, a flicker like a silhouette crossing the dawn horizon between trees. As he grew, year by year, that flicker became more pronounced.

Silver didn't accept the cow yet. "Use your human words."

"Sorry, Alpha." Edmond hung his head.

Silver picked up the cow by the least damp part, set it on its feet beside her, and walked it over to him. For this lesson, it would have been better if she could have divided the cow into parts and given Edmond one, but she'd make do. "Thank you, Edmond. Even though an alpha always gets the first share of the kill, it's her job to make sure every member of the pack gets at least a little bit of the rest. That's part of being an alpha. You can have all of this one."

Edmond left the cow and trundled over to watch the adults talking and laughing together near the entrance to the den, shedding extra clothing before leaving for the hunt. "I wanna go. It's not fair. I'm *always* in human."

"So am I," Silver pointed out. Unfair, as the child said. But seen from a child's perspective, it was also simple fact, easier to bear somehow. "Forever. At least the Lady will call your wild self when you're older."

Edmond considered her for a moment and then threw his arms around her neck in a hug. Silver laughed in surprise, cupped her good arm around his back, and breathed in his scent. She knew what she was doing with this cub, at least.

Then it was time to go. Silver handed Edmond over to Susan, who would be staying with all of the children too young to have their wild selves yet, and slipped outside with the rest of the pack. Everyone's scent was wound tight with anticipation, shift so very close in the full, and Silver avoided Dare. Touching him, feeling that anticipation in his muscles rather than just smelling it, would call to her own impossible-to-fulfill impulse to shift. She could hurt herself if she gave in to that, so she avoided Dare, and he let her. He understood why, and she'd make it up to him after the hunt when he'd run off the energy.

Out at their hunting lands, Dare lingered with his tame self dominant as the others piled up their clothes and dashed off into the trees on four feet. He gestured for Tom to remain when the young man would have done the same. "Hey! You know better than that. Shifting's good for you, but you don't need to be running."

Tom lifted his head high with annoyance, but Dare tipped his head to Silver, and Tom relaxed. Silver suppressed a smile. She didn't mind looking lonely as an excuse to keep a young pack member sensible. She held out her hand, palm down, and Tom padded over and ruffled his own ears with it.

"See you soon," Dare said. He switched to his wild self with joyous relief and pounded after the others. Silver knelt and scratched all around in Tom's ruff until he looked ready to fall over from enjoyment. A breeze ruffled up her hair as well as his, carrying the crispness of the growing green that surrounded them. Evergreens young and old, generous underbrush, and a stretch of grass at their feet where they flattened the plants traveling in and out. Rather than chasing individual scents, squirrel or crow or many other animals, Silver let the whole fill her up with a scent quietness. They'd be back among the humans soon enough, with layer upon layer of smells, pleasant and unpleasant.

She listened with half her attention to the soft noises of stalking and pursuit that reached her now and then, waiting for the louder burst of activity that would mean the prey was caught and everyone was circling back to divide it with both their alphas.

Instead, a different sound assaulted her ears. Silver knew the particular note of it, though she couldn't quite touch the knowledge. It meant someone was calling out for her mate. Tom pulled away from her, eager. Silver sighed. "I'm sure he's heard it himself, but yes. Go get him. At a moderate pace."

Silver stayed with the strident noise, until the pack trotted out of the trees, Tom curving around to join the general group on the opposite side from Felicia. Dare carried a raccoon in his mouth, and he dropped it at her feet. Silver bent, smoothed an unmatted section of its ring-circled tail, then straightened again. That's all she wanted of it when she was held to this form. Dare tore off a mouthful and then left the kill to John and the rest of the pack as he came to see who was calling.

The noise finally ceased as Dare switched wild self for tame, but he picked it up anyway, absently wiping blood from the corner of his mouth with the side of his thumb. As he had perhaps predicted, the noise began again. Someone was very determined to speak to him.

"Alaska," Dare greeted, and his scent grew surprised. Silver had a sense of the other side of the conversation, but it made her head hurt to listen to people who weren't there. Dare could tell her about it afterward.

Frustration flooded Dare's scent, and his wild self laid its ears flat. He nodded once. "Yes, all right. I'll come and help. No strings attached." He snorted. "Yeah, well, next time don't let it get this far—or happen in the first place." He didn't bother with a good-bye.

Silver slipped to his side, eyebrows raised in question. He gave her a thin smile. "We should discuss this at home. Get Susan in on it. John!" He raised his voice and the beta trotted over and began his shift as Dare spoke to the rest of the pack. "We've got to go back early and take care of something, but the rest of you can stay and run. Oh, and Tom. You should come with us." He said it lightly, as if it was another excuse to keep Tom from exertion, but Silver flicked him a sideways glance. She guessed he actually wanted Tom for something. Interesting.

The rest of the pack drifted back into the trees, hiding their curiosity better than Felicia, who lingered, perhaps hoping for an invitation of her own. Dare ignored her, and she finally slipped off with the rest.

When they arrived home, Susan met them at the door with Edmond at her heels, worry clear. "You're back early. What happened?"

John kissed her forehead, hand on the side of her neck to reassure, though he knew no more about this business than Silver did, yet. "Dare got a call from Alaska."

Susan pulled back to look at them all properly. "Why would any Were be calling during a full moon? I'd have thought they'd be too anxious to be on four feet to bother with long conversations."

"For Alaska, I suppose the full's the only time his pack would be in human long enough for any kind of conversation." John shrugged, then settled a comfortable arm across his wife's back. "They do everything backwards like that."

Tom laughed and slipped over to prop up a wall at the back, to listen but not join the decision making.

Dare drew a deep breath and grimaced. Down to business. Silver slipped her hand around his, and he nodded in thanks before he explained. "One of the Alaska pack fathered a child with a human, but they were too busy running around in wolf in the wilderness to even realize it. So now he's a year old, and they need someone who can act like a normal human to sweet-talk the mother out of custody. They're worried enough they're willing to accept my word we won't try to pull the pack under Roanoke's authority." The irony in his tone matched Silver's own at that thought: as if they wanted to have to deal with all the stubbornly independent troublemakers rather than letting them sort themselves out and band together out of the way.

"Is that all they want him to do? Just talk?" Death sat down and flicked an ear.

Silver suspected a similar thought must have occurred to everyone, because wild selves' ears swiveled to Susan, even though she hadn't said anything yet. They should have known better. Silver knew Susan was too practical to object based on her own emotions toward her husband and child.

Edmond was holding on to Susan's leg, confused, and she

petted his head. "If everyone's expecting that I'm going to demand you let her in on the secret, I'm not stupid. It depends on the person." She flicked a quick smile over at her husband. "No killing, though." She held up a hand that she wasn't done when Dare raised his eyebrows at her. "With modern methods for investigating murders, you'd create more problems than you'd solve. Lady above, give me some credit."

Dare nodded once, conditionally accepting a beta's advice. "Too bad," Death murmured. Silver gritted her teeth, certain his next dart would strike straight at the core of what was currently making her stomach twist into knots. She would never have cubs, not with the poison in her blood, and this man did not care enough about his to even know he existed.

"Some prey is too easy," Death said and stood again, drawing a wisp of shadow with him. "And you haven't figured out the good part yet."

"Actually getting out to meet the pack will probably mean a lot of travel in wolf," Dare said, tone too careful. Silver shoved away thoughts of cubs to look up at him. Lady damn it, he was right. Unfair once more, but better she support the inevitable in front of others, even others as sympathetic as those gathered here, rather than railing against it. It would turn out the same in the end, but one path would leave her with more authority.

"I'll stay here," she said, even voiced. "Watch over things at home." Dare kissed the top of her head. In his scent and in the grip of his hand on her neck, she felt a promise that there would be time for her to rail against the unfairness in private before he left. Thank the Lady for understanding mates.

"And I have a job for you," Dare told Tom, who had been looking decidedly confused as to why he was here. "Help Silver with anything she needs. I know you have your day job, but—"

"I can help cover those times," Susan spoke up. "I mean, I know it's a status thing, to have a low-ranked assistant rather than needing a high-ranked Were to do everything for you, but—"

Silver cut Susan off with a growl and crossed her arms, using her good to hold the bad up. "I don't need *that* much help. It will be fine." She'd have protested the need for an assistant at all, but that was another of the inevitabilities she'd decided not to fight. They seemed to be piling up tonight.

"As a human, you've never quite been in the hierarchy anyway. I wouldn't worry about it," Dare said with a shrug.

John coughed. "We could make Felicia earn her keep. She doesn't have a job."

"Alternately, we could put two badgers in a sack and shake them up." Death dropped his jaw in a canine grin. "One would be in no danger of boredom with that either."

Silver gave a little hiccup from swallowing her laugh. It was rude, but she wanted to be helped by Felicia about as much as she wanted to be in the bag with Death's badgers.

Dare snorted. "Silver's going to have to deal with her enough as it is."

Silver set her hand on her mate's elbow. "And you'll have Alaska to deal with. You should have another with you, for safety and for status." She looked at her cousin. "Don't you know some of the Alaskans, from your time as alpha?"

John shrugged. "For a given value of 'know.' I've had drinks with a couple. They come down here to stock up on gear sometimes." He edged closer to his wife, scent turning uneasy. "But we can't both go. That would leave you without muscle."

Susan punched him in the arm. "Except for all the other pack fighters, dumbass. Besides, do you really think Silver and I can't take care of ourselves?"

Silver laughed at Susan's reaction, but her cousin did have a partial point. She and Susan could take care of themselves, but visible muscle made things simpler sometimes. "We'll get Pierce to rearrange his time working so he can glower in the background for any official meetings. With him and the others, we will be fine." Dare hadn't voiced his thoughts on the subject, but his muscles relaxed under her fingertips at that.

Tom bounced on his toes. "And I'll help!" Silver had to smile, because Tom certainly had the enthusiasm and protective instinct, but not the strength and experience. There was no need to make him feel bad about it, though. He had his value as her assistant.

"Everyone can help." Dare smiled at Tom too, then tipped his head meaningfully away. The young man scooped up Edmond and took himself off deeper into the den.

When he was gone, Dare allowed himself a frown, and concern crept into the undertones of his scent. "It's not a physical attack that I'm worried about, anyway. There's going to be no real way to hide from all the sub-packs the fact that I'm going to be out of communication range for an extended period. I know the older, more traditional sub-alphas still listen to me better than you, Silver. You might want to keep in regular contact with them, remind them that you're watching."

"Watching like a hawk." Silver grimaced. She'd definitely do it, but that didn't mean she enjoyed dealing with those yapping purse dogs. "I'm sure they'd love the opportunity to extend their own sub-territory boundaries."

Dare chuckled. "Like you won't notice because it's far away. Exactly." His laugh slipped back into a frown. "And then there's my daughter. If I'd known I was going to get called away, I never would have confronted her and flushed that prey so early." He hesitated, scent twisting with the sour taint of old emotional wounds. "Do you think she really would go back to Spain . . . ?"

Silver clasped her mate's hand, firmly. "No. She made her choice to stay with you. Right now, she's a child looking for her adult place in the pack. She's being a little sulky, that's all."

Dare jerked a nod and then his attention sharpened, apparently with a new thought. "Speaking of Spain—you'll probably want keep track of any new Were who show up in outlying packs while we're away. My absence would make an excellent opportunity for Madrid to slip someone in to gather information."

John raised his eyebrows. "It's been three years, Dare. That's an awfully long time for him to be plotting revenge for you humiliating him, without doing anything about it."

Silver rather agreed with her cousin about the length of time, but she also trusted Dare's judgment, so she stayed silent, searching her mate's face for hints of his reasons.

Dare shook his head. "Madrid plays a long game. He gathers information for years before acting on it. I'd estimate he's due to try for a better source by now. I'd recognize any of his pack he tried to send, so while I'm away would be a perfect time." He dropped her hand and paced a few steps.

"Wouldn't Felicia recognize someone he sent too?" Silver

cupped the side of Dare's jaw, stilling him from further pacing. It would be good to be on their guard, but she thought Dare perhaps underestimated the effect of distance. She had no doubt Madrid would carry a grudge against Dare until Death took his voice, but Madrid was very far away. Revenge at such a distance took more energy than most people had. "I'll ask her about any strangers. Promise." She pressed her thumb to her forehead, sealing the promise in the Lady's name.

"Fair enough." Dare kissed her forehead where she had touched it. "I promise not to worry about it, then. Much." They both laughed and Dare took both of her hands. His squeeze, though it looked equal, felt uneven to her, conveyed in a muffled fashion by her bad hand. "Don't feel like you have to enforce anything with Felicia until I get back."

Silver squeezed back, one-handed. The situation couldn't be clearer: this was her time to learn to deal with Felicia properly. "We're alphas of all of Roanoke. I can handle one sulky cub. If she doesn't choose to go roaming, Susan can help me judge her progress."

"Thank you." Dare gave her a wan smile. "If you can think of some time-consuming task to give her as well, don't hesitate. When I was that age, half the restlessness came from not having something to focus my energy on."

"I can think of *plenty* of ways to provide her that," Death said in the voice of a past enemy, the one Susan had killed for them. Silver took his point. Lady ensure that circumstances wouldn't step in to provide excitement once more.

———

After the hunt, Felicia went straight back to her room, absently picking pine needles out of the ends of her curls. She wanted to know what was going on, but she wasn't going to seek out her father and ask him.

She stopped with her hand on the knob, sniffing. Everyone's scent was all over the pack house, but her father's had just reached her more strongly. Lady, was he waiting for her? Lovely. She jerked the door open a little harder than necessary.

Her father sat at her desk, working on a laptop. She thought it was hers for a moment, since she'd left it there, but a quick scan found it closed and sitting neatly on a flat spot in the piled blankets on her bed.

He tapped a last few keys and looked up. "John and I have to take care of some things up in Alaska. Our flight leaves pretty early tomorrow morning."

Felicia shucked off her shirt and dumped it beside the door. Scent marking her space like that was a little rude when someone was in it, but she hadn't invited him in. She left her jeans beside the bed before removing the laptop and forming the blankets into a nest. She'd sleep in wolf tonight, she decided. "So this is when you tell me to listen to Silver?"

"If I have to tell you to listen to your alpha, you have deeper problems," her father said. He closed his laptop and stood. "Just don't"—he sighed—"poke at her because you're angry at me, all right?"

"I'm not angry at you." Felicia jerked one blanket off the bed entirely. She actually was a little. He'd smell that. But it wasn't him so much as being European and not having a pack company job to look forward to and not really knowing what she was doing, searching for a job. And now Tom was talking about *friends,* and that *was* her father's fault. "I don't have any problems with Silver."

"Good." Her father paused at the door, maybe thinking about saying something else, but he left it at that.

Felicia bit her lip. She couldn't let him go with that kind of good-bye. She threw her arms around him for a quick hug. "Watch out for helicopters. They said on TV they hunt wolves that way up there."

Her father petted her hair. "I will."

6

Over the next week, Silver didn't know if Felicia was being particularly effective in her efforts, but she certainly worked hard at something Silver didn't understand. Susan pronounced herself satisfied with the girl, even impressed with her intensity, so Silver put off their talk. Cowardly, she supposed, but as long as the girl was working on something, why push her harder?

A distraction arrived at the end of the week, in any case. Portland spoke with Silver over a distance to warn her that she wished to meet with a Roanoke but didn't mention the reason. Silver didn't press her, but the omission made her all the more curious when she opened the door to the den that morning and invited Portland and her beta in. Pierce stood just inside, watching. He didn't have John's build to hulk even with his wild self dominant, but he watched with an intensity that the visitors couldn't miss, ears tight on them.

"Roanoke," Portland said, and they embraced on the doorstep. Two less familiar alphas might have shaken hands to test each other's grip, but this was an even deeper offering and testing of trust. Portland was a short woman, black of hair and dusky of skin, and her wild self had a hint of reddish sand mixed among the gray. Silver paid close attention to that wild self to find what Portland was hiding in her tame self's body language, because she was hiding something. That was clear enough.

"My beta, Craig." Portland motioned the man forward. He was square jawed and stubborn looking, tame and wild self alike.

"And you without any hackles to raise," Death said. He came to sniff the newcomers as Silver's wild self should have, had she still been alive.

Silver drew a deep, calming breath. Death wasn't wrong. She did not like Portland's beta at all. She had to dig mental fingertips into the name to avoid losing it in a rush of anger. Before Dare had bled the worst of the silver from her veins, this man—Craig—had been in favor of killing her. Her own memories of that time were too jumbled to remember that, but Dare had let it slip once to explain his avoidance of the man.

But as Roanoke, she had to set that aside. She had only words to hold against this man, not actions. Not even words she'd heard herself. So she would be polite but wary.

Death's attention lingered on Portland's wild self, which surprised Silver. She would have expected him to nip and harass Craig's. Death held his nose close to Portland's flank for several moments, then sneezed and wandered off. When he opened his mouth, his voice was a wail of a newborn, slicing right through defenses to the pure emotion beneath. Protect. Protect the cub.

Silver closed her eyes. That child was dead. She'd heard Death use that voice once before. One of Portland's, lost during shifting. She opened them again and gestured to dismiss Pierce. This was definitely private business, and he knew to wait within easy distance, should she need him. When he was gone, she spoke. "You can't be very far along. I can hardly smell it."

Craig jerked in surprise and Portland smiled in satisfaction. "I told you she'd figure it out." She patted his shoulder teasingly but sobered quickly. "That's why we need to talk to you."

"Come in." Silver gestured for them to precede her deeper into the den. She hung back to speak to Tom, who was waiting just out of sight, curiosity quivering beneath the surface of all his muscles. "Get some food and drinks, then chase people out of earshot," she told him. He bobbed a nod and bounded off. She had to call the rest after him. "Including you!" He waved to acknowledge it without turning around, and she had to laugh.

They all sat and Silver and Portland made strained conversation about the weather and how it was affecting the prey populations in Portland's territory until Tom had set down the food and drink and disappeared. Silver only sipped at her drink, but Portland nibbled and nibbled, probably not even realizing how much she was eating.

Silence fell, compacting under the weight of important things to follow. Craig broke it first. "I have a petition for you, Roanoke."

Portland jerked straight backed. "You said that you wanted to discuss it, not—" The rest of her words trailed off into a rolling growl, and her wild self bared its teeth and snapped at Craig's.

Silver straightened too, stalling through her assumption of a formal expression. She and Dare had continued a tradition of Roanoke under other alphas: A Were of any rank could formally present them with a petition and be heard in full, their alpha barred from making any arguments until the petitioner was finished. It had come up only a few times, and she'd never before felt so biased. She'd much rather believe anything Portland said than Craig, but that didn't matter. She needed to hear him out. "Do you wish to make your case privately?"

Craig hesitated and glanced over at his alpha, who didn't give him time to answer. "You mean for a formal petition I can actually be kicked out?" Portland glared first at Craig, then at Silver.

Silver wanted to grimace, but she kept up her formal mask. "If the petitioner requests it. Or if keeping silent proves difficult for you at any point." She pressed her lips together, then unbent as much as she dared. "It's to keep low-ranked Were in a bad situation from being intimidated out of getting help. Obviously, there's no intimidation here." She raised her eyebrows at Craig for confirmation, and he dipped his head in a nod and even exhaled on a note of humor.

"She can stay." Craig waited as Portland crossed her arms and settled back, scent indicating she was seething inside. He grew even more expressionless in his own version of formality. "I am petitioning to have Michelle removed from the position of alpha."

Death laughed. Silver closed her good hand into a fist in her lap, hidden from view. Oh, how she'd love that fist to connect with his square jaw. "What?" She didn't growl, but she put that vibrating rage into her tone. How dare he ask such a thing? "Why?"

Craig set his hands flat on his thighs. "Alphas come under a great deal of stress. Stress that could trigger an unwanted shift and harm the child."

Silver could see the thought so plainly on Portland's face she voiced it for the other woman, though with less anger. "Stress like having an unsupportive beta?" Death's smugness deepened so markedly that she examined the words and winced internally at how badly she was doing at listening as an unbiased alpha. When she shoved emotion aside, this did not seem to be as similar to his opinion of her in the past as she'd thought. She'd supposed his suggestion to kill her had been laziness and a wish to avoid trouble, unleavened by empathy. This wasn't avoiding trouble, it was causing it—in pursuit of what goal? Was Craig really motivated only by worry for the safety of his alpha's cub?

"Are you trying to say that no woman can be alpha without choosing between the position and having cubs?" Silver spoke quickly to dispel her last jab with a more logical argument. Female alphas were clearly the real issue here.

Craig drew in a deep breath and glanced at Portland with a flash of concern so deep and surprising that Silver reevaluated her earlier assumption of his lack of empathy. "That depends if the other female alphas have lost children before."

Portland choked something back, and Silver was grateful for the excuse to stall before giving her response. She knew

Portland had lost a cub to an early-term shift, but she hadn't thought of it in quite those terms until Craig voiced them. These things happened, but they happened to some women more than others, and only the Lady knew all the causes and factors. "I will have to think about this."

Silver hated the words even as she said them, but she couldn't think properly with both of them staring at her, and Craig was right: it wasn't just about being a female alpha, it was about being a female alpha who had already lost one cub. Portland smelled frustrated but didn't protest.

"And consult with your mate?" Craig dropped his head in acknowledgment without waiting for an answer, as if his question was only a formality. If anything, that made it worse.

Silver shoved to her feet, the violence of the movement cutting off Portland's reaction. A small part of Silver whispered urgently that she was supposed to keep her temper because she was Roanoke, but the rest was all icy clarity for her next words. "Think very carefully. Are you telling your alpha that she cannot make a decision on her own?"

Silver took one step, another, and touched Craig's chin to make him meet her eyes. She didn't bother to measure her dominance against his, as one might normally. She overpowered it, smashed him flat as he gasped. She'd told him she'd consider his petition, and yet he still felt the need to bully her. She walked with Death in the place of her wild self, and he *dared* to say she could not make a decision on her own?

Craig twisted his head away from her, panting. "I can make this big, Roanoke. I'm not the only high-ranked Were in the sub-packs who feels this way. Not by a long shot. Children are too precious to endanger them for posturing about status."

His voice was a frightened whine, but his words stopped Silver short anyway.

She stepped back. She could believe that he'd get support. Lady, she didn't want to, but she could. Were had few children and they all felt the longing, if not as strongly as she often did, denied the chance for her own. And what a convenient excuse for the packs that disliked being united under Roanoke to agitate for their independence. The Western packs had been united for only three years, and even the original Roanoke sub-packs had their share of troublemakers, always bucking for more power.

Thinking about defending against all that made Silver realize she knew her answer to the petition, even without time to think further. You couldn't let fear for yourself, or fear for your cubs, keep you from living your life. At some point, you had to leave it in the Lady's hands. But having made the decision, now she couldn't voice it. She couldn't match dominance with everyone across the entirety of their territory, one by one. And if she lost one sub-pack, others were likely to follow. Better she and Dare work together, Dare using his skill with words on them, persuading and ordering where necessary.

"So don't posture," she told Craig. "Mention this to no one and I'll consider your petition. Yes, and discuss it with Dare." She cut him off as he drew breath for a further objection.

That didn't stop Portland, however. She stood and crossed her arms, anger rolling off her in waves. "Roanoke, how can you—"

"Roanoke?" Tom's voice was loud, to be heard over their argument, but his wild self had its tail tucked far between its legs. "One of the patrols found an unknown Were. He was at the—"

He said a word Silver knew she should know, but at the moment, that was about as much use as looking up at the tiny dot of a bird against the clouds and knowing it could be eaten. Both hypotheticals, when they were impossibly far out of reach.

"The place where people arrive from far away," Death said. "Another visitor for you. Wouldn't want you to get lonely, with your mate gone, would we?"

"Have the patrol bring him in," Silver told Tom. He bounded off. She wished she could escape this situation so easily. "I'll have to ask the two of you to find accommodations of your own while I deal with this. Rest assured, we are not done with our discussion."

She held her arm wide to the exit, and Craig left without fuss. Of course he would, he'd gotten what he wanted. Now she would be mired in talk and argument when her voice was already heavy with the weight of the decision she wanted to make.

Portland hung back. "Roanoke, please." Her voice was low, thin with the frustration of the choice her beta wanted to force her into.

"If this could be fixed with a pronouncement, Portland, I'd make it." Silver massaged her temple as she walked with Portland to the exit. "We need to work things around carefully, all right? Leash your temper." She glanced ahead to make sure Craig wasn't lingering to listen. "What does the father think?"

"You just heard." Portland tipped her chin ahead of them.

Silver stopped short to stare at her. "Lady preserve us, tell me you're joking." When Portland shook her head, Silver smacked the back of her head, as she would a cub. "Why do I have to *say* this to any of you? Don't play chase with your beta! Look what happened to Sacramento and hers. Did watching that fall apart teach you nothing?"

"Sacramento's girlfriend was crazy," Portland said challengingly, but her wild self's tucked tail admitted her guilt. "We're not lovers anymore, anyway. We were already drifting apart, before—" She dropped her hand but stopped before touching her abdomen. "And arguing about it finished off the intimate parts of relationship."

She sighed. "However much of a cat he's being, it's not about him wanting to keep a woman from holding authority. I'm sure of that. He supported me without reservation when I challenged for the alphaship back in the beginning. I think the idea of having a child has just got his voice so twisted up, he doesn't know what he's saying anymore."

"Mm," Silver murmured, still dubious. That was a nice excuse. He loved his child too much. What about loving his child's mother?

Once she'd seen Portland out, Silver returned to the den and found some more substantial food. She waited for the unknown Were to arrive and ate while staring into nothing in particular. As a healthy den, their home had a deep glow of the Lady's light about it, and Silver drew on the sight of it as a comfort.

Felicia arrived home and lingered just out of sight, probably catching up on all the gossip from Tom or one of the others. Silver felt irrationally like her decisions were being judged by the young woman, being compared to what Dare might have done. What Dare might have done didn't matter—they were equal alphas, and he wasn't here right now. Still, the itchy feeling of a judging gaze lingered. When things died down, Silver would have Felicia lay out today's accomplishments in finding herself occupation, even if Silver couldn't understand all of them. Just because Felicia had been out of the den didn't mean she'd been working.

Silver had time to finish her food, clear it away, and set her chair to face the entrance with Pierce standing near, an alpha relaxing ready to deign to offer an audience, before the new Were arrived.

He was younger than she'd expected, only a few years older than Felicia. He was dark in coloration in both tame and wild selves, as Felicia was, though his wild self was more dark gray than black, in a wash along its back and head.

He knelt before her and tipped his head to one side to show his neck, formal in his respect. Too smooth by half, Silver decided, as he lifted his head to smile at her. His wild self held its head high, pleased with itself. But arrogance didn't necessarily mean evil intentions. "Roanoke. My name is Enrique. My birth pack is in South America—" He said a name of a place, but it meant nothing to Silver, especially tinted into something warm and exotic by his accent. Not North America, not Europe, that was the important part. If he was telling the truth. Silver could smell no particular lie. Dare had warned of Madrid sending someone, but to an outlying pack. Silver doubted Madrid would be so foolish as to send someone to Roanoke's home pack.

"We are very isolated. I want to see more of the world. I hoped you would give me permission to . . . explore?" The stranger hesitated over the word.

"Roam," Silver suggested. She glanced at Death, to read his

reaction to the young man, but he was apparently dozing, watching events through half-open eyes. "Felicia? Do you know this man? Is he someone Madrid could have sent?"

Felicia started. "What? No." She shook her head a beat later to emphasize the answer, though her face still showed confusion at the question. Her wild was on high alert, ears high and nose straining forward at the young Were. Silver narrowed her eyes at it. Was Felicia trying to hide something?

But then understanding dawned. Young was the important part here. Young woman, young man. Silver gave the face of Enrique's tame self more careful attention in that light. He was handsome enough, she supposed, though his self-satisfied air was too much a barrier for her to class him as truly attractive. Felicia smelled sharply of excitement and anticipation under her surprise.

"You may roam Roanoke territory," Silver told him, and motioned for him to rise. She needed to get back to dealing with the problem Portland's beta presented. "So long as you don't cause trouble, and you seek permission again before you settle anywhere."

"Thank you." Enrique smiled even brighter and sought out Felicia immediately among those of the pack who had gathered to watch. Silver rubbed at her temple. A new chase might put Felicia in a better mood, but it wouldn't keep her nose to the trail of her father's orders. But if Silver needed to drag the young woman back on track, she would—Dare would come home to a united Roanoke and a daughter with work, if Silver had anything to do with it.

————

Felicia could hardly wait to speak until she'd pulled Enrique out to the backyard. She dragged him across the wild grass to the bushy trees planted at the fence to block nosy neighbors. It wasn't completely private, but it would do. She faced the house and watched for any windows edging up to indicate one of the kids was eavesdropping. She used Spanish too, just in case. *"I can't believe I lied for you. Lady. What are you doing here?"*

She pressed fingertips to her temples. She hadn't even thought about the lie, it had just slipped out, which was probably why Silver hadn't smelled it. She'd seen her childhood reflected in Enrique's face so strongly, she couldn't stand the thought that he'd be sent away before she could at least talk to him.

"What kind of greeting is that?" Enrique laughed. Felicia remembered him being hot when she'd been back in Madrid, but Lady above. He'd cut his hair shorter since she'd seen him last, turning curls into lush black waves. Just standing here smelling him, she wanted to run her fingers through it.

He opened his arms, and after checking for observers again, she embraced him. Inhaling his scent filled her voice with all the tones of home, but she quickly pushed away. *"Lady, you're so lucky my father wasn't here. He'd have seen right through you even if he didn't recognize you from when you were a child. Chilean? Seriously? That accent never even watched a TV documentary about Chile. You didn't smell even a little like you were lying, though. How'd you manage that, when it was a planned lie?"*

"You think that was luck? I knew Dare would never let me near you, so I was bumming around in Mexico until he was out of town or you went traveling on your own. Mexico City has too much to do with keeping his people out of the human violence

to worry about lones. And Silver's too crazy to understand place-names. You only smell like a lie when you're worried about it."

Felicia snapped off a twig and tapped the flat needles against her upper lip, as if in absent thought, to discreetly use the evergreen scent to block out his distracting one. She needed to remember that he was—or had been, at least—part of the Madrid pack that had kept her from her father when her mother died, and then tried to use her as a pawn against him. Even as she reminded herself of that, though, memories kept intruding of nipping at his tail in childhood games. *"My father wouldn't let you near me to say what? Why are you here, Enrique?"* Her chest tightened at a sudden thought. *"Is everyone all right? I haven't e-mailed anyone since just after I decided to stay here, but I noticed everyone's still posting status updates. I mean, it's stupid stuff, since it's where their human friends can see, but it means they're still online, with enough time for the stupid stuff."*

Enrique clasped her upper arm briefly, but his expression twisted. *"It's not that bad for most of the pack. After what your father did, Madrid lost everything outside the city limits to Barcelona, except for one hunting ground. But inside the city, we're reasonably safe. Madrid himself makes sure of that."*

Felicia looked down at her feet. What she'd helped her father do, Enrique could have said. But her father hadn't injured Madrid, he'd only humiliated him in front of the other European alphas. If Madrid didn't have the physical strength to keep his territory after that, it wasn't her father's fault. But being constrained to a single city sounded pretty frustrating to Felicia. No wonder Enrique wanted to get out. But he'd chosen to get out to here, not actually to South America, or anywhere else in the world. She let her silence indicate her first question still stood.

"As for why I'm here—they didn't treat you fairly." Enrique bowed his head, granting her a greater angle of respect than she really deserved. He was presenting himself as a lone and she was pack, yes, but he was also a few years older and more experienced. *"I told Madrid that, I told my parents that, but I finally got tired of arguing. So I left. I figured you'd be old enough now that your father would finally let you out on your own a little, so I could talk to you."* He hesitated. *"I do think . . . if you came back, it would be different. Madrid obviously couldn't show weakness to me, but he knows how he treated you was wrong—"*

"No." Felicia tossed her twig at his chest. "Never in the Lady's cycle am I going to go back because things might be different this time. I'm not that stupid." She didn't realize she'd fallen back into English until halfway through, but she went with it, emphasizing how little accent she had compared to him.

Enrique held up his hands. *"I completely understand. I didn't come to try to coax you back or something."* He dropped his hands, but to her waist, fingertips settling lightly over her hips. Easy enough for her to pull away, but one of his thumbs happened to slip under her shirt hem and slide over bare skin above her jeans, and she got distracted. He smiled, a slow expression. "Like I said. Time to get out and see the world and its beauties."

His accent wasn't so bad after all. Felicia knew his compliment wasn't particularly special to her, that he'd say that to any Were he wanted to charm into a game of chase, but she smiled anyway. "You just wanted to get out of the city."

Enrique shook his head, amused, as if that accusation was too patently untrue to deserve a reply. He wasn't that much taller than her, something that must have been true before she'd left as well, but she'd never had a chance to realize it so viscerally as when he leaned in to kiss her.

"Does that line work on South American girls?" Tom stuffed his hands into his pockets after closing the back door, but the way his strides ate up the distance across the yard spoiled his nonchalant act. "If you're here to roam, go roam."

"Why do you care, Tom?" Felicia jerked her head away from Enrique and stepped out to block Tom before he could get too close to Enrique. Tom looked over her shoulder and tried to catch the other man's eyes for a dominance contest anyway, but she held up her hand to block that too. "It's not like he's impinging on territory *you* wanted."

Tom's eyes flicked to hers and then away. His mouth twisted like he'd bitten into something rotten and he turned away. "Fine. Whatever."

Felicia watched him slouch back across the yard, fighting a sick feeling in her stomach. She hadn't meant to hurt him. She couldn't have anyone watching her with Enrique too closely, though. It would soon become noticeable that they already knew each other. Besides, Tom going all hackle-y when he'd passed up that right was damn annoying.

A chuckle behind her jerked her attention back Enrique. *"He doesn't appreciate what he's passing up, if I understood that right,"* he said. This time, Felicia smacked him. Enough was enough. She wasn't going to be swayed by a gorgeous face and a bunch of empty compliments.

He dropped his head, acknowledging the rebuke. *"I would like to see the local sights, though. If you'd be willing to show me?"*

Felicia looked back at the house a final time. Tom was out of sight again, probably back at Silver's side, dancing loyal attendance on his alpha. It seemed lazy to take the afternoon off, but other than filling out yet more applications, she could only wait around for calls for interviews. And she'd already sent an application this morning.

Besides, Enrique would know how hard this job search thing was for someone raised European. It would be nice to talk to someone who actually understood. "Sure, I'll show you around. There are a couple places worth seeing in human, we can do those first. Let's go grab your bag from inside so no one thinks you're planning to stay here, and we can explore Seattle." She extended her hand to tug him along back to the house.

7

Death chuckled, and Silver frowned at down at him for a beat before she realized he was reacting to Felicia departing very much in the roamer's company. She'd have thought that was a foregone conclusion, not worthy of his scorn. She raised her eyebrows at him. "Don't you have less inevitable things to mock?"

"Tom doesn't think so." Death strode to the side of the room where Tom's wild self sprawled at the tame's feet. The tame slouched against the wall, waiting in case she should need anything. Death nosed the wild self's sandy-furred head, and it moved only slightly to the side before flopping its muzzle on its paws again. Silver winced. She promised herself she'd spend some time with him, maybe offer his wild self a good brushing, once she dealt with Portland. But before then, she needed his help.

She crossed to Tom and stooped to give his wild self's ears a ruffle. That self wasn't dominant to feel it properly, but it still should soothe him subliminally. "I need you to call Dare so I

can talk to him." Craig and Portland were a problem Silver
would have to solve on her own in his absence, but they could
at least discuss strategy together.

Tom nodded emphatically, some of the dejection going out
of his muscles at the prospect of something helpful to do. It
didn't take long for a frown to creep back in as he held his
hand up to his ear, however. "Lady damn it, it's going straight
to—" Tom cut off and his eyes flicked to Silver's face. She
knew the look of someone trying to phrase a concept so she'd
understand. She gritted her teeth and tried not to let frustration seep into her scent. It wasn't Tom's fault.

"It's not that he's not answering. He's not even in range
to . . . hear me calling. I guess it's not that surprising, up in
Alaska." Tom held something out to her. "But you can leave
him a message. He'll hear it when he's next in range."

Silver hesitated a beat. She couldn't leave her message with
what Tom held without him hearing. "Don't tell anyone else
about this," she said, closing her hand tightly around his wrist
to underscore the order. Tom swallowed and nodded.

"Dare . . ." Silver tried to picture him here before her, but she
hated speaking at a distance in the first place, and speaking to
nothing was even worse.

"But you speak to me all the time. Wouldn't Dare consider
that the same?" Death murmured. He padded over and sniffed
at what Tom held. "Tell him things are much more exciting
around here without him. He should travel more often."

Silver laughed, and the sound broke her awkward silence.
"Death sends his regards. Something's come up." Quickly, she
outlined the situation with Portland and her beta and then
nodded to Tom.

Tom straightened and took an abortive step after her as Silver turned away. She paused. He smelled like he was bursting with an opinion. She suppressed the beginnings of a smile. She might as well make sure he didn't strain himself. "Yes?"

"Craig is fucking prey-stupid! I don't think Portland—or Sacramento, or any other female sub-alpha in the future—should have to step down just because she's pregnant."

Tom practically vibrated with his earnestness. She'd needed that reminder badly, Silver realized. Plenty of Were would agree with Craig, but plenty of others wouldn't. She went on tiptoe and cupped the side of Tom's neck to kiss the opposite corner of his jaw. "But don't go telling him that. I need to handle this myself, puppy."

Silver settled back and examined matters with her new, calmer perspective. She didn't know when she'd hear back from Dare, so perhaps it was best to continue as if he would not receive her message in time. A long delay strengthened Craig's position. She already knew her decision about his petition. She could invite him and Portland to dinner tonight to announce it. Eating would keep everyone calmer and let her ease into it.

"You're released for the evening," she told Tom and gave him a playful shove on his chest. "Find Susan for me, would you?"

"Yes, Roanoke!" Tom bounded off.

Silver slipped farther into the den and paced as she waited for her beta's mate—or perhaps her beta, now John was away with Dare—to arrive. She could feed herself well enough with any of the food stored here, but preparing it for guests was different. She frowned, chasing after even a flicker of the knowledge she needed. Death sat and mocked her movement with his utter stillness. "Stare at the food a little harder. I'm sure it will grow so scared as to form itself into a meal on its own," he said.

"Silver? What's wrong?" Susan's entrance made Silver jump, focused as she was on proving Death wrong. He was right, though. Much as she wanted to control every aspect of the meal herself, much as Susan didn't deserve to be ordered around like a low-ranked Were, she couldn't see clearly enough to do it.

"I'm going to invite Portland and her beta for dinner. I . . ." Silver hesitated and the shorter woman came to rub a hand along her back. She leaned her whole body against Silver's back a beat later, cheek against her hair. The gesture wasn't entirely natural, and a little too low ranked for her place as beta, but it was much closer to correct for their status than the hugs human women usually offered each other in the same situation. Susan was good at noting and learning those differences.

"If the human can tell I'm tense—" Silver exhaled in a laugh.

"You're allowed, you know." Susan stepped back and Silver turned to face her. Susan presented a picture of stability, much as her husband did. Silver wouldn't have expected it from someone so young, human or not, but over the years, Susan had settled into an enviable confidence in her value as a fresh perspective on Were problems. "I'm happy to organize everyone to get it cooked if you'll guide me through the etiquette. I'm guessing this isn't a casual cookout for friends."

"No." Silver let her shoulders drop with relief. Since Susan had offered first, she wouldn't have to figure out how to ask her. "You already know I get served first. The most important thing is not to serve Craig anything. Give him an empty—" The word escaped Silver for a moment, but she was used to that. She focused on the important part of the sentence, and it popped out on its own. "Plate, and serve Portland more than she can eat. She can choose what he eats and how much."

Susan's eyebrows rose. "What'd he do to fuck up that bad?"

Silver shook her head. "It's not a matter of punishment. That's the most formal of pack eating etiquette. No one bothers with it usually, but it's there when you want to remind someone of his role."

She drew a deep breath. "And I want to remind him of it because he wants Dare and me to force Portland to give up her sub-alphaship because the stress might make her lose her child." In the silence after saying it, Silver examined the statement, but she'd captured the important part. It struck her as darkly funny that so much trouble could be summed up so quickly.

"Oh! She's—" Susan touched her own stomach, but she continued without waiting for Silver's nod, tone sharpening. "Seriously, though? That's bullshit. John said you guys can miscarry if you shift after the early part of the pregnancy, and I assume what counts as 'early' varies from woman to woman. But if Portland knows she's pregnant, where's the problem? She can just avoid shifting."

"In theory." Silver held her good arm across her chest, as close as she could get to crossing her arms. "If he does decide to start howling up support, he's got a stronger argument to call on. I understand pregnancy makes human women emotional." Silver smiled in answer to Susan's sharp bark of laughter. She could see the memory of Susan's own experience in her expression. She squashed her own wish that she could speak from experience too before it could become more than a whisper in the back of her mind.

"It's the same for Were. In the full, when you're emotional, a shift can get *so* close—for most women, it's just a part of life, but a few can trap themselves in circles." Silver illustrated with a fingertip. "She worries about shifting by mistake, and that worry brings the shift closer, and then she worries more . . ." Silver drew a deep breath, unconsciously waiting for Death to mock her, but he remained silent, leaving her to catch and hold a ghost of a bloody memory in peace. "When I was young, still with my birth pack, one woman lost her baby very late that way. It was . . . ugly."

"Jesus," Susan hissed. Her eyes flicked to Silver's and she pressed a thumb to her forehead, the Were gesture of respect to the Lady. Silver smiled thinly and echoed it, flattered that the woman would offer it to her. Susan had her own God, so the gesture clearly wasn't on her own behalf.

"But Portland won an alphaship—and *held* it. She's in no such danger. And you can't live your life based on that kind of fear anyway. It's in the Lady's hands." Without looking, Silver flexed her hand at her side in sheer frustration and felt fur under her fingertips. She didn't look at Death, just buried her hand deep in his ruff.

"Craig has threatened to pull the other packs into it." Silver growled low. "You were here when we first united the packs, you know how some of them are itching for an excuse to declare independence again. They'll see this as a Lady-sent opportunity."

Susan tapped her fingers against her hip, a thinking gesture. "What, because you plan to make a decision to preserve a sub-alpha's power, rather than decreasing it? Dumbasses." She shook her head before Silver could correct her. "No, I know. With those kind of power games, it doesn't matter what decision you make, just that they can get others to agree you were wrong."

"And people will have plenty of emotion about this issue to blind them." Silver looked up into the sky, where the Lady might be, were they not in the den, were the sun not glaring away Her light. "But I am not—we are not—going to lose the packs over this. If I have to set my teeth in each of the sub-alphas' throats personally."

"Amen," Susan agreed intensely, then ducked her head in vague apology for the human expression. Silver waved it away. She understood the sentiment.

After a beat of thoughtful silence, Susan's head came up. "Is Craig the father?" She snorted in amusement at Silver's surprised nod. "It just makes sense. He's worried about his child, but as the father he feels like he can't control any of that, so he's clamping down in the only way he sees to keep the baby safe. He's wrong, of course, but I can see why he's doing it."

Silver nodded slowly. She could see that now too. But understanding Craig's motives was useful only if the insight allowed her to change them. "My cousin didn't try that with you, did he?"

"John? Nah." Susan laughed and ran her fingers through

her hair. "But I could feel him wrestling the whole time with the urge to wrap me in blankets and carry me around everywhere. Knowing about the shifting thing actually explains a lot in retrospect."

Silver seized Susan's hand as an idea took hold of her mind just as tightly. "You should talk to them. Neither of them has had a child before. You can help reassure Craig with your experiences."

Susan set her other hand on top of Silver's. "But I'm human. I don't shift."

"Humans are fragile. They can lose a child for any number of reasons, can't they?" When Susan opened her mouth to be more precise, Silver squeezed her hand. "Fragile compared to a Were woman, I mean. It doesn't matter what the actual danger is. You can assure him that the emotions are manageable."

Susan laughed, lopsided smile growing. "Manageable, yes. Fun, no. I'll certainly do what I can to reassure him. Anyway"— she squeezed Silver's hand back, then disengaged hers—"for now, we have a meal to organize."

Silver nodded and tried to tease apart her unconscious assumptions for anything else Susan might need to know. "Make something without much meat in it. We want to remind everyone that we're thinking, speaking people, not instinctive fighters feasting on a fresh kill."

Susan huffed another laugh. "And let's hope it works."

Felicia pressed the parking sticker to her window before slamming the car door and waiting for Enrique to swing on his backpack. She didn't know why he couldn't leave it in the car, but when he was ready she grabbed his hand to tug him toward the entrance to the Ballard Locks. High, decorative fences framed both sides of the gate, foliage pressed so thickly against them it was hard to see inside.

Already, the smell of salt water surrounded them, probably noticeable even to humans. Sometimes it was thick and heavy enough to worm annoyingly into her nose, but today the wind was fresh and carried the promise of the distant open ocean.

"I'd take you to the real coast—last time Father and Silver visited Portland, they took me along to Cannon Beach, and the Northwest coast is very different from the American beaches they usually show on TV—but we'd have to drive all the way out on the Olympic Peninsula. Puget Sound isn't bad." Felicia realized she was babbling and cut herself off. It didn't matter if Enrique liked this particular place or not. He wanted to see the sights, and she was showing them to him. And her impulse to prove how much better North America was than Madrid was stupid. She didn't have to justify her decision to stay to anyone.

Enrique took a measured look both ways along the train tracks bisecting the Locks' parking lot and then stepped down between the rails. "*Smells salty to me.*"

Felicia balanced a foot on each rail in turn and then jumped to the concrete curb on the other side. "Well, Puget Sound *is* ocean, it's just protected by the peninsula—" Felicia tried to draw a map in the air and gave up after a moment. Inside the park, she hurried him through the boring landscaped neatness of the gardens to the locks themselves. Walkways lined the tops of the system of concrete and wood walls and gates, pedestrian as well as boat access changeable as gates opened or shut. Algae lined the inner surfaces in green and brown.

No boats were coming through at the moment, but once they crossed a couple gates, they reached the spillway on the other side. Even on such a small one, the water cascaded out beneath concrete arches with impressive white fury. Felicia pointed everything out, shouting over the roar of the water. Enrique listened patiently without saying much.

He finally perked up when the spillway ended and they turned down concrete stairs to a tiny enclosed fish ladder. The water was murky, but the dark shadows of several salmon shimmered occasionally. Enrique went down to stand with his nose practically touching the window. "Kind of scrawny." Fish dismissed, he glanced at a father and his two children. The girl bounced at the window while the boy slept in a stroller. Felicia supposed that Enrique had chosen English to avoid catching their attention. Not that a little Spanish would stand out around here, but she understood the impulse. You had to hide so many Were things, the instinct was ingrained.

"I'm pretty sure you'll get arrested if you try to catch one." Felicia smacked Enrique on the shoulder. They left the ladder to the girl, now running along the windows to count every fish.

Outside, Enrique seemed inclined to just watch the water for a while, so they climbed up to the open area on top of the fish ladder and skirted a metal curled tentacle sort of sculpture to lean on the railing together. He settled a hand loosely over her back, and when he didn't push any further, Felicia let him keep it there. It was comfortable, standing that way.

"So you really do like it here?" Enrique said at length. They stood far enough behind the spillway that they could hear each other, but the risk of anyone else overhearing was very low.

"I do." Felicia lifted one hand and set her spread fingertips on the railing. The metal had sucked up warmth from the sunlight though the air temperature was still quite mild. "Even when Father's being so—" She growled. At Enrique's inquiring look, she expanded. "I have to get a job or get kicked out to wander. Roam. You know, what Silver gave you permission for. I guess it's something a lot of the North American kids do before they settle down to a job. But they don't have Were companies here, like we did."

"You're supposed to get a job dealing with humans all day?" Enrique's eyebrows went up.

"Everyone else has one! I'm not going to whine like some low ranker about how it's too hard for me." Felicia pressed her lips closed. She'd wanted someone to be sympathetic, so why was she suddenly defending North American customs? "It's not going to kill me, it just jumped me from downwind." She'd applied to a dozen places already. No interviews, but Susan said that sometimes took quite awhile. All she needed was for someone to call her back and then hire her before her father got home. That would show him.

Enrique nodded. Felicia got the infuriating impression that he was agreeing that it was important to her, not that she was actually right. "I have something for you, since you're staying," he said and stepped away from her to swing his pack around to hang in front of his body. He rummaged around and pulled out a white stuffed canine of indeterminate species, rather gray and floppy by now.

"Blanca!" Excitement made Felicia's heart loud in her ears

as she accepted her childhood puppy and buried her face in it. It was stupid, but she'd always felt like she could catch the memory of her mother's scent in it, inhaling deeply in the darkness of the most lonely nights as a child.

And now it smelled wrong. Like dust and Enrique, layered over the particular "dead" smell of possessions without owners to infuse them with their scent. Even without the hint of her mother's scent, it should have smelled intimately of Felicia herself. Felicia clutched it to her chest as tears pricked in her eyes.

"What's wrong?" Enrique tried to take the puppy back so he could check it over, but Felicia jerked away.

Felicia sniffed back moisture and tried to decide whether to admit the real reason she was upset. It slipped out anyway. *"It doesn't smell like Mama."* Something about saying it out loud connected things in her mind with a disconcerting feeling of them snapping into place. "But it never should have in the first place. I had a Blanca before Mama died, but it should have burned with her and everything else in the house." The words came out breathy and too quick.

Felicia held out the puppy at arm's length. Was this Blanca a lie? She reached back to her memories, but she'd been three when she and her father returned to find their house burning with her mother inside. She remembered terror and the smell of smoke, but if her toy had been one way before and another after, she couldn't tell.

"Weren't you staying with your uncle when it happened? You would have had Blanca with you." Enrique gently pushed Felicia's hands so she cradled the puppy against her chest again, then looped his arms at the small of her back.

Felicia bowed her head over the toy between them as she focused all her attention on what her nose was telling her. That had been a lie her family told her, to cast guilt on her father for not running inside to try to rescue her mother. She trusted her father now, and he'd told her that he'd stayed clear because she'd been with him, been in his arms. He'd chosen to take care of her rather than throw himself away in a hopeless rescue attempt. The question was, was Enrique repeating a lie others had told him, because he didn't know any better? Or was he part of the conspiracy to taint her father in her eyes? "You know that's not true," she said and then drew in a deep breath.

Enrique's scent soured with guilt. He knew what he'd said was a lie, Felicia was sure of it.

"Lady," Felicia hissed. She tore out of his arms and stomped away.

"Wait!" Enrique's stride was longer, so it took him fewer steps to eat up the distance to put a hand on her arm. *"Yes, I heard everyone talking about your father's version of events when they came home from the Convocation without you three years ago. But I don't want to spoil your puppy for you, Felicia."* That all tumbled out in one breath, and he only paused to draw a new one when she didn't go any farther. *"I think—I'm not sure, I was only five or six—but I think they wrapped the new one in a forgotten coat of your mother's every night to try to make it smell right."* He gave an awkward huff of laughter. *"I didn't see why you should get so much attention, but then you were so sad, it broke my voice even then."* He reached out and petted Felicia's hair.

Felicia allowed it for a few moments, turning the idea over

in her mind. She hadn't imagined it, then. Blanca really had carried her mother's scent and thus a small part of her. Not a lie. She was embarrassed by how much that cheered her. She knocked away Enrique's hand. "I'd have been much less sad if they hadn't thrown my father out soon after, so I lost both parents."

Enrique's expression darkened and he slipped his knocked-away hand into his pocket with exaggerated care. "He killed seven Barcelona Were after they surrendered. Madrid was right to revoke permission for him to stay in our territory."

"And they killed Mama! You think he lives a single day without thinking about that mistake? I've lived with him for three years, Enrique." Felicia balled up the hand not holding Blanca. "It . . . *drives* him in a way I'm not sure I even fully understand, but it makes him a far more honorable man than Madrid—either the former one who kicked my father out, or the current one who decided to use me as a pawn in his territory-expansion games."

"That's not what Madrid meant." Enrique's scent was such a mixture of annoyance and guilt and concern by then that Felicia couldn't separate out what applied to his current statement.

The two of them were fast running out of path in the park before it turned into a regular city sidewalk at the top of a flight of stairs. Felicia considered continuing, but back across the locks was the only path over the water to their car without traveling far out of their way to the next bridge. She turned and stalked back the way they'd come. Enrique followed. "Oh, so when he told me all about how terrible my father was, and then brought me along to snarl in his face and distract him at a crucial moment, that wasn't a calculated strategy? It wasn't a strategy, that moment was when he was about to unite North America so they were strong enough they might be a threat to European packs? It was all just coincidence?"

"But you chose to stay," Enrique said with amusement sharp on his face. "Whatever Madrid's motives, I'm sure he didn't expect that." He kept his pace slow, and Felicia finally slowed too so as to not leave him completely behind. "Can I ask why?"

The change in Felicia's pace made it a little easier to think. "Why I stayed?" She didn't wait for his confirmation. "Because Father wasn't lying. He loved me. No one could have saved Mama, and he stayed out of the fire to hold me."

"How do you know?" Enrique's tone was gentle, not challenging, so Felicia only growled instead of punching him.

"Because his actions matched. Like Silver says, it's easier to lie with words than actions. People just . . . follow him. They also believe he doesn't lie." Felicia sorted out Blanca's legs as they crossed over the locks so she could cradle it like a real puppy. "I'm not coming back, Enrique."

"I know." Enrique patted Blanca's head. "If I end up back there anytime soon, I can pack and mail the rest of your stuff."

Felicia snorted. "All my clothes are from when I was fifteen. I don't think they'd fit, even if I wanted to wear them." She looked down at herself. She wasn't sure, but she thought she'd lost some puppy fat since she'd moved to North America. "My jewelry, though . . ." Her jewelry was all recent stuff without too much meaning—anything she might have inherited from her mother had burned with her—but Felicia was curious what Enrique would do. Would he get it for her? She wouldn't actually mind having the pieces that were gifts from her uncle and Madrid.

"Of course." When she hesitated in the gardens, Enrique held out his arm to invite her in the direction of the car. "C'mon, I have an idea for what to do next."

"What?" Felicia pulled out her keys as they crossed the tracks. "In human, or in wolf? You don't want to go to the Space Needle, do you? There are other things in Seattle, you know." She shook her head. "I was going to try to get at least one more application out today, anyway. Maybe you should keep going on your own."

"And if you don't send it today, you'll miss a deadline? Come on, you need a break. Ever been drunk?" Enrique grinned at her over the top of the car, showing enough teeth for it to be a challenge. It took Felicia powerfully back to when they were kids, just after their Lady ceremonies. He'd grinned like that before daring her to outrun him, or catch the rabbit before him, or dart over the border with Barcelona's territory farther than him.

Felicia narrowed her eyes at him. What was he up to now? "It's too much of a pain in the ass for a werewolf to get drunk. We metabolize it too fast. Why bother? I've been buzzed, sure, but—"

"That's true if you try to get drunk on *wine*. There are other ways." Enrique laughed. "I'll show you. Trust me."

Felicia pulled out her phone to check the clock. She supposed that application could wait until tomorrow morning. Besides, she'd lied to get a chance to spend time with Enrique, so she shouldn't waste it. "Why not? Try anything once." It piqued her curiosity, anyway. Humans made so much of drinking, and all she'd ever gotten out of it was a little warmth and light-headedness. She got in and tucked Blanca away in the center compartment between the seats before starting the car.

At the store, Felicia accepted the large bottle he handed to her and read the label while he considered his own choice, frowning deeply over all the American brands. *Citrus vodka.* Enrique tapped the cap as he passed. "I think you'll like it. Better for a first-timer than straight whiskey." He selected his own bottle and headed for the cash register.

Felicia grabbed at his arm as she remembered something. "Do you have ID? Mine says my real age, so they won't sell it to me."

Enrique stopped and frowned at her. "You're eighteen, aren't you? My math isn't that wrong."

"It's twenty-one in America." Felicia laughed at Enrique's wince, because of course he'd heard that before, she guessed. The United States caught her in weird ways every so often, even now.

Enrique dug out a driver's license and handed it over. She examined it carefully and held it up to the light. "New Mexico?"

"It's what they offered me." Enrique shrugged. "I know it's not as nice as yours probably is, but it has worked so far." He took it back and held it with two fingers in the same hand as the bottle. "You are lucky *I'm* twenty-one."

The clerk glanced at his license only long enough to match the picture with his face and check the date. They waited to open the bottles until Felicia drove them back over the lake to the east side. Apparently being drunk was more fun when you could shift if you wanted, and they'd planned to end up in wolf eventually anyway. She was most familiar with which parks would be empty enough for that near the house. She considered taking him to the pack's hunting lands, but that was still too connected in her mind to what happened to Tom.

She pulled off the road at the park she'd chosen as the sun grew low in the sky. She took her bottle and leaned against the trunk of the car to watch the sunset. The road formed a gap in the tall trees wide enough for them to get a good view. Even in summer, cloudless skies were worth appreciating. Enrique joined her in leaning, posture gorgeous and confident.

Felicia sipped from her bottle and coughed. "That's *strong*," she said. It did sort of taste citrusy, but wow.

"*That's the point.*" Enrique relaxed into Spanish. "*You don't get drunk if it's not strong enough. C'mon, drink up.*" He tapped the bottom of her bottle and hovered his hand nearby until she lifted it for another swig. This time, she was expecting it, so it went down a little smoother.

By the time Felicia got halfway through the bottle, everything was warm, delightful, and hilarious. She returned the favor by pestering Enrique until his bottle was similarly low. He got more and more relaxed, rather than silly like her. Felicia laughed at the way he oozed deep into his lounge against the car, then tucked herself against his side. She didn't care if she was being silly. This was fun.

"*So is Silver really as crazy as all the rumors say she is?*" Enrique asked. He settled his bottle against his chest and looked up at the Lady's face, comfortable.

"*She's not crazy! Well, she is. But it's this weird not-crazy kind of crazy.*" Felicia gestured with her bottle and made it slosh. She giggled. She'd spill it if she wasn't careful. "*When she's at home or somewhere familiar, you'd never be able to tell. And she gets really uncomfortable when she's somewhere new or complicated, but she's still supercreepy. It's like she can't see the world, but she can see people extra well. You can't get away with anything. Seriously.*"

"*But she can't really fight, can she? I noticed she didn't use one arm, even though Madrid said she did at the Convocation.*"

Felicia grinned, thinking back to when she'd watched Silver do that. "*She can move her fingers, if she wants to. That's what she did when she held that silver chain on the former Roanoke.*" Felicia curled her own fingers halfway to her palm to illustrate. "*She can't shift. But you're underestimating her if you think she can't fight just because she can't shift. She's got creepiness on her side.*" Felicia giggled again. "*Never underestimate the power of the creepy.*"

"*So creepiness makes her the mate of the alpha of all North America?*" Enrique shook his head. "*I don't even understand how that works. How does one alpha control that many people?*"

"*Two.*" Felicia held up two fingers and her bottle sloshed around more as her grip loosened. She switched to holding them up on her other hand and tipped the bottle up to drink. "*Two alphas. And the sub-alphas are the key thing. Papa and Silver don't have to keep track of every single Were themselves, they just make sure that all the sub-alphas do. It works pretty well, actually. Papa's good at it.*" Felicia frowned. "*Even if he's infuriating.*"

"*You just called him Papa,*" Enrique noted. He looked up at the moon again, so Felicia couldn't tell if he was teasing her

for being too old to call her father Daddy, or if he was confused by it. She was a little confused by it herself. It had just
slipped out. She'd better not ever let her father hear her say it,
though. He was too infuriating for that.

"So?" she said to Enrique, trying to sound nonchalant. "I'm
drunk." She grinned at him. "I don't know even half of what I'm
saying right now."

"So I guess you get along with him, then? Even when he makes
you get a job or go roaming?"

Felicia kicked at a rock, part of the gravel they must have
put under the road surface. "I think everyone expects me to
roam. I don't really want to go to a stupid job all day all the
time, no, but it's not like I want to travel around with everyone
snarling at me because I'm some evil European, either. I earned
my place in this pack. I want to stay."

Enrique reached over and tilted her head so he could kiss
her hair. "You're not evil. North Americans are just rabbits."

Felicia shoved his shoulder, and he shoved back, developing
into a brief tussle like they were children again. She was no
rabbit. She stole a swig from his bottle and he pulled it back
out of reach. She liked the taste of hers better anyway.

The talk of Europeans made a question that had been nib-
bling at her float back to the surface. "Are you seriously here
because you think you can talk me into coming home, Enrique?
Tell me the truth."

"The truth? Can you keep a secret?" Enrique waited while
Felicia pressed her thumb to her forehead as a promise on the
Lady, then swigged from his bottle and sighed. "All right. Yes,
I want you to come home, but not just because everyone misses

you. Madrid has made some decisions I don't agree with. I think he'll listen to me and maybe change course if I prove myself by bringing you back. And he'll listen to you, if you support me."

Felicia twisted to face Enrique and wished she hadn't. Better not to move too quickly right now. *"Decisions?"* Anger bubbled up that Enrique thought she'd support him just like that, but it did depend on what kind of bad decisions her former alpha was making. She nodded to show she'd hear him out at least.

"I know I said it wasn't bad for most of us at home, but it was enough to drive me mad. One of the fighters is always there, always watching you. I can take care of myself, I should be one of the fighters, but there's no room for advancement with everyone always in the city, never out on patrol. Some of the families with young kids even joined Barcelona to keep them safe, so there are fewer people to protect too. We need to take the fight to Barcelona, not keep letting them bully us, but Madrid won't hear of it."

Felicia took Enrique's hand when she smelled his old, soured anger, even over the alcohol. *"How badly were you hurt when you tried to take the fight to them all on your own?"* Enrique was more than old enough to be the protector, not the protected, unless he'd gone and done something stupid. His wordless growl was enough to confirm her guess. *"You really think I'm going to help you do that again?"*

Enrique jerked his shoulders in a shrug and pulled his hand away. *"It doesn't have to be a head-on attack. Just something besides hiding in the city."* He held his bottle against his chest, as if to shield himself from her wrath. *"I want you there be-*

cause you're you, though. Not just for that. You're not angry, are you?" Enrique glared down at his bottle, as if it was the one that had just spilled the secret.

Was she angry? Felicia cradled her bottle more contemplatively. Thinking in straight lines took concentration at the moment. She was sure she had the truth now, at least. And she knew she didn't want to support Enrique in that fight, or even send him back to it alone.

But he was here now. She'd liked North American life when she got to know it. If he stayed for a while, maybe he'd start to come around to appreciating North America too, especially if she gave him a shove or two. Life back home in Madrid sounded like shit, so why shouldn't he settle here? She'd show him all the good things about North America that she'd discovered. And if he stayed, he'd be around to commiserate about the North American idiosyncrasies that no one else saw.

Meanwhile, she needed to be subtle about her real motives. *Wait quietly enough, for long enough, and your prey will walk right by,* Madrid had often told her when he was teaching her to hunt. It had seemed a stupid strategy at the time. Only later had she grown enough to see the less literal meanings.

"I'm not angry with you. It's not going to work, but I'm not going to tell on you or anything." Felicia paused, maybe a little extra long, as she considered that. That sounded pretty good. No hint of her ulterior motive. She wagged a finger in his face. *"Don't think you can wear me down, though!"* Hopefully he'd think just that and stick around so she could do it to him instead. She toasted him with her bottle and tossed back some generous swallows to celebrate her decision.

Enrique pushed away from the car, relief showing clear in his expression and scent. *"Enough talking, anyway. Let's go run."*

Balancing to get undressed was a little difficult, but Felicia found a tree to lean against and managed it. They had to be well into the trees anyway, to avoid the risk of being seen from the road or parking lot. She took one last swallow from her bottle and then nestled it carefully on top of the pile of her clothes.

Enrique had already shifted, and he trotted over, darkly gray and shadowed to match the evening. Shifting made the alcohol sit badly in Felicia's stomach, but the nausea settled out once she was safely on four feet. She still felt warm and silly. Enrique led the way in an easy lope, and Felicia bumbled after. She couldn't laugh in this form, but she panted in amusement. She'd never actually catch any prey like this.

She wondered what Enrique was thinking. A line of red cedar or hemlock trunk here and a tangle of encroaching blackberry there felt familiar after seeing many like them while living here for three years, and she was in no state to note details. It was home to her, but of course it would be strange to Enrique.

Enrique seemed intent on something, though it wasn't prey, because he ignored several promising trails they crossed. As Felicia's head cleared a little, she realized he was paralleling the road that twisted up the side of the nearest hill. Cars flashed past regularly, the two-lane highway probably providing access to any number of expensive homes buried up in the trees. Enrique paused on the top of a slope down to the ditch flanking the pavement and watched the cars for a while. Most of them came down far too fast, enjoying the speed of the hill and trusting their fancy technology to keep them on the curves. Felicia flumped down beside him, muzzle on her paws. This was boring. What was he doing, counting them?

Without warning, Enrique jogged along the slope until it offered a diagonal trail down to the pavement. He waited, ears pricked, until a car growled around the curve immediately above them. Then, as its headlights swept down onto them, he dashed across the road. Brakes squealed, and the car slewed wildly into the oncoming lane as the driver panicked, but there was no sound of impact.

Felicia felt like her heart stopped. In her imagination, she saw Tom's expression of canine shock as the car zoomed around the bend toward him instead. She hadn't actually seen that moment, but it clawed at her voice anyway.

Over on the other side, Enrique looked fine, of course. When her thoughts started moving again, Felicia realized he'd been gauging the cars' speeds carefully earlier. He'd had this planned to the split second and looked mightily pleased with himself, tongue hanging out as he panted.

The sound of another engine interrupted from above them, and Enrique jerked his head in invitation for her to take her turn at the game. Her father or any other older Were would be Lady-darkened furious that they were showing themselves to humans, but any teen knew that humans saw monsters in the dark all the time. Catch the light on your eyes and run away before they could do more than grasp your size, and no one was hurt.

But she was in no mood to play along. Not this time. Not with Tom's expression in her mind. Besides, the driver who had seen Enrique might turn around and come back. They should get out of here. Felicia headed into the trees, toward her clothes. Enough.

Enrique arrived when she'd shifted back and was frowning at the bottle she'd lifted off her clothes. She'd liked the part of the evening where she'd been drunk better, but that wasn't really just because of the alcohol.

Enrique shifted and came up to kiss the back of her neck, hands on her shoulders. He chuckled. *"They'll be calling the local news right now, screeching about the . . . what would it be here, the chupacabra?"*

Felicia rolled her shoulders to dislodge his touch and swigged from her bottle. "Bigfoot, up here. Well, Bigfoot's dog, maybe." He kissed her again, in the curve between shoulder and neck this time, and she twisted to face him. Now she was starting to feel embarrassed about her strong reaction back there. Enrique hadn't been in any danger, and she wouldn't have been either. She was plenty fast enough to outrun a car she was expecting. "I don't . . . like playing with cars right now, okay?"

"Okay." Enrique said it easily enough, eyes on her face. He touched her bottle, and she took the suggestion, finishing it in a couple gulps. Then he took it away from her, set it down, and kissed her deeply.

It was a great kiss, or maybe the alcohol hit her bloodstream right then, but Felicia tingled all over. She felt vaguely like she'd been more conflicted about Enrique's gorgeousness sober, but her whole body throbbed with the attraction to his scent surrounding her now.

She shoved him against the papery bark of a red cedar trunk and devoured his mouth. Why not? He was hot, and he wanted her. And she bet he wouldn't run away even if her father did show up this minute and forbid him. Not like stupid Tom. Enrique brought his hands up, smoothed her hair, tangled fingers in the waves.

And he didn't try to get away.

Felicia pulled back from the kiss, though not away from her press against his body, and tried muzzily to pin down the instinct that made her hesitate. Playing chase was no fun if the other person just sat there, waiting for it. Was he not actually that interested in her?

Or was he too interested? His scent made it seem like he was so ready for them to have sex that he wasn't bothering with the chasing part. That made Felicia uneasy, though she couldn't really put her finger on why.

Whether or not she knew why, it completely killed her mood. She shook her head and put a hand on his chest to push away from him. "You're not going anywhere, are you? We don't have to do *everything* tonight. Leave something for later."

Enrique growled under his breath, but he turned frustration into humor with a smile after a beat. "If you don't want to scare the humans, what do you want to do, then?"

She tried hard to think, but the alcohol was hitting in earnest. Her thoughts kept flitting away like butterflies. She needed to catch one, and the image of herself snapping her jaws after them made her laugh again. "Let's go dancing!"

Enrique held out his arms, striking a pose from the Were version of flamenco. Felicia shoved his chest. "No, in a club, stupid. Come on!"

Enrique pulled a face. "With humans? I know North Americans are weird, but that's too much."

Felicia shoved him again. "That's what I thought at first too,

but it's actually a lot of fun. You have to at least try it before
you make up your mind." She looked at him with a parody of
an imploring expression that hadn't really worked on anyone
since she was six, and he snorted and nodded. She grinned.
Now, *this* would be fun!

Getting dressed and back to the car took awhile and a little
more alcohol. When she tried to get into the driver's seat,
Enrique chuckled a little worriedly and swung her away. *"No,
none of that. Tell me how to get there."*

"You were drinking too," Felicia said after several moments
of intense thought. It was like those stupid commercials on
TV about drunk-driving accidents, she realized. She'd never
paid attention when she'd thought she couldn't get drunk.

*"And I'm used to it. A drunk werewolf's reaction times are
pretty near a sober human's, but that doesn't help if you make
stupid decisions."* Enrique tweaked her chin and guided her to
the passenger seat. *"Okay, let's go find this club of yours."*

8

When Silver welcomed Portland to her home this time, she dispensed with the formal greeting and motioned her inside. Susan had turned Edmond over to one of the teens to watch for the evening, and she stood close to Silver's shoulder, supportive as any Were beta would be.

"Did you find somewhere comfortable to stay?" Silver asked the question but didn't pay attention to Portland's answer. She watched Craig instead, to read his manner going into this meal. He stood farther back from his alpha than Susan did to Silver, evidence of Portland's displeasure with him, probably expressed at length in private. His confidence remained, however, clear in the prick of his wild self's ears. He'd gone into this expecting that it would be a long, rough chase, Silver was sure. Well, she and Susan would do what they could to guide him off that chase, rather than providing the obstacles he expected.

The sound of someone wanting to speak at a distance

interrupted them once more, making Silver grit her teeth. This time, Susan spoke to whoever it was. "She wants to see the Roanoke?" Susan sighed where a Were would have growled and looked at Silver, eyebrows slightly raised. "Sacramento flew in to see you. Does she have permission?"

"How coincidental." Death grinned. Silver didn't need him to raise her suspicions. One female sub-alpha was dealing with a petition that could loosely be said to bear on her gender, and suddenly the other female sub-alpha shows up?

Silver speared Portland with a look. "You told her about the petition?"

Portland's head and her wild self's tail dropped. "I spoke to her, but only because I wanted her perspective." She brought her head up to bolster the sincerity in her scent. "I never imagined she would decide to come up here. Roanoke, I am so sorry."

Silver hesitated, lips pressed tightly together. She didn't need another dominant personality in this situation, especially one as volatile as Sacramento could be when she thought she needed to defend her position as a female alpha. Silver could readily believe that coming up had entirely been Sacramento's own bad idea.

But that volatility seemed like a reason to keep Sacramento close now she knew about the petition. She could easily polarize the issue and prompt one of the more traditional male alphas to be the first to declare independence, if Silver didn't handle her carefully. Having her close would give Silver the opportunity to channel her away from anything rash. "As long as she's here, I will see her." Silver changed her focus to speak to Susan directly rather than passing a message through her. "Is there time for her to arrive before the meal is ready?"

Susan nodded. "She can just make it. Have her hurry up," she added at a distance to the patroller who had found Sacramento, then dropped her hand. She smiled wanly at Silver. "I'd better make sure they set another place." Susan slipped farther into the den to deal with the food.

Awkward silence reigned over drinks as Silver sat with the others and the meal's components grew slowly into harmony in the scents surrounding them. Silver had intended to use this time to steer the conversation to Susan's experiences, but now she was scrambling for neutral topics. She silently urged the food to cook faster, but of course they couldn't begin until Sacramento arrived anyway.

Now she knew Craig was the father, she wondered how she'd missed it before. Protectiveness oozed from him, and every time Portland moved, his attention snapped back to her, checking and rechecking for new threats.

A knock sounded and Silver pushed herself up. Portland and her beta followed Silver to the front door. Susan opened it and Sacramento strode in, completely ignoring her. "Roanoke," she said, and dropped her head with barely the respect necessary for Silver to not toss her out in the dirt again.

Sacramento was as rigidly controlled in her appearance as ever, perhaps in overreaction to the empty-headed beauty-obsessed part Silver had heard she'd played before she assumed the alphaship in her own name. Her blond hair was pulled too tightly back, making her face stark and hard even at rest. Her wild self snarled and snapped at Craig's.

Her tame self stopped in front of Craig. "I hear you think no woman can be an alpha and also have a child," she said, and caught his eyes to measure their dominance. She was tall enough she hardly had to tilt her head. Craig snarled back.

"Sacramento." Silver closed her fingers onto Sacramento's upper arm, digging fingertips in until bruises formed and healed like little stains under the pressure of her hold. Sacramento had no right to challenge Craig over this, that was usurping Roanoke's authority. "You forget yourself." She tugged downward until Sacramento took the hint and went to one knee.

"Oh, go the rest of the way and cast her out for her presumption." Death laughed. "Might teach her a lesson. Might also turn her against you and your mate's authority. Never know." He shook his ruff until it settled down to look exactly as it had before, bottomless black on black.

"Portland was at fault for mentioning this issue to you." Silver's glance at the other sub-alpha must have been as furious as she felt, because Portland dropped to her knee too. Craig followed, as etiquette required. "When I told her beta to mention it to no one, she was not excepted." Silver focused on Sacramento again. "But you have no right to enter so disrespectfully. Do not compound your fault in this further. It is not your place to speak to Portland's beta about it."

Sacramento dropped her head. "Roanoke." This time, properly respectful. A start, at least.

Death snorted. "And how long will that last?"

Silver set her hand on the back of Sacramento's neck and squeezed, fingers digging in briefly to remind the sub-alpha of her authority. Only then did she allow Sacramento to stand. "You're just in time for the meal."

As Silver led them all in to eat, Sacramento tried to get Portland to hang back for a private word with a touch on the other woman's arm. Portland shook her head, lips thin, and pulled away. She went in with Craig.

When they were seated, Susan arrived with the last dish of food. Silver was too busy watching everyone to appreciate all the scents now matured to deliciousness, but they at least blunted the edge of Sacramento's anger and embarrassment. Silver felt not a drop of sympathy. If Sacramento didn't want her alpha angry at her, she shouldn't have sprinted forward on a chase without considering where it led.

Susan set the dish for Silver to choose her own portion, then lifted it to portion it out for the others. Susan hesitated, and Silver casually angled the first two fingers of the hand resting on the table toward Portland. Portland had held the position of alpha longer, though there was no official difference in rank among the sub-alphas. One had to decide an order at group events *somehow.* Susan gave the two sub-alphas about equal portions without further hesitation.

When Susan settled into her seat and Craig's plate remained empty, he winced but didn't seem truly embarrassed until Sacramento smirked. Craig's wild self snapped at hers, and Silver braced herself to say something, but Portland nudged her plate close to his without hesitation and transferred a generous portion over. Craig subsided.

Portland broke the awkward silence first. "Have you heard from Roanoke Dare about how things are going in Alaska?" Craig's head came up and Portland frowned him down. He wanted to know what Dare thought about his petition, of course, but Silver suspected from her frustration that Portland hadn't intended the question to be about that, so Silver answered it rather than growling at them.

"He's too far to hear calls at the moment," she said. She ate slowly, too distracted to pay attention to the taste. "I assume earning the mother's trust will take time, in any case."

"The mother? I heard he'd gone to Alaska, but not what for." Sacramento said, leaning cautiously forward to see Silver better around Portland.

"One of the pack sired a child without realizing it. Dare has gone up to talk the mother into some solution."

"Or kill her," Death contributed. While everyone ate, he gutted a rabbit of his own with dignified deliberateness.

Silver ignored Death. "So, as I say, he'll need to earn her trust. I don't expect him back soon."

"Lady above, I don't understand why Were men can't refuse a game of chase when it comes to human women," Sacramento grumbled. "They're so awkward when they can't smell what you enjoy."

"Speak up, I don't think I heard you with my human ears," Susan snapped and scraped up a mouthful from her plate with an angry clatter. She glanced guiltily over at Silver, but Silver just leaned back and said nothing, making sure the others saw her do it. Her beta had her permission to answer an insult, and they should be aware of that.

"Not *you*." Sacramento flushed and her wild self pressed its ears flat with embarrassment. "You're not—you're different."

"Nice of you to say so." Susan's tone was thin, but she took her next bite with a composed expression.

"And how would you know what human women are or are not like, Sacramento?" Silver said and raised her eyebrows. Clearly she had experience of her own with them and shouldn't talk. Awkward silence fell to ensnare them once more. Again,

Sacramento had fouled her timing—Silver wanted to give Susan time for her frustration to cool before asking her to be persuasive.

Perhaps Silver would have to begin it, then. Hopefully everyone's bellies were full enough for them to think logically. "Being a sub-alpha is not the same as being an alpha alone, you know," she said, setting her elbow on the table and resting her chin on her knuckles to feign nonchalance she didn't feel. "Portland can always come to me or Dare with any problem at all."

"But will she?" It seemed to Silver that Craig's voice had picked up an extra rumble from the disuse this evening. "She's never been one for appearing weak that way."

"It's not weakness. It's a lack of stupid pride." Silver lifted her shoulder on her bad side. She'd noticed that people reacted the most when her dead arm's muscles failed to move the way their instincts said they should. Sacramento winced. "An alpha is no alpha without his or her pack. And a pack dies out from inbreeding without the neighboring pack. We all need each other. I cannot have cubs, I'm sure everyone is aware of that by now. But I will do anything—anything—to keep another Roanoke cub safe."

"I can't believe you're even bothering to argue with him." Sacramento settled back and crossed her arms, an unyielding expression returning. "If I demanded that you force one of the male sub-alphas to step down for a similarly stupid reason, I bet you'd dismiss me out of hand."

Silver wished she could have put her face in her hand. Why couldn't Sacramento see she was doing more harm than good? "Dismissing anyone without an explanation rarely helps. Do not mistake explaining for arguing." Explaining, as Silver was doing to Sacramento at this very moment, rather than dismissing her.

Silver caught Susan's eye, silently urging the other woman to break in now, rather than give Sacramento time to dig herself deeper. Fortunately, Susan caught her signal. "I don't really think it's that big a deal anyway. Everyone makes jokes about how pregnant women are crazy, and sure, things are a little out of whack, but it's manageable. Especially with support." She lifted her hand as if to indicate the den in general. "You guys have it good with the pack thing. I only got the edge of that, with John, and it still helped enormously."

Sacramento put her hand on Portland's. "Yeah, not just your pack. Anything I can help you with, just ask."

Portland laughed, shaking her head at the seriousness of the offer. She lifted Sacramento's hand and kissed it gallantly. Sacramento's scent flared briefly with attraction, no surprise to anyone, but Portland flushed slightly as her scent did the same in answer. Craig stilled, then looked pointedly away from the two of them, and the moment stretched long enough that even Susan's eyebrows rose slightly.

Just what they needed. Before Silver could start worrying about that particular wrinkle, Portland set Sacramento's hand down and continued on like the moment hadn't happened. "I certainly don't feel crazy yet."

"How about morning sickness? Has that started? Or do Were even get it?" Susan grinned when Portland shook her head and started describing the malady in gleeful detail. Portland seemed happy to have a voice of experience to question, and even Sacramento began to look intrigued, but Craig remained quiet. Hard to tell if the details were having any soothing effect on him at all.

Silver glanced around. Everyone's plates were empty by now, so that seemed like a good excuse to lead into giving them her decision. "Come. We can go sit somewhere more comfortable."

Craig stacked Portland's plate with his own and lifted them both automatically, but Sacramento set hers in front of Susan. Sacramento started to turn back, perhaps to lean in for a low-voiced comment to Portland, but Susan caught her across the knuckles with a spoon with a sharp crack. Sacramento squeaked in shock at the pain. "I'm not your low-ranked servant," Susan said, tightly controlled. Silver suspected it sounded like anger to the others, and while she knew anger definitely played a part, she also knew Susan was controlled because she was fighting against her instincts. The physical aspects of Were culture didn't come easily to her.

"I outrank you, human or not." Sacramento turned back to face Susan squarely.

"Do you? I'd always got the impression that the relationship between the Roanokes' beta and their sub-alphas was something of a gray area that was still being negotiated." Susan lifted her chin.

"The Roanoke beta is in Alaska." Sacramento snorted. "You're just his wife."

"I'm stepping up in my husband's absence. If you have a problem with that, we could fight it out." Susan smiled without warmth. "I'm a good shot, as you may recall."

"All right, enough, both of you." Silver's tone came out more sharply commanding than she'd intended. Susan had used a human weapon to kill the former Sacramento in defense of their pack, but that wasn't something she should be throwing at the current Sacramento. "Susan, go ahead with the others. Sacramento, a word if you please?"

Silver waited until the others were well gone. Silver's patience with the sub-alpha was now officially exhausted. "What crawled into your water supply and died?" she snapped.

Sacramento, who had been watching Portland leave, jerked back to face Silver, tightly tailed hair swinging with the movement. "What?"

Silver gestured sharply at Sacramento. "I have to think that you're possessed of some inkling of the concept of subtlety, however minor. Weren't you playing chase with the last Sacramento, influencing him without his knowledge? I find that hard to reconcile with a Were who thinks the best way to influence her alpha to rule her way is to argue with her and repeatedly insult her beta. Your pack is happy, you're perfectly capable of adult decisions when leading them, so what is it about defending a woman's right to be alpha that makes your mind turn off?"

"I—" Sacramento swallowed, and her head dropped. "Maybe I did overreact when Portland called me. I just . . . this is how it starts, don't you see? Allow men one excuse for getting us out of power, and soon it will be something else, and another thing, until women have no power again."

"Not all men are against you. Not even most." Silver petted Sacramento's hair, as much as she could with it caught up so tightly. "Dare isn't looking to take anything from you. We're with you, both you and Portland, but this needs *finesse*. You have to understand that and stop fighting me. I have no wish to see my power taken away either."

"Well, you don't exactly have to worry about it, at least in this case, do you? No one's going to try to force you out for being pregnant like they're doing to Portland, and they might me someday." Sacramento ran her hand over where Silver's had just been, as if Silver had disturbed wisps that needed smoothing.

"I suppose not." Silver could hardly hear her own words over the pure, shaking rage that bubbled up into her chest. How dare she? How dare Sacramento throw that in her face, imply that she couldn't understand other women's problems because she couldn't have cubs of her own?

The rage pooled deeper, and deeper, until Silver's muscles shook with it, but she held it back from poisoning her voice. "Have you managed to pick a new beta yet, Sacramento?"

Sacramento stared at her, perhaps not yet believing what her nose told her about the change in Silver's body language. "Not yet. Why?"

"I suppose, then, if you don't get out of my sight and my home this instant, I'll have to hand your territory over to Reno." When Sacramento didn't move, Silver raised her voice. "Get out!"

Sacramento continued to stare at her, a little wide-eyed now, then retreated to the entrance with as much dignity as she could muster. Portland and her beta arrived a moment later, attracted by the shouting. Silver tried to wrestle her anger down, to find the tact she'd planned to use, but all of that had deserted her. The best she could manage was an even tone.

"My decision is that Portland will remain alpha unless she gives me another reason to demote her." She gestured to the door.

They left. Silver waited, shaking, letting the rage free into her voice because she didn't need to speak further. Susan approached, and Silver held up her good hand. She didn't want to talk to anyone, *deal* with anyone, she wanted to be alone. She slipped out into the chilling air of the twilight, Death padding at her heels. She would have ordered him away too, but she knew he'd never listen.

Even outside, she was surrounded by humans, too many humans who shouldn't hear her scream frustration to the stars hidden somewhere up behind the remaining sun's light. Silver kept walking until she'd left the majority of the humans behind, her thoughts circling the same paths with each step. How dare Sacramento? How dare she? Eventually, she slowed, and her exertion was not enough to warm her in her thin shirt as true darkness fell. She shivered, and sense began to return.

"Finesse, hm?" Death drew even with her, using her brother's voice. He also borrowed her brother's particular tone of exasperation. *Are you done yet?* "You're a master of irony, at least. Barely a minute after your lecture on subtlety."

Silver scuffed her toes along the ground, kicking up a twig and rolling it along until the bark started to abrade. "Some alpha I am. Dare goes away, and I start falling apart within a month." A crow cawed cheekily at her, and she stopped to glare up at him in the branches above. "You're lucky I have only my human teeth, rude little bird," she told it, and gave a laugh that walked the edge of tears.

"By all means, give up, then," Death said. "Fade back to be-ing the alpha's mate instead of the alpha's equal."

"No!" Silver snapped, and the crow rose in a flurry of wings. "I allowed my anger to get the better of me, yes, but who's to say that it might not have come to this anyway? Craig did not look likely to change his opinion, no matter what I did. Let him tell who he wants, and I'll deal with it. If any of the sub-alphas want to declare independence, they'd have found some other excuse eventually, if not this. Dare and I knew when we united Roanoke that it would be a hard trail to walk, keeping it that way."

Death followed the crow's flight with his head. He didn't say anything, which seemed the only response Silver was likely to get. Her resolution about dealing with Craig steadied her but didn't touch the tight core of her current pain. She knelt beside Death and set her cheek against the soft fur over his shoulder, and he stood steady and let her. "It hurts so much sometimes, to know there will never be a cub that's a little bit of Dare and me. I love him so much, and I think to-gether, we could—" Silver swallowed. "It doesn't usually hurt so badly, but sometimes it jumps up and takes me by the throat."

"You could stop flinching from acting as a mother to Dare's daughter." Death used his more habitual voice now, rumbling low against her ear.

"Easier said than done," Silver murmured and sighed. "But you're right. It's about time to call her home. She doesn't need to be staying out all night with that young man." Silver straight-ened and started the walk back to the den.

9

Felicia had to punch Enrique on the shoulder before he remembered to present his ID at the entrance to the club, even though he'd seen her do it just a moment before. Then it took him forever to realize the bouncer was trying to get him to hold his wrist out to receive the stamp for being legal to drink. It glowed under the black lights as the stream of people carried them toward the dance floor. Beyond it, stairs led up to the balcony level with the bar.

Even at the door, the sound and scents had been a physical pressure, but as they neared the speakers around the dance floor, the atmosphere enveloped them, every sense blanketed with the overwhelming presence of music and sweating humans. Felicia drew in a deep breath and stood still for a few moments, letting it wash into her. Like surrendering to a huge ocean, letting it take her and pull her under, the sound relaxed something knotted deep within her.

Enrique shook her shoulder, pulling her out of it. *"I'm heal-*

ing deafness just standing here, I can feel it," he shouted into her ear. *"I don't know how the humans can stand losing more of their dull senses . . ."* He dropped his hand to put both over his ears, and his breathing grew faster.

"Calm down!" Felicia cupped Enrique's face before leaning close enough to be heard again. *"I don't know how the humans do it either, but you have to let it overwhelm you. When you're hearing and smelling so much you can't hear or smell anything more, then you can stop hearing or smelling at all, and just feel."*

She pulled him onto the dance floor, starting to move as the deep bass seeped into the very voice in her chest. Here, she could forget everything, not think, just feel. Move with the beat, with the music, just one of the huge pack the humans formed, all moving together. Surrender to the pack.

Enrique moved too, but only to glance around with increasing panic. Felicia watched him, certain the beat and the pack mentality would catch him up soon enough, but his eyes started showing white around the edges. She didn't have to tug him off—the moment she started to move toward the edge of the floor, he fled in front of her. When she caught up to him in the clear space—clear compared to the dance floor—below the balcony, she put her hand on his arm and pointed up the stairs. *"Why don't you get a few more drinks in you? Unless you're too scared. Then we could go."* It was a low blow, but Felicia felt Enrique's reaction was a little over the top. Sure, back in Madrid they hadn't done anything like this, but the experience wasn't *that* terrible. Besides, he'd made her just as uncomfortable earlier, dodging cars.

Enrique bared his teeth at her in a humorless smile, showed

his stamp to the bouncer at the bottom of the stairs when prompted, and marched up. Felicia watched the lights wash over the heads of the crowd, making them a screen for the play of the neon colors and flashes and dots and beams. She started moving with the beat again. No need to wait for Enrique to continue dancing.

Her phone vibrated against her hip, and Felicia flipped it open. Good thing it had the vibration on as a default, because she'd never have heard the tone in this place.

SILVER'S ASKING WHERE YOU ARE, the text message from Tom read. Felicia frowned at it for a while. Did she want to tell Silver where she was? It was none of her business—well, that wasn't technically true. It was her business as alpha, if she chose to make it her business. Probably better to tell her. Silver couldn't possibly object to her being at a club, and that way she wouldn't start imagining anything worse. Felicia replied with the name of the club and slipped her phone away again in time to see Enrique coming down the stairs. Finally.

He must have chugged more than one drink, because the smell of alcohol rolled off his breath as he leaned close, hand on her back. He nipped at her ear, her neck, and his hand slipped lower to squeeze her ass. She smacked him. If she hadn't wanted to play chase earlier, she definitely didn't want to be doing it in public, in front of all these humans.

Enrique grinned. *"All right,"* he said. *"Now I'm ready to dance."*

He wasn't very good at dancing. The alcohol had taken the edge off his panic, but he mostly stood and swayed. A significant number of men on the floor were doing the same, however, so Felicia didn't bother him about it. The energy of the group was more than great enough to carry a few swayers along with the rest.

Time stretched and sped or slowed, Felicia couldn't tell. She had no idea how long she and Enrique had been there when Tom appeared out of nowhere. She squeaked embarrassingly when she twisted with the beat and found him right there beside her. Not that anyone could hear her, but it was the principle of the thing.

Felicia had to rely on flashes of Tom's expression under different colors for his mood. She thought she saw frustration at first—no wonder, if Silver had forced him to come out here to find her for no reason—but it faded under the wash of music, the same way her frustrations had. She smiled watching it happen, and he smiled back, even began to move with the music.

Tom had been the one who introduced her to dancing in clubs, and the memory of the pure excitement of that first night and the closeness they'd shared back then, in the early heady weeks of their flirtation, drew her close to him. They danced that way, closer and closer, until Tom suddenly jerked away. This time, she could read his thought easily in his face: he'd remembered her father's orders.

Well, fine. There were other men to dance with here. Felicia turned and hooked her fingers into Enrique's belt loops to draw him in as close as Tom had been. He may not have understood dancing, but he understood grinding, and he slid a hand to the small of her back to hold her to him as they moved. She cupped her hands along the sides of his neck and brushed kisses along the line of his jaw.

It wasn't that Felicia wanted to make Tom jealous. She was

curious what his reaction would be, that was all. He'd given up so easily when her father ordered him, she wondered how strongly he'd felt in the first place. She couldn't tell now, either, because when she turned them with the music so she was looking around Enrique's shoulder, Tom was blank faced. He moved just enough with the music to avoid bumping the elbows and hips of gyrating dancers around him.

Tom waited that way until a change to a less popular song prompted several people to push to the edges of the floor, probably headed for drinks. One of them decided to shove between Felicia and Enrique rather than beside them. The moment she and Enrique were apart, Tom stepped in close enough to be heard. He kept his body angled away like he wanted no chance that they'd touch accidentally. "Silver wants me to take you home."

Several excellent arguments for why Felicia wasn't going to be escorted home like a naughty child occurred to her, but they lost most of their effect when she imagined shouting them in short phrases near his ear. If she was going to talk him out of it, she would probably have to do it outside. She gestured him toward the door. Enrique slung an arm over her shoulder and she shoved it off. It was hard enough to weave through the crowd alone without being tethered to someone else who would get caught on obstacles.

The noise trailed off slowly as they approached the door, but silence as well as cold hit them like a slap when they finally squeezed outside. Felicia shivered and allowed Enrique to keep his arm over her shoulders when he tried the move again.

"*You aren't planning on going back inside, are you?*" Enrique said, voice too loud at first after the noise inside. As he got it down to normal, his tone turned lightly teasing.

A scowl flickered on Tom's face for the first time that night, and it took Felicia several seconds to trace it to the Spanish. Now the shock of the temperature differential had faded, it wasn't actually that cold out here, but she still felt light-headed. That was the annoying thing about drinking: before Enrique had shown her how to do it properly, she usually got maybe fifteen minutes of fun buzz before she dropped back into the light-headed unfun part. She suppressed a laugh as she remembered her earlier solution: drink more.

"I was thinking of going back, yes. The night is young." Felicia drew a breath of Enrique's discomfort in the open air and suddenly felt guilty. She hadn't realized he minded it *that* much. Or had she? She'd been drunker at that point. It still seemed to her the new experience should be good for him, but now her judgment was a little steadier, it didn't seem particularly likely to make him more enamored of North America and the Were culture here. "I suppose we could call the hunt finished for the night, though." At least with Tom around, she wouldn't have to deal with the awkwardness of the playing chase question again.

Enrique turned them both in the direction of the car, but Tom increased his pace to get in front of them. "Unless you're going to tell me someone spilled a drink—several drinks—on you both, you're not driving anywhere. I'll drop him off and take you home, Felicia."

Felicia started to correct Tom, that Enrique hadn't had as

much, he'd been perfectly fine on the way out here, but then she remembered the drinks he'd had upstairs. He might have caught up with her.

"I'll need my pack from her car," Enrique said, so thickly accented he had to repeat it in the face of Tom's blank look. Tom nodded and fell in behind them. Neither of them was the quickest or most steady walker at the moment, so when Tom spotted the car in a lot a block away, he strode ahead and waited there impatiently for them.

When Enrique leaned into the backseat, he rescued not only his pack but his unfinished bottle as well. He made sure the brown paper was pulled right up onto the neck and handed it to Felicia with a grin. She swigged from it as they walked back to where Tom had parked his pickup on the street. The taste wasn't that bad, really.

The pickup had a couple sideways-facing tiny jump seats behind the main seats, and Felicia climbed in back to sit behind the driver without waiting to be asked. Enrique could probably have fit half of himself in one of those seats. She propped her feet on the opposite one and finished off the bottle. That should hopefully take care of the light-headedness. She didn't bother with her seat belt.

"Have you ever been properly drunk?" Felicia thumped her hand on the back of Tom's seat. He just grunted, so she supposed he was concentrating on his driving, but she couldn't see out the windows very well from her angle, so she got bored quickly. She repeated the question to try to get him to talk to her.

"Yes," Tom said shortly. "Not with a random stranger, though."

"He's not—" Felicia put her hand over her mouth. Lady. She'd almost screwed that one up royally. Even if she hadn't already lied to Silver, Enrique should have a clean slate if he decided to stay here, so people needed to get to know him without judging him as an evil European. "—a stranger anymore," she finished after a bit of thought.

"I noticed," Tom said, dryly.

Enrique choked on a swallowed laugh. "Stop here?" he asked, enunciating each word carefully to avoid an accent. He pointed somewhere Felicia couldn't see. Tom pulled off into a parking lot and Enrique jumped out with his pack. He folded the seat down and offered her a hand in invitation. Felicia didn't even really think about it before climbing out. Home was boring. Enrique looked like he had another idea for more interesting things to do.

She wasn't sure what things they could be, though, since Enrique had directed Tom to one of the polite parks with lots of picnic tables and open space underneath scattered trees rather than proper underbrush with animals to hunt. In the darkness, it smelled primarily of charcoal smoke from a grill between two tables, now cold.

"Felicia— " Tom managed to rival her father for pure exasperation in his tone.

"Come on, I can't just go home and stare at the walls now." That sounded whiny without Felicia meaning it to, so she was more careful for the next part. "There's nothing to do at home. You could join us." She steadied herself on the doorframe. "I'm sorry I'm being frustrating, Tom. Just come have a little fun, and you can tell Silver it took you a long time to find us."

"It'll be lots of fun," Enrique said and smiled. Felicia noticed he stood straighter, like he was showing off how much bigger and stronger he was than other men. He reached into his pack. He pulled out a whip, coiled tight for travel, and looped it more loosely for use. Memories of home in Madrid caught her like a hand squeezed around her voice. She knew that whip, nearly as intimately as she knew the one that had been hers. Enrique ran his thumb over the handle, where interlaced strips of leather formed a raised spiraling ridge down the length. It may have looked nice, but it was his fighting weapon, worn and well used with a weighted handle, not one of the ones for fancy tricks. Felicia had borrowed it sometimes to practice with the longer reach. She remembered the feel of that ridge.

Tom stiffened and took a few steps forward as if he couldn't quite believe what he was seeing. "What—"

"Don't worry. Just target practice." Enrique stepped to an overstuffed trash can beside a picnic table at the edge of the gravel parking lot. He rescued a juice and a water bottle, both with some liquid remaining, and set them up on the table. It took him several seconds to balance the heavier one on top of the other without it falling off. Felicia giggled. He wasn't going to be very good when he was this drunk.

Enrique made a big production of rolling his shoulders, bracing his stance, and adjusting his grip on the handle. He cracked the whip a few times. Felicia jumped at the first, a purely reflexive reaction, then snorted. That was showing off, without the skill needed for targeting. Just when Felicia was sure he was too drunk to hit the side of a mountain, he used a sidearm stroke. The whip's tip lashed out and the bottom bottle clattered onto the ground beside the picnic table. The top bottle clumped down onto the table and sat solidly, completely unaware of what had just befallen its friend.

"Even drunk you're unfairly good at this." Felicia stuck out her tongue and Enrique saluted her. This time, when he flipped the whip, he wrapped it around the remaining bottle, tugged it toward himself, and caught it. Felicia clapped.

Tom came out of nowhere and knocked her hands down. She hadn't even seen him move. Lady, this being drunk thing kind of sucked sometimes. "How can you applaud that kind of—" He snarled, pure contempt in the sound. "It's disgusting."

Felicia stared at him. She didn't . . . she didn't understand. "He's knocking bottles around," she said cautiously. And showing off how much manlier he was than Tom, but it wasn't like Felicia was comparing the two of them. She hadn't thought Tom was that insecure.

"Yeah, and you're telling me he doesn't practice bottle tricks to keep his hand in for using it on people?" Tom snarled again.

Enrique laughed and coiled his whip. "Pussy."

"But—" Felicia's voice died in her throat and left her feeling sick. She'd never been as good as Enrique or the older Were, and she was three years out of practice, but she'd been pretty good with the whip herself. Both for tricks and in practice bouts with other people. Madrid had trained her himself, and she still remembered the way he'd laughed the first time she scored him properly, right across the cheek. She'd been so proud, drawing the alpha's blood.

Lady, what would Tom think of her if she admitted that? She took a deep breath and told herself sternly not to be dramatic. She'd been a kid, learning what they told her to learn. Tom would understand that.

"Did you see your father after Madrid caught him at the Convocation?" Tom gestured several jerky slashes across his own chest. "He'd healed all the damage, but he hardly had any shirt left. You could tell what they'd done."

Felicia pressed her lips together. Of course she'd seen what they'd done to her father. That's why she'd sneaked in and set him free. Madrid had said they wanted to talk to him, not that they planned to hurt him like that. But a few quick strikes to defend yourself against an armed enemy, that was completely different from lash upon lash inflicted on someone tied up, as they had done to her father. The whip was the tool, not the method. "It's different—"

Tom cut her off by seizing her shoulder and pulling her aside. "Skill like that with a whip . . . Is he Spanish? I thought you guys were suddenly very close. Has he threatened you so you don't tell anyone?" He clasped her other shoulder too, and Felicia could see in his face that he was building up the story in his mind. "Whatever it is, I can help . . ."

"Well, I don't know what weapons South American packs do or don't use, but he's not from Madrid." Felicia lifted her chin and looked at Tom straight on. She was doing this to help Enrique, and it was none of Tom's business. She'd explain to Tom later about weapons being tools, when he wasn't so wound up.

Tom hesitated a beat, then let his hands slide away. "If you're sure."

"It's not like I'd be unsure about whether I'd known someone since childhood," Felicia snapped. The lie slipped out easily once more, but worse guilt twisted in after it. The alcohol on her breath should keep him from smelling it, but that wasn't the point. She'd lied to Tom. Lied to him for a good cause, but she'd have sworn on the Lady this morning that she would never have lied to him by choice.

Tom shook his head and returned to his truck. "Fine. You can come or you can stay and watch his fancy tricks, but I'm leaving." He slammed his door and started the engine. Felicia took too long trying to decide if it would be better to go with him or give him space to get over his initial disgust at seeing the whip, and by then he'd driven away.

Enrique came up to her with his whip tucked away and pack slung back over his shoulder. He leaned to kiss her hair. *"Don't let him get to you."*

Felicia jabbed an elbow into his stomach. She'd had to lie for him, and why? Because he wanted to show off. If he wanted to play chase so badly, he needed to earn it by being attractive himself, not by trying to make rivals seem less so. If he hadn't brought out his whip in front of Tom, his nationality would never have been in question. Maybe later she'd be ready to give Enrique another chance and go back to convincing him to stay, but right now her head hurt and she was angry with him.

"I'm going home, Enrique." She pulled out her phone. She'd call a Lady-damned cab and be done. If she didn't have enough cash left, she'd put it on the pack credit card.

Enrique waited while she arranged the pickup without touching her, then he offered her an apologetic grimace. "If we go to your car instead, I will be fine for driving by the time we get there," he offered.

Felicia scrubbed her face and calculated the cost in money to get another cab out to the car in the morning, or the cost in disapproval to get someone in the pack to drive her out. Enrique's solution did seem the better one, even if she wasn't very happy with him at the moment. "You can't hang around once we get there. And I don't want to see you again tomorrow, either. If you're going to pull shit like this with my friends, I don't want you around."

"You might want to reconsider." All traces of apology disappeared from Enrique's face, and it took on a blankness that seemed to Felicia to be a reflection of one she'd seen often on Madrid's face. He didn't gloat, but you could sense the emotion below the surface when he let whatever he'd been pretending fall away. "I still need your help with something."

Felicia shivered. Adrenaline flushed through her and pushed the fuzziness back for a few moments. What was this? "Enrique . . ."

He pulled out his phone and found what he wanted with a couple practiced swipes. He turned the screen toward her and smirked. That wasn't a very Madrid expression—but that almost made it worse. Felicia could dismiss the resemblance as her imagination when it was too perfect, but this Madrid as interpreted by Enrique's smugness made too much sense.

The type on the screen was too small for Felicia to read at that distance, but she could see by the arrangement of text that it was an e-mail. She took it and adrenaline left sharp cold in its wake as she read. It was an e-mail from her address to Madrid. It talked about how she didn't fit in, how she was thinking about coming home, about how she missed her friends in Spain. It sounded just like something she'd have said. A niggling at the back of her mind finally broke through her confusion to point out she *had* said that, or nearly that.

Three years ago, when she'd first decided to stay with her father, she had e-mailed one of the other teens in the pack. She hadn't said exactly this—it was all twisted up somehow, reflected wrong like a flawed mirror. But she'd said she missed them. And she didn't feel like she fit in here.

She kept reading and suddenly couldn't breathe. SOMEONE NEEDS TO DO SOMETHING ABOUT SILVER. SHE'S NOT WORTHY TO LEAD. IT WOULD BE EASY ENOUGH. SHE HATES NEW PLACES, THEY CONFUSE AND UPSET HER. AND NOW IS THE TIME, WHILE MY FATHER IS AWAY SO SHE CAN'T LEAN ON HIM.

"I didn't . . . how did you—?" She'd thought panic had cleared her head, but now she still couldn't think right. Felicia clutched at the phone and flicked back up through menus to find that the e-mail she'd read was only the latest of half a dozen apparently from her address. She hadn't sent that e-mail, or any others. She hadn't written anything of the kind, anywhere. She'd only just told Enrique about Silver and new places . . .

In the park before they'd gone running, and then to the club. The club where he'd vanished upstairs for a drink. Had he really been panicked at all, or had that all been an act so he could get time alone to send the information he'd tricked out of her? Send it to—

"Madrid." Felicia returned to the full text of the latest e-mail, tried to match it to her faint memory of her e-mail three years ago. It truly was a work of art, and while she'd never seen anything of any length Madrid had written before, he was artful enough with spoken words. He must have been the one who had created this forgery. "Madrid may have sent you to get me alone, to get . . . material out of me for this stupid forgery, but it won't work!" She was yelling by the end. She shoved at the phone violently back at Enrique's chest. If only smashing it would have destroyed the e-mails. "No one will believe you! Everyone knows Papa's gone. And I must have the original e-mail somewhere, I can show them . . ."

Enrique took the phone away from her and tucked it back into his pocket with exaggerated gentleness. "But you were so helpfully specific about Silver's weaknesses. You told me they were already trying to get rid of you; why would they see this as anything other than a Lady-sent excuse?"

He tried to take her hand, the soothing gesture spoiled by his continuing smirk, and she slapped him away. "Why would I write you guys in English, then, purse dog?" She had the feeling of snapping after a retreating prey's tail, forever just too short, but she had to try.

Enrique raised his eyebrows. "But you did."

Felicia slashed her hand. "Three years ago, yes, I guess I did. But that was because I wanted to prove that even if I was whining about missing home, I was committed to Papa and English and my new home. If I'm your coconspirator, that's stupid."

Enrique pulled his phone out again and reread the screen with pretend deliberation. "I don't know. It sounds awfully bad. Do you think they'll even think about the language? You lied to hide me. Twice." He looked up at her and smiled with too much teeth. "Perhaps your father is desperate to try to keep you, but he's not here."

Felicia pressed shaking hands over her face. She could imagine everyone's reaction. She could imagine it perfectly well. She'd lied, and she *had* told Enrique everything he'd put in the e-mail. And the e-mail sounded like her because it was her words, just twisted.

Felicia's stomach heaved, perhaps more from the alcohol than anything, but she swallowed it down. She needed to think about this later, with a clear head. Maybe a way out would be visible then. Meanwhile—"Why? I know this isn't just revenge, fucking with me to punish me."

Enrique patted her cheek and pulled away before she could bite at him. "We can talk about that tomorrow. I told you, I need your help with something. Don't worry, no one will get hurt, we're just going to change the balance of power a little."

Change the balance of power: translation, get her father and Silver out of it. Felicia could guess that much. She thought about demanding more details, but a headache was gouging painful fingers into her head, and maybe tomorrow she'd see a way out of it and it would all be moot anyway. She let jagged silence fall. Enrique smiled and didn't break it either.

It continued as the cab arrived, as they rode back to the lot and then drove back to the house. When they crossed from the light pollution of downtown Bellevue—business signs, cars' headlights, eternally lit windows—to the comparative darkness of the neighborhood with only soft orange streetlights, the darkness seemed oppressive to Felicia rather than freeing as it usually did.

When they pulled into the driveway, Silver was sitting on the front step. Her white hair shone under the porch light, and her fingers drifted above the concrete beside her, like she was petting something Felicia couldn't see. It was far from the craziest Felicia had seen her act, and tonight she almost could imagine a tangle of shadows hulking there.

Felicia didn't want to talk to anyone right now, not when she had Enrique's leverage tightening around her like a leg trap and a headache pounding behind her eyes, but she especially didn't want to see Silver. She hadn't meant to give Enrique her weaknesses. She'd been just talking. While drunk and stupid. Very, very stupid.

"See you tomorrow," Enrique said brightly as he got out of the car.

Felicia shoved her door open and growled wordlessly in response. She waited until Enrique had collected his bag and headed off into the night before turning to the house to go in and sleep it off in wolf. She felt too Lady-damned sick to deal with any of this right now. Lady grant things would be better in the morning. Please.

Death stood and moved out of the way as Felicia walked carefully up to the den's entrance. She stank of the stuff people drank to relax, or not be themselves for a while, though Silver knew few Were who bothered with it. Maybe with a wild self as well as a tame, it took twice as much to manage not to be them.

Silver's eyes widened—Felicia's wild self held its ears flat and had its tail tucked between its legs. Now under the drink, she smelled something that might have been fear. What had that young man said to her? What had he done? Silver shoved to her feet and went to her immediately. "What's wrong?"

"Silver, don't." Felicia rubbed her temple as if her head pained her. "It's nothing, okay? Everything's fine. I showed the roamer the sights, he and Tom snarled at each other, and now I just want to sleep."

"Roanoke," Silver corrected her absently. She caught Felicia's arm. Everything was not fine, a night-blind, nose-blind human could see that. "Tom was angry when he got back. But was it more than snarling? Did the roamer do something? Did he chase after you said no?" Silver couldn't touch the lump in her pocket with her hand busy, but she knew her silver chain was there by the feeling against her hip. Felicia could defend herself, but Silver and this young man would still have words, if he had begun a chase Felicia didn't invite. Silver metal would help make him listen.

"No!" That didn't smell like a lie, at least. Felicia jerked her arm away and stood stiffer, more challenging. Had Silver imagined the fear earlier? Maybe it had been only guilty anticipation of her alpha's reaction to disobedience. "It's nothing you need to worry about," Felicia said.

"I'm your alpha, and you have work to do. You can't be out playing all night. And when Tom is carrying out my orders, you need to follow them." That slipped out before Silver considered it properly, automatic in response to that challenging stance.

Felicia bowed her head just low enough to be respectful. "Roanoke. I'm sorry for not coming home on time." She stomped into the den.

Silver swallowed a call after her and stood alone outside. Alone but for Death, of course. The distant roar of the humans' rivers had faded for the night, but it never truly left this place, full of dens rather than trees. What did she do now? Would a mother follow Felicia, badger her until she broke down and admitted what had happened? Or would a mother treat Felicia as an adult and figure that if things had gone wrong and needed to be repaired with Tom or anyone else, the young woman could fix them herself?

"You forgot sitting back and letting it get so bad she breaks herself. A broken daughter cannot protest when you pick up the pieces." Death tipped his muzzle up to look at the stars, broken pieces of the Lady's first child, before she made the Were. "Though pieces cannot always be put back together."

"Stop it," Silver said without heat. Death knew her better than to think doing nothing would ever be an option for her. Even waiting was better than doing nothing, because it meant you had a plan ready for when the situation changed, as it inevitably did. Dare would do the right thing, but Dare wasn't here, only her. And she wouldn't do nothing, even if what she did was the wrong thing.

"Get to it, then," Death said and jumped off the step to be about his nightly hunting. He did that while she slept, and Silver took that as a good suggestion. Time to sleep, and she would speak to Felicia again in the morning.

10

Felicia had never been in such pain in her life. She hadn't thought it was so bad when she woke up, just a dull pounding inside her skull, but it didn't *end*. She didn't understand how something so dull and weak could become so terrible. It didn't ease even for a few seconds. She'd been hurt, sometimes quite badly, roughhousing as a child, but that pain faded quickly with healing. She put her paws over her head and muzzle and tried not to think about what the pain was making her stomach do. Why couldn't she just die and get it over with?

She couldn't lie under her bed in misery forever, though. Felicia finally crawled out. When you were injured normally, you were supposed to eat and shift, so she supposed she should force herself to do those things in case they helped. She shifted back to human and pulled on yesterday's underwear and jeans because Susan didn't like it when they walked around nude, even in the house. She made it as far as a bra and decided she didn't care about anything else.

Downstairs in the kitchen, she realized breakfast involved all kinds of work when you showed up after the main meal had already been cooked and cleared away. Despite her stomach's protests, she thought food would help, but what food? Felicia collapsed in a chair at the kitchen table and put her palms over her eyes to block out the indirect sunlight sneaking through the windows. Thank the Lady the kitchen didn't face east. Even seeing hurt.

"Here." Someone set something in front of Felicia. Susan, by the voice and scent. Felicia reluctantly opened her eyes to find a glass of water and a couple brown pills. "I'm not surprised you guys don't have any of your own in the house, and Lord knows I have to buy in bulk for cramps. Take those two, and I can give you more in four hours if you need them."

Felicia stared at the pills, not comprehending. Medicine? She supposed that did make sense for pain, but what good would human medicine do for pain that could defeat Were healing? She gave Susan an incredulous look. The older woman wasn't dressed as formally as she usually was for work, but she still looked self-assured, brown hair subtly and elegantly styled.

"You're not at work?" Felicia wasn't sure of the time, but she knew it was later than that.

"I'm taking a half day. Edmond has a preschool thing later this morning." Susan turned Felicia's palm over, put the pills in, and then directed her mercilessly through the process of swallowing them whole. Felicia did it, because that was easier than not doing it.

Susan nodded once and then sat down in the chair across from her. "Your first hangover, I take it. Your father explained

the Were version to me at one point—the headache is caused
by dehydration, and since you didn't drink any water, your
healing can't do anything about it. Finish that." She nudged
the glass closer. "A couple more during breakfast, and you
should be back to normal."

Felicia glared balefully at Susan and decided that hearing
for too long also hurt. She chugged the water and set the glass
down with a clunk. Susan nodded approvingly and got her
another. "Fun night?" she asked, not bothering to hide the
amused irony in her voice. She sat again, chin on her hand.
"Don't get me wrong, you have my sympathies. I remember
one real fucker of a hangover I had in college, freshman year."

Felicia eyed at Susan. "You don't swear," she protested, and
then winced at herself. That sounded prey-stupid out loud.
But it was true, she'd never even heard Susan use any human
swear words before.

Susan laughed, the bright sound stabbing into the pain at
Felicia's temple. "I'm twenty-eight, puppy. Just because my
impressionable young son is usually around doesn't mean I've
transformed into a prude."

Felicia grumbled under her breath and started drinking
the second glass of water with smaller swallows this time. She
was sort of starting to feel better.

The concern in Susan's face eased, and she petted Felicia's
hair reassuringly after filling the glass for a third time. "When
you missed breakfast, Silver was worried about you, but I told
her to let you sleep. I gather that roamer was trouble after all?"

The easing pain made room for the rest of Felicia's problems
to come crowding back in. She'd lied to protect Enrique, and
now he had e-mails as well to prove to the others that she was

on Madrid's side, helping him to work against her alphas. If Felicia tried to tell her side of the story, say, to Susan right this minute, would anyone believe her?

She doubted it. Everyone had seen the way she'd welcomed Enrique, seen the way she was fighting with her father and Silver.

Susan was waiting for her reaction, so Felicia drew breath without really knowing what her words would be. "It was nothing. Just a wild night and now a hangover, apparently. And boys being boys. I wish Silver would let it go."

Susan raised her eyebrows in an expression of extreme dubiousness. Felicia kept her expression blank. Susan couldn't smell anything on her, and she refused to crack in any other way. Maybe no one would believe her, but that didn't mean Enrique had her cornered before his shotgun. It just meant she'd have to deal with him alone. It didn't matter that he'd been taking lessons from Madrid; he was alone here in North America, and she must be able to outsmart him somehow.

Felicia's stomach growled, and she realized that while she'd been worrying, the last of her physical headache had seeped away. She pushed to her feet. She'd be able to think of a plan to thwart Enrique better if she wasn't hungry. "I'm going to make bacon. Did you eat already?"

Susan snorted and gestured no thanks to the offer. "Oh, to be a Were," she said, watching Felicia get out the pan and meat. Felicia supposed she was referring to how many strips she was squeezing into the pan. Susan never seemed to let herself eat much.

Felicia had expected Susan to go about her business, but the other woman stayed at the table, angled in her chair to watch Felicia cook. "I have a question for you," Susan said when the initial sizzle of the bacon had died down. "I think the vocabulary is a little out of Silver's realm. But it pertains to pack business, so I'll need your word that you'll keep whatever I say private."

Felicia turned around to rest her hip against the counter, holding the spatula idly. There was supposed to be a spoon rest but someone had probably washed it recently and forgot to put it back. "Okay." Susan waited, so apparently Felicia was supposed to be official about it. She pressed her thumb to her forehead. "My word on the Lady."

"Do you know if Portland's bi?"

Felicia waited for the rest of the question, but Susan didn't add anything else to make that make sense. "Buying what?" Susan exhaled on a slight frustrated laugh and Felicia's mind finally caught up with the human slang. "You mean bisexual?"

Susan nodded. "Attracted to both genders."

"To play chase with, or settle as a mate with?" Felicia thought back to the times she'd met Portland. She certainly hadn't heard about the woman having a mate since she was in North America. "I don't think she's the type to mate same, like Sacramento, if that's what you mean."

"Hm." Susan frowned down at the table and tapped her fingers a couple times. "But is she the type to sleep with women normally? Play chase with, I mean. Not literally nap together."

"Why wouldn't she be?" Felicia felt like she was missing three-quarters of this conversation. Was that a human thing? "You're not planning to claim that humans only play chase with people they think they might settle as mates with, are you? Even given how much stuff on TV is made up, I know that's not right."

"Some religions claim that's what we should do," Susan said with a low laugh, and then waved away the comment and Felicia's further confusion. "But no, what I mean is that many people think of themselves as attracted to either the opposite gender, or the same gender, or both. And by attracted, I mean for anything. To fuck, or to settle down with. Either."

Felicia rubbed her temple. Her headache might be gone, but humans were still weird. "But you can decide to play chase with someone for so many reasons. You might have a reason to have sex with all kinds of different people. That's different from the specific kind of person you'd want to settle down with long term." She found a paper towel, laid it on the counter, and started lifting the bacon strips onto it. Once the bacon cooled, she'd hold the towel in her hand so she didn't have to get a plate dirty.

"Huh." Susan thought about that for a while, and then stood to snag half a strip and eat it despite her earlier refusal of the offer. "So that's how Were think about it." She licked her fingers. "Have you ever played chase with a girl, then?"

"Back in Spain." Felicia shrugged. Adela had been her first, because she'd wanted to try out sex with someone she'd have a better chance of understanding. Then she discovered that Adela had blabbed details of her clumsiness to all the other young people in the pack. There hadn't been a second time, even when the teasing died down fairly quickly. She'd realized much later that the others had probably been sympathetic due to embarrassing first times of their own. "Haven't you?"

Susan hesitated a beat, perhaps considering telling Felicia

that it was none of her business—since Susan was higher ranked, that was true, but she could still ask—and then shook her head. "I was never much of a partier in college, in any sense, that party I was talking about earlier being a notable exception. Turned me off the idea."

Felicia chomped through her bacon. She couldn't say she was surprised. Susan had always seemed the kind of person who settled down early, rather than chasing for an extended period. The boring kind of person.

Tom came into the kitchen, an empty mug dangling from his fingers. Felicia started to hold out her paper towel and the last few remaining strips in offer, but Tom walked by without looking at her. He rinsed his mug in the sink and refilled it from the office-size pot of coffee someone always made for everyone in the morning.

"Tom, look . . ." Felicia crammed the last bacon strip into her mouth and dumped the paper towel in the food waste bucket. "About last night—" She couldn't admit that she'd lied to him, couldn't tell him he'd been completely right about Enrique, but at least she could apologize for everything else.

Tom concentrated more than really necessary on not spilling any coffee, and Susan glanced at her watch and left the kitchen, presumably off to the preschool thing. Having made that promising beginning, Felicia stalled out for several moments. "I grew up seeing people use whips, you know."

"I know." Tom turned around and stared down into his coffee, hair falling into his eyes. "It caught me off guard. I don't blame you for it. You're not like that."

"And I know Enrique was showing off to try to needle you." Felicia examined her hands for any remaining bacon grease.

Maybe he'd also meant to lead her into another lie, but he'd smelled a lot like he was posturing like a stupid boy. Her lie was probably just a bonus.

Tom grimaced and sipped his coffee. "After you danced with him."

Felicia's head snapped up. "I didn't mean—" She cut herself off. She had meant to see Tom's reaction, but she hadn't really thought it through beyond that. She hadn't realized Enrique might take it as an invitation to be challenging at Tom. She'd never intended that.

"It's fine. Dance with who you want. I mean, I think that someone who shows off with whip tricks isn't exactly a decent kind of a guy, but what do I know about non–North American standards." Tom shrugged.

Felicia clamped her jaw shut against instant agreement. Never mind not decent, Enrique was a fucking cat, working hard on digging down to Madrid's low level. But she couldn't say that, so she shrugged, as if she disagreed but couldn't articulate a defense.

She thought she'd done pretty well with the gesture, but Tom's attention narrowed to her face. "Where is he from, again?"

"Chile." Felicia hid her reaction to having to renew the lie with movement, sliding her hand down Tom's wrist to clasp his fingers. "I'm someone he can speak Spanish to, that's why we ended up talking so much. I'm sorry, anyway. I was being prey-stupid last night too." She dropped his hand before he could pull it away. "I know, we're keeping things to 'friends.'" Saying that so casually, like she agreed, stung. But she'd needed to raise that issue to distract Tom from his suspicions about

Enrique. She slipped out of the kitchen. She needed to deal with Enrique, and fast. Then she could repair things properly with Tom.

Silver had a morning of relative quiet while Felicia slept late, and Craig undoubtedly howled to everyone he could think of. When the pack drifted out after the chaos of breakfast, Silver claimed the room and sat with the remains of her food and Death, thinking. When she heard Felicia in the next room, she left the young woman to Susan. The need to create a strategy for keeping the packs united was more pressing at the moment.

"I want to avoid arguments if I can." Silver spoke in Death's direction, but he only flicked an ear. Apparently she was on her own in planning this. "Letting them whine at me makes it seem like I might change my mind. But if I dismiss all of them out of hand, that will create resentment."

"Roanoke?" Tom leaned through the doorway. He smelled of frustration again. Perhaps with Felicia. "Do you need me for anything?"

Silver tipped her head to invite him over to sit. "I can use your help for talking at a distance, yes. But first, are you all right? You and Felicia . . ."

Tom pulled out a chair but leaned with his hands on the back rather than sitting. He rolled his shoulders in a gesture more awkward than a shrug. "We're not great." Amusement sparked up suddenly. "She needs to get over herself, you know?"

Silver laughed, as much in relief at Tom having found the

humor in the situation as anything else. "You mean the Lady didn't build the world as a foundation for a young Were's feet?"

Tom ducked his head, pressing his grin down to a smile. "It's not that she's selfish. I mean, I like her. Really like her. She's gorgeous. And wicked smart. But I think coming here at the age she did, and with what everyone says about Europeans, she wants way too much for everyone to *like* her. And then if someone—like that roamer—pays her a lot of attention . . ."

Silver raised her eyebrows. "That's extremely perceptive."

Tom dropped his head even more, embarrassed. "Not really. It's amazing what you can figure out if you shut up and actually listen."

Silver nodded. Tom could take care of himself, clearly. She let silence settle for a beat to mark the change of topic. "As for what I need your help with, I'm sure the sub-alphas will all be asking to speak with me soon. I'd like you to answer, to emphasize how I don't need to defend my decision." She held up a finger. "Except for the troublemakers. Sacramento's here, at least, but I want to talk to Billings or Charleston if either calls." She reviewed their sub-alphas in her mind and added a few more names after consideration.

Tom flopped into the chair. "Are you sure you want to talk to them at all? I know you don't like it when people aren't here in person."

"This isn't about what I like." Silver flattened her palm on the table.

Death flicked another ear. "So you say now. Let's see if your resolve survives all of the sub-alphas." Silver ignored him and went to draw herself a drink.

The first sub-alphas wanted to speak to her before she fin-

ished the last of that drink. Tom spoke to them. Silver sat and
listened with thinned lips and tried not to doubt herself. She'd
decided not to speak to all of them, and that was the end of it.

Susan joined them after the first few conversations. Silver
looked up as the woman arrived, but she shook her head. She
hadn't found out anything more about the roamer. Silver
hadn't really thought she would, but it had been worth trying.
Susan was closer to Felicia's age than Silver was, but she was
mated and a mother, which Silver suspected would put her in
an entirely different category in Felicia's mind.

"Let me," Susan offered, when it came time to answer a call
from the next faraway worried sub-alpha. She held out her
hand to Tom, but it was Silver's turn to shake her head.

Susan frowned, but Silver waved her away more emphatically. "If they can't take the hint when the alpha refuses to
listen to their whining, it won't help to speak to the beta." She
tossed Susan a wan smile. "With two strikes against her. A
woman—"

"And human." Susan smoothed her hair, though it wasn't
out of place, and brushed an errant wolf hair from her thigh.
"All right. I'll see you tonight." She squeezed Silver's shoulder
and slipped out of the room.

"Billings," Tom said a moment later, wincing, and held something out to her. Silver didn't take it yet. She'd told Tom to do
this, but Lady, she didn't want to talk to the man. Nothing for
it, however.

She accepted whatever it was and held it close so the conversation wouldn't carry to others in the house. She closed her
eyes to make talking over such a great distance a little easier.
The lack of smell was still disturbing, but at least she could

ignore the fact she couldn't see him. "You have some issue to bring to your alpha's attention?"

A pause, then: "Roanoke Silver. Yes. I've heard about your recent decision about the petition concerning Portland, and I think perhaps you haven't considered all the implications."

Silver gritted her teeth against the condescension in Billings's voice. He was one of the traditional sub-alphas. He'd held his position for half a century, if she remembered correctly. He liked to cloak his outdated attitudes in politeness, as if any other participants in the argument would realize their childishness and be shamed into accepting his adult wisdom. "On the contrary. I considered them for much longer than I normally would have on a less contentious issue."

Billings didn't interrupt, but he picked up again a beat too quickly, as if he hadn't really listened, just allowed a pause to provide that illusion. "We are not humans, electing leaders. Holding an alphaship is a matter of strength, pure and simple. I would never argue that female Were aren't strong, but their strength is not an alpha's strength. It's the strength to refrain from shifting and carry children to term, and protect them from harm as they grow. I would never challenge a mother for her child, but she's not suited to being an alpha. Especially not at the same time."

The calm of incredulity led the storm of Silver's anger. To hear it said so baldly, so unapologetically—she could hardly process it for a moment. How dared Billings? How *dared* he? Knowing Were thought that was one thing, hearing it said to her face was quite another.

Silver twitched her bad fingers once and the effort needed for even that small movement focused her mind. In some ways, Billings's sheer effrontery also helped her set her emotions to one side. He made no points in gray areas that she might have to allow him, as she had allowed Craig his about Portland's previous child. She could tear the throat out of Billings's argument.

But how? With one of the men who shouted and blustered, as she suspected Charleston would, she would refuse to argue. Instead, she'd reassert her position on the basis of her authority, making it her authority as a whole that he had to accept or reject. Other sub-alphas, she would try to persuade, but she wasn't sure about Billings. Ironic that he would be the one she had to speak to first. It would be foolish to meet his illusion of logic with the unyielding wall of her authority, and she doubted he'd actually listen to any arguments she made to persuade him.

"Why do you insist on framing your thoughts in their terms?" Death asked, exasperation only thinly veiled. "Must a blind Were argue colors?"

Silver froze and opened her eyes to stare at Death. He stared right back. Of course. She should have thought of it herself earlier. "Who is alpha to the Lady, Billings?"

Silence, which Silver let stretch long enough she was sure Billings could have searched his memory for her words even if he hadn't listened to them at first. "What?" he said finally.

"Who is alpha to the Lady? The Lady is a woman, after all. She had the strength to create all Her children—all of *us*— and to lead them too. Death was Her partner once upon a time, Her equal, as much as the one who came before all else can have an equal." Silver paused to give her next words the true bite of teeth to the jugular. "Are you calling Her weak,

Billings? Or are you implying that She loved some of Her children less, that She would deny them part of Her strength? That is not the Lady I know. Perhaps you know another."

Death bared his teeth, sharply pleased, and Silver smiled back as Billings's silence once again stretched. "You should still reconsider. A leader needs to do what's best for her people, or she won't be leader long," he said shortly, and then Silver had the sense that he was no longer within range to hear her in his distant place. His last threat about not following her as alpha had been less veiled than she'd expected. Under the politeness did lie bluster in the end, then. Interesting.

Tom released a huff of breath, some of his habitual bounce returning to his manner. "That'll show him." He grinned at her.

Silver threw him a wan smile in return, even as she shook her head. "It won't be so easy. When he has time to twist it around, he will be back, howling the same song, working himself up to declaring independence. But hopefully he will stop and think for at least a little while."

An unexpected scent assaulted her nose and Silver turned in confusion. It smelled like flowers, but flowers that had died in sweating misery, squeezed to their last drop so humans could smell it over the miasma of unpleasant odors that so often accompanied them.

Felicia tried to slip past the room, shoulders already braced, probably from stares others in the den had given her. She was *wearing* the scent of agonized flowers. Silver couldn't help staring herself. What in the Lady's name did Felicia think she was playing at? Covering over her scent that way might as well have been a snarl in everyone's face. Unconscionably rude. Silver pushed to her feet. Was this in response to her questions last night? If so, it was even more important she continue asking them.

Silver planted herself in the doorway and coughed. Felicia lifted her head, caught Silver's look, and flushed. "I"—she cleared her throat, uncomfortably—"was just going out."

"Smelling like that?" Silver crossed her good arm over her chest. "What are you thinking?" Her voice grew sharper than she'd intended, the edge she would have loved to turn on Billings twisting free.

Tom interrupted her with a diffident touch to her arm. "I'll go take her to wash it off," he offered, head very low. He'd take her aside and explain how lucky she was to escape the alpha's wrath, Silver was sure he meant.

She drew a deep breath to try to read Felicia's emotions underneath, but she only made herself sneeze. Lady-damned flowers. She waved Tom to go ahead. Let him deal with it for now. Clearly, she needed to let her mood calm after dealing with Billings. Tom grabbed Felicia's wrist and towed her away.

Death sneezed too. "I was wrong the other night. The most subtle one around here is clearly her, not you."

Silver rubbed her face. Just what she needed to be doing. Handling a tricky political crisis and a young hormonal mystery while being choked by flowers.

11

Felicia gritted her teeth as Tom pulled her through the living room and into the backyard. Clearly her plan had backfired. It had seemed like a good idea at the time to give herself a little cover for any further worry about the situation with Enrique that might leak into her scent.

Tom rounded on her. "Perfume? Seriously? Where did you even get that? What are you trying to hide? If you're trying to tweak Roanoke Silver's tail, I'd think again. She's got a lot to worry about right now, so she's not going to be as sympathetic to you as usual."

Felicia scrubbed at her cheeks. They felt so hot, they were probably betraying her emotions as much as her scent might have. "I'm not . . . look, there was this winter gift exchange last year at school, I got the stuff and I never remembered to throw it out. I just want people to stay out of my business for a while. I didn't know Silver had something going on, but I don't care

what she does, as long as she doesn't poke her nose in my business."

Felicia brought up her wrist and sniffed where she'd splashed
it. She sneezed violently twice. She hadn't realized this damn
stuff was so strong. Obviously, unscrewing the misting top
had been a mistake. It seemed such a pain in the tail, though,
pressing and pressing for almost no liquid at all. She'd assumed it would diffuse the longer she wore it. No such luck so
far.

"Well, stop fucking around and no one will be worried
about you enough to be in your business," Tom snapped. He
seemed to surprise even himself with his tone's harshness. He
looked at his feet, returning to the puppyish droop he usually
got when upset.

Felicia scrubbed her wrist on the hip of her jeans. She'd
have to shower a second time and start again with the stuff.
Maybe like two molecules of it this time. Calculating perfume
amounts kept her metaphorical voice from tightening up at
Tom's worry, and her from blurting out everything about
Enrique. She really did have a reason for all of this; she just
couldn't tell him.

Lady damn it.

The sound of a car came from close enough someone must
have turned into their driveway. It made a convenient reason
to cut short the conversation, so Felicia raised her eyebrows at
Tom to show her curiosity, then headed into the house. Tom
followed her toward the front door. A knock sounded before
they reached it.

Silver had already opened the door on Portland's beta when

they arrived. "Will you let Portland know we should get going?" he said, a sense of betrayal in his tone and body. Felicia couldn't smell anything over her own perfume, but he hadn't shaved this morning, and the stubble on top of his already square, rugged jaw make him look exhausted and hard. He turned and started for the end of the driveway without waiting for an answer. There was no sign of an extra car, so Felicia assumed he'd taken a cab and now planned to wait at the curb.

"Portland's not here," Silver called after him. "Why would she be?"

The beta jerked to a stop and looked back slowly. "She didn't come back to the room last night, and her phone's off. I assumed she was speaking to you privately and stayed over, but it's past when we planned to leave for the airport. If she's not here—" He cut off and looked in the direction of the main road, like something about one car among the many had caught his attention. Maybe his senses were keener when picking up a vehicle familiar to him, because a moment later a sleek BMW did turn into the side street.

Portland pulled into the driveway and swung out gracefully to her feet. On the passenger side, Sacramento stayed seated. Portland gave her beta an apologetic grimace. "Hey, Craig. Sorry I was late this morning. I promised Allison we'd give her a ride to the airport. Had to pick her up. Got your text, but not in time to save you the trip out here." She said it matter-of-factly and settled the black waves of her hair back over her shoulder. That hair always filled Felicia with envy, since it curled so attractively even after air drying as it undoubtedly had that morning. Portland might have been nonchalant about her excuse, but Felicia didn't need to smell the woman to guess that Sacramento would be freshly out of the shower too, and both of them would have little hints of the other woman's scent all over them.

Craig clenched his hands to what must have been the point of pain and looked from one woman to the other. The way his expression softened from anger when he looked at Sacramento to hurt when he looked at Portland screamed jealousy to Felicia.

Susan's questions abruptly made much more sense. Felicia suspected what Susan had really meant was, "Is Portland really interested in the chase itself, or just in having one right under her beta's nose?" Portland seemed uncomfortable and a little apologetic, but watching Craig, Felicia had a pretty good guess as to which *he* thought it was.

Just like when you danced with Enrique. Seems even stupider from the outside, doesn't it? a little voice in Felicia's head commented. She swallowed to try to loosen the tightness closing around her voice. And that had been something she'd done on her own, not something he'd blackmailed or manipulated her into. She was never doing it again, the Lady as her witness.

Craig stomped over to the passenger side and yanked open the door on Sacramento. "You have no business poking your muzzle into any of this."

Sacramento put out her feet and kicked at Craig when he didn't move back to give her room to stand. He retreated enough for that, no farther. She stood up so she was toe to toe with him and jabbed a finger into his chest. "You misunderstand, beta, who's chaser and chased."

"Not beta anymore." Portland's voice was arctic. She held up her thumb and forefinger close together. "Just another Were who's this close to walking the two hundred miles back home."

Craig looked over Sacramento's shoulder, expression crumpling at the demotion. "Michelle—" he begged, but she shook her head. Craig growled, a rumble beginning deep in his chest and bursting up. "What are you planning to do, join territories with this cat? She can't even manage to keep a competent beta."

"Another thing we have in common, then," Portland threw back, but Sacramento had already seized a handful of Craig's shirt and tilted her head to catch his eyes for a challenge.

"Inside. In wolf. You'll answer for this," she ground out.

"Gladly." Craig stepped aside to allow Sacramento to lead the way, ignoring Portland's order to wait as she strode around the car.

Silver stopped Portland with a hand on her arm before she caught up with the other two. "You can't stop them from following their dominance fight through, now they've made the challenge," she said thinly. "If you didn't want this, you should have thought about it earlier, Portland. For the love of the Lady, how old are all of you?"

Portland looked at the ground. "I just wanted to relax with a friend. It wasn't supposed to be related to any of this—that was the whole point."

Felicia had been so caught up watching—what did the humans call it so aptly?—the train wreck, she had to move aside quickly to avoid getting run into by the challengers. They headed for the living room, which was the obvious choice. It had heavy bookshelves around the edges, but otherwise all

the furniture was movable, leaving a large space without anything to crash into. Felicia had always suspected the blood-
camouflaging dark brown carpet hadn't come with the house
but had been added later. It had certainly cleaned up well after
the few minor dominance fights among the lower ranks she'd
witnessed since she'd been here.

Felicia grabbed one side of a couch and Tom lifted the other
when the drag marks she was making in the carpet became
obvious. Sacramento and Craig began to strip, leaving all the
furniture moving to Felicia and Tom and then other pack
members as people snuck in to see what the excitement was
about. Pierce stepped in to direct the helpers and then push
people back from a large enough space.

Craig shifted a little more quickly, but his emotions had
probably been boiling up all morning, just waiting for an outlet. He was much heavier than Sacramento in wolf. In human,
her challenging attitude, clothes, and hairstyle made her stat-
ure less important, but in wolf her smaller size stood out. She
made enough noise to make up for it, snarling and snapping
at the air, lips pulled far back from her teeth.

Craig didn't bother to growl. He gathered himself and went
straight for her. Sacramento danced neatly out of range of the
snap of his teeth. Craig seemed to have expected as much,
however, as he just lunged at her again. Lunge and dodge, lunge
and dodge.

Portland lifted her hands to her mouth, one in a fist, first
knuckle against her teeth, the other clasped around it. She'd
blanked her face, but Felicia could imagine what was going
through her mind—she was probably urging Sacramento on,
as the more likely of the two to get badly hurt, as if a concerted

effort of thinking would transfer some of Portland's strength to the other woman.

Silver glowered, weight forward like she longed to throw herself between the combatants to stop the challenge. In Spain, the same as here, everyone watched challenge fights in human to remind them not to interfere, but Felicia had never seen the point of that before now. Interfering was something you just *didn't* do, but she could tell Silver longed to.

As the fight dragged on, Felicia noticed that Craig never extended himself very far. He was saving his energy, not blundering all out after his more nimble opponent. Maybe Craig would win after all. That didn't seem right, but then again, who was on the right side of this argument? Craig had been rude to Sacramento, yes, but his alpha and Sacramento had both been thoughtless about how their chase would affect him. But maybe Craig had been thoughtless in whatever had brought them to Silver, Felicia didn't know. It all seemed like a stupid reason to fight.

Sacramento dodged in the wrong direction and Craig's teeth ripped into her shoulder, releasing a gush of blood to mat the fur of her leg before it healed. She gave a canine shriek at the surprise rather than the severity of the wound, and Portland's next breath sounded more like a sob.

Felicia imagined herself standing there, in Portland's place. What if Tom had challenged Enrique, when she'd danced with him right under *his* nose? She stole another quick glance at Portland. She imagined her face would have looked similar.

The shoulder wound healed quickly, but it still disturbed Sacramento's rhythm and seemed to drag at her energy. She

stumbled and Craig got her down on her side. Portland choked
down a curse. Sacramento squirmed away, momentarily re-
covering her earlier speed, but she was flagging, and he was
just plain bigger, heavier, stronger. Enrique wasn't big by the
standards of someone like Craig or John, off with her father
right now, but that wasn't the point. He only had to be heavier
and stronger than Tom if they fought, and Tom was so rangy
in wolf.

An idea was taking hold of Felicia, as much as she tried to
push it away. It was all Silver's fault for making her even consider it. She couldn't interfere, she *couldn't,* yet she had to do
something. And if it looked like an accident, who would ever
know? The combatants would have to stop if they knocked
into a bystander. She rocked slightly on her feet as she watched
the rhythm of the fight. Close to the end now, with more
stumbles from Sacramento, and another rake of Craig's teeth
over her leg.

There. Felicia saw her moment, and she moved around the
side of the room as if looking for a better vantage point just as
Craig body-slammed Sacramento straight for the wall. Sacramento smashed into Felicia on the way there, and everything
was suddenly pain and fuzziness.

The wall. She'd hit the back of her head on the wall and slid
down it, Felicia realized a breath later. The weight on her
eased as Sacramento rolled off over her legs, and Craig's next
bite came right for her face instead of Sacramento's flank.

Felicia yanked her head to the side and Craig tried to change
his angle, but his teeth still grazed her cheek, cutting a line of
pain. Warmth splashed over her jaw and shoulder. It stopped
a moment later, but facial wounds always bled enthusiastically

before they healed. The warmth faded quickly to the chill of wetness all down her shirt.

Craig changed back first, while Sacramento was still scrambling to her feet, panting. "Lady!" He stayed kneeling and swiped his thumb through the blood on Felicia's cheek to check the skin underneath, his expression creased with concern that surprised her, especially with how naturally it sat on his usually dour features.

Felicia pushed his hand away. "I'm fine. Bad timing." That was true too. She'd expected to get knocked over, not slammed into the wall head-first. And bitten.

Craig pushed to his feet. "Probably light-headed from how much you stink, girl." Felicia never would have expected an apology from him, but at least he seemed mostly exasperated rather than angry. Thank the Lady. She wanted to get up and flee the scene as soon as possible, but she definitely was light-headed *now*. Better not to get up when a concussion was healing.

"Idiot," Sacramento snapped after she shifted back. She rolled her shoulder several times, testing the muscles in human. She sounded angrier than Felicia had expected. "Lady-dark European idiot. Is that how they taught you to behave at fights in Spain? Now the challenge is invalid."

"And for good reason. Enough, both of you." Silver caught the combatants' gazes in turn and held each until their heads dropped. "Portland, one of my people will take Sacramento where she needs to go." The combatants gave each other a last poisonous look and then started collecting their clothes. Silver pointed to someone in the crowd, deputizing him to take Sacramento to the airport, Felicia assumed.

Sacramento pulled on her clothes and jammed on her shoes the more quickly of the two and disappeared with her ride. Craig wasn't far behind, but his phone chimed, interrupting him with his second shoe in his hand. Tom's beeped a few moments later. That one Felicia was familiar enough with to identify the sound as a text message.

What now? Felicia wished everyone would leave so she could pick herself up in peace. Fear was trying to sneak tendrils into her thoughts. They wanted to kick her out for being an evil European, as Enrique had said. Felicia squashed the fear. Sacramento had been tossing around "European" as an insult without thinking, same as many North American Were did, that was all.

At least the rest of the pack had slipped away, probably assuming she was in for a chewing out once the text messages had been resolved and the guests were gone. That seemed pretty likely to Felicia too, unfortunately.

Craig finished reading and glared at his screen, so Tom was the one who spoke first. "Roanoke—"

"I did not intend this any more than Michelle did." Craig tipped his phone to Portland. "Though maybe it's only fair."

"The patrol at the airport. Someone else to talk to you— well, to Portland, actually." Tom glanced from one player in the drama to another, wincing. Felicia waited for him to give a name, then realized he wasn't bothering because Silver wouldn't recognize it anyway.

Silver's lips thinned to bloodless white. "And based on past experience, better to have Roanoke as the mediator," she snapped. She pointed into the living room. "Go. Wait somewhere else. Tom will make you comfortable."

Portland leaned close to her beta as they exited. "Who?" she growled, very soft.

"Someone else who can't give advice without showing up," Craig said and clenched his jaw against any further words. Felicia had no doubt Portland would keep at him, but intervening walls muffled anything further from her.

Peace, finally. Except for Silver's steady, disquieting gaze on her where she was still slumped against the wall. Felicia's head felt safe, so she pulled herself up using the windowsill farther on and checked the wall and carpet for blood. Her shirt seemed to have sopped it up, fortunately.

"You're a mess," Silver said, after watching her climb to her feet. She came over and frowned at Felicia's cheek. After Craig's wipe, it was probably one big smear. Silver carefully smoothed her hair aside and Felicia leaned forward slightly to give her better access. Maybe Silver was trying for the silent, disapproving kindness Felicia's father often used to such great effect. Felicia certainly had to swallow an apology. She felt like apologizing for being clumsy was admitting she had been— which she hadn't!—but she didn't want to admit her real reasons either. Lady, she'd actually interfered with a challenge fight. On purpose.

Silver licked away the blood, starting at her hairline and then over her cheek. Felicia drew a shuddering breath. Maybe she should have objected to Silver using a gesture better suited to a child, but she appreciated the sentiment.

Guilt bubbled up about other reasons she didn't deserve Silver's sympathy, but Felicia ruthlessly squashed it again. She'd been tricked by Enrique, but she was going to fix that. Once that was taken care of, the lies would have been harmless ones. Anyway, Silver was her father's mate, and people always kept some secrets from their parents.

Silver stood back and considered Felicia's appearance. She nodded as if satisfied. "Thank you."

Felicia frowned and started pulling off her shirt. Wiping the remaining blood off her shoulder with the clean parts made a good excuse to not look at Silver for a little while longer. "Bad timing," she said, low and probably unconvincing.

"I'd have done the same thing if I could." Silver's gaze angled to the side, and she got her small listening-to-the-air-make-a-joke smile on her lips. "But they're less likely to believe the alpha stumbled than a cub. Neither of those two winning would have improved the situation, so better nobody win." She snorted. "One of the strange truths of leadership."

"Oh." Felicia rubbed the back of her head, though the bump was long healed. She hadn't done it for any reasons nearly as good as that one sounded. She'd just been trying to shut up her guilty conscience about the dominance fight she could have started herself. "Whatever."

"Felicia." Silver hesitated a beat. "That new roamer, if there's anything he's done—"

Why couldn't people stop asking her questions? Then she wouldn't have to lie to them. "He hasn't done anything." She jerked away from Silver. She needed to go shower again and figure out how much of the perfume to use. Now she'd started, she'd probably better continue, or it would seem even stranger to people.

Dammit, it had seemed like a good idea at the time.

———

When she was done with Felicia, Silver sought out Tom and pulled him aside to find out more about the latest visitor. He had no idea, of course, which made Death laugh. Even when he stopped, the dark of his eyes danced against the dark of his fur. Silver considered crying, but in the end she laughed too. "If this continues, I'm going to demand Dare find us a larger den," she told Tom. He probably needed the laugh as well. He had the look of a young person taking on more than was really his fault. As one grew older, it became clearer that the world never provided a straight trail.

Tom jerked his head up to peer at her, as if she was trying to trick him. He seemed to decide yes, it really was a joke, and his until recently habitual grin returned. "Maybe a—" Whatever word he used, Silver didn't understand, but she nodded in agreement. After dealing with all this, perhaps she deserved whatever outrageous thing he'd just suggested. She'd tell Dare to ask Tom about it, when next she spoke to him.

Whenever that was. Silver's worries settled back on her shoulders like she always imagined it must be for dogs pulling things in harness. The weight of pulling everyone else forward always pulled you back. Acting as a mediator was important, but Silver also wanted to know this Were's motives. Was it one of the sub-alphas, who thought to reverse the Roanoke's decision more directly by changing Portland's mind? It would have to be one who knew her well.

At least she could address that question when the Were arrived. Felicia presented a more intractable mystery. Silver padded to where she could hear the running water as Felicia washed up. She closed her eyes and leaned her head against the wall. Soothing water, a gentle sound.

How was she was supposed to know how to treat Felicia, when she wavered from child to adult and back again? Silver was certain Felicia had intended to stop the dominance fight when she made that misstep.

"Or are you certain she did it intentionally because you wanted so much to stop the fight yourself and could not?" Death murmured. His tail slid by her leg as he paced by. She didn't open her eyes.

"Whatever else you accuse her of, you can't include a lack of intelligence," Silver said, keeping her voice low. "A failure to use it when in the grip of strong emotions, yes, but I suspect someday she'll have the same ability to read people her father does. That was well done."

"But does she care for your opinion?" Death snorted.

Silver made a fist and set it very precisely and gently against the wall. "Probably not. But in some things, she doesn't have a choice. I'm her father's mate, and I'm responsible for her at the moment. I'm not going to let her hurt Tom. Or herself."

Death chuckled, long and deep. "When you find a way to keep the young from hurting themselves and those they love, you can become rich teaching it to every parent."

The water trickled off into silence, so Silver straightened. The visitor should be here soon. With her luck lately, the visit would end in screaming, tears, or a bloody fight.

The visitor arrived with her Seattle escort soon after Silver reached the entrance to the den. Her scent seemed familiar, as did her dark hair and strong, round face. When she turned her head to thank her escort and Silver caught her profile, the memory clicked. Silver and Dare had traveled quite a lot when they first united the North American packs, and this woman had been one of the many pack members they met in—Silver had to search hard for the name—Salt Lake City's territory. But she'd not been of any particular rank in the pack, which made this visit even more surprising.

Of course, Silver couldn't remember the woman's name. Names were slippery, people's names especially. She'd left collecting them to Dare in their travels. Silver nodded in acknowledgment when the woman stepped up and dropped her head low. "Roanoke," the woman said, respectful. Silver supposed Portland would know her name, since this woman was here to see her. If Silver was lucky, Portland would use it before it became clear Silver didn't remember.

"I don't mean to intrude, it's just Michelle's pack said she was still out of town, and I wanted to see her as soon as possible. We can—" The woman gestured over her shoulder, clearly offering to meet somewhere else.

Very interesting that she called Portland by her name, not her title, when she wasn't high ranked. "No, come in. Have something to eat." Silver stepped out of the way in invitation. Maybe the food would make things go a little smoother this time.

"Eliza?" Portland stepped into sight from inside the den, surprise and anger stiffening her steps. Craig hung well back. Wise man.

"I thought I smelled—Craig called you? Why in the Lady's name did you come all the way out *here*?" Portland stalked to stand before the other woman, glowering at her.

"I didn't tell her where we were," Craig said, from his safe distance.

"He didn't need to. Of course you'd talk to the Roanoke in

person. But why in name of the Lady's kind mercy did Mother have to find out about this from Salt Lake, who heard it from Billings, who heard it from Lady knows who? Even when someone told me about it directly, why was it your beta, not you?" Eliza crossed her arms. "You tell me that, Shelly."

Portland's lip lifted like she was holding back a snarl at the name. "Find out about what?"

Silver exhaled on a note of dry amusement. Sisters, of course. She should have seen the resemblance before. They were of a height, with the same dark hair and warmly dusky skin, but Eliza was built rounder and more generously. Their wild selves were nearly identical, Eliza's perhaps slightly less red. The way Portland was fighting against a reaction too strong for a simple nickname made Silver think Eliza was the elder. In childhood, the older one would probably have been able to talk circles around the younger, leaving her to fume impotently and creating a pattern that lingered now.

"About the baby." Eliza's expression softened and she held out her arms and pulled Portland into a hug. The younger woman endured it without her muscles yielding an inch. "Lady. We're all happy for you, truly, but why couldn't you tell us?"

"I was waiting to see. No point getting people's hopes up . . ." Portland turned her head away and pulled out of the hug.

Silver could clearly see the expression Portland hid from her sister, hurt fighting with frustration. She went forward and gripped Portland's shoulder, trying to distract the woman before the hurt turned savage.

Too late. "You should know about that," Portland said. Her words thudded into dead, dangerous silence. Death laughed, a baby's burbling laugh, with a different tone from the one he'd used before.

Portland swallowed. "Eliza, I'm sorry . . . but you have to understand, with everyone coming at me about this all at once—"

"Lady!" Eliza shoved Portland and spat the word. "Why do you always have to be so defiant about everything, Shelly? I know Mother can be annoying with how much she wants grandchildren, but only you have to turn it into a big drama, hiding it from us. And Craig said you were refusing to step down as sub-alpha for the good of the child?"

"Enough." Silver left Portland to interpose herself between the sisters. Nothing good could come of anything else said with voices twisted with such emotion. "You've relayed your concern." She gave Eliza an alpha's stare. "Now is the time to give her solitude to think."

Silence stretched, charged. Silver smelled the same from both sisters: pain twisting into anger, not true rage. Pain born from love. She presumed they'd both lost babies and were dealing with it in their individual ways, unable to understand how the other could find healing through a process so different.

Eliza pressed her lips together until they went white. Silver silently begged her to know when to retreat from cornered prey, but she could tell Eliza wouldn't. "But Shelly needs to—"

"She doesn't need to do anything." Silver felt Portland marshaling a retort behind her and held up her hand to forestall the woman. Eliza had a better chance of listening if the explanation came from an outsider, not family.

"Go hunt the void, Eliza. I'm not stepping down!" Portland snarled. "A woman *can* be alpha."

Of course, that strategy required Portland to actually listen to her alpha. Silver twisted to glare her down in turn, which released Eliza.

Eliza stepped around Silver to jab a finger at her sister. "I knew you'd make it some kind of talking point, an *issue*, when it's your baby's life we're talking about. This is about doing what's best for your child. Please." Her tone softened, grew strained. "If *one* of us could just have a baby . . ."

Portland's face crumpled. She whirled away from them both and stormed out of the den. Eliza bit her lip, but her scent spoke of satisfaction with having gotten her point through.

Silver smacked the back of her head, swallowing down enough of her own frustration to keep her voice steady. "Next time your alpha says enough, listen. Step back. You've hurt your sister enough."

Eliza squeaked at the blow and finally seemed to take in her surroundings. She dropped her head low. Silver didn't have time to drive home her point, however, as Craig slipped into the room and tried to follow Portland.

Silver held out her arm to block his path. "No. I know someone who wants to be alone when I see it." She speared Craig with a more direct look. "And I doubt you would be particularly welcomed even if she did want company."

Craig growled under his breath. "I'll wait for her where we stayed the night." He stalked out of the den.

Eliza slipped after him and stopped him with a hand on his arm. "Thank you for bringing this into the open. Michelle can be so stubborn sometimes. She needs someone to bite her in the tail. I knew this alpha thing would never be good for her."

Craig turned an incredulous look on the woman. "I supported her when she challenged for alpha."

Eliza waved that away. "I know how Michelle gets, trust me. I think she's been alpha more than long enough to prove that she can do it, so now she can get on with her life."

Craig's wild self snapped at the air, but his tame remained expressionless. "Ah." He pulled away from her and strode off without further comment. Eliza looked taken aback but left in her own direction a moment later.

Silver stood in the den's entrance for a few moments after they were both out of sight. She should have acted faster to keep Eliza silent, but if a Were was truly set on stupidity, she'd find some way around her alpha's orders to the contrary. Perhaps the conversation would have been even worse if Silver hadn't done as much as she had.

"If you're curious, I'm sure you could find out in the second round," Death said. He stretched and padded into the kitchen.

Silver winced. There wouldn't be a second round, not if she could help it. The longer she kept everyone apart, the longer they'd have to cool down and think about their words again. Hopefully. She followed Death inside.

Some while later, when the sun was past its height, Silver left the den and stood outside at the start of Portland's trail. It began in the same place hers had, when she'd stalked off in anger recently. She'd told the others to leave Portland alone, but her instincts urged her to do otherwise herself, now time had passed.

Death didn't even bother setting his nose to the trail, just stared along it like he could see Portland all the way at its end from where he stood. "It is an alpha's prerogative to inflict her advice on her pack members, even they want to be alone," he said mockingly.

Silver snorted. "Oh, shut up." She followed the trail, as Death had undoubtedly known she would. This time, with Portland's pain to focus on, her voice felt steadier. Her inability to have cubs was immutable. She could deal with it now, or set it aside to come to terms with later. Portland had to sort out her emotions much sooner.

Eventually she found Portland seated, curled around her knees, wild self pressed against her side. Her hair had tumbled down all over her arms and shoulders. The sun had mustered heat by now, and Silver could imagine the delicious warmth her hair's dark color collected and fed to her skin.

"Roanoke," Portland said finally, without looking up. Silver stood in silence and waited to see if more words would come, given space. "When I left the house, I wanted so badly to run. On four feet. It helps me straighten out my thoughts. In the last full, it was different. I knew I'd want to. I expected it. This took me by surprise." She jerked her head up, suddenly fierce. "I wanted to, but I wasn't *tempted*. Not even for a minute. I just thought about how nice it would have been."

Silver nodded. She believed Portland. She knew all about wanting to shift but not letting herself *want* it, lest she hurt herself permanently trying to touch a wild self that was gone.

Portland dropped her head again, reassured, and was silent for another few beats. "My sister and mother always hated that I challenged for alpha. They didn't understand . . . why I would even want to, I guess. They called me defiant a lot."

"A good alpha has to understand how her pack might think, how they might fear responsibility. But those pack members don't have to understand anything; they just have to be as they are. Sometimes they are curious and make an effort to figure it out, but sometimes they don't." Silver settled her bad hand more comfortably in her pocket and then mirrored it with her good. "*They've* never felt the drive to lead, so obviously no one else would."

Portland gave a pained little laugh. When she didn't lift her head again, Silver sat down beside her.

"But maybe this time she's right." Pain and self-doubt had a death grip on each of Portland's words. "Maybe I am making a political issue of my baby's life."

Silver winced and looked up at the sky, bright with clouds like scattered fur, searching for the right words. "May I tell you a story?" Portland didn't answer in words, but her small noise sounded positive, so Silver began.

"Once, after the Lady retired from the world and left Her children alone, there was a Were woman who wished for a child with every tone of her voice. She prayed, and she played chase with many different men, and still she couldn't conceive. The years passed, and where others might have turned to finding joy in the pack's cubs, she refused to give up. Finally it happened. She conceived. She praised the Lady every moment.

"And she lost it at the first full."

Portland tightened her arms and ducked her head lower as if she could block out the very idea. Silver didn't pause, because that wasn't the point of the story. She didn't want to lose Portland there.

"Grief stricken, she ran, away from her pack, away from the Lady she felt had betrayed her. From the deep forest, she heard the cry of a baby, and she followed the wails without quite knowing why. Humans lived nearby, she knew it would be a human child, but still she could not pass without discovering what had made it sound so desolate, as desolate as she felt.

"She found a human man there, weeping silently at the grave of his wife, while their infant cried from hunger. The woman saw the baby and her voice sang with longing. It was not her child, no, but it was a child who needed her. She prayed to the Lady, that She, having given the woman nothing else, would at least give the woman her milk, and She did.

"The woman spun a tale of mischance and a dead family, and offered her services to the man. He accepted gratefully, and the woman made a human life. That life came with a son, and in time she grew close to the human man and so had a lover. She was happy."

Portland lifted her head enough her eyes were visible, dark brown filled with suspicion. She knew how these stories went, just as Silver did.

"For a while, at least. At first, she thought she would not shift at all. But if she had been able to spend each full in human, she might have kept her child. So she told the man of crippling headaches and that she must lock herself alone in a room and not be disturbed for an entire night, or an entire day. She let her wild self pace the room as often as she needed, and that was enough.

"For a while, at least. For years she lived that way, with her son and the human man. She even agreed to become his wife, because the human ritual pleased him. But she missed the trees. She missed running, she missed hunting, she missed feeling more than the packed dirt of a house floor beneath her paws. She began to think: what would it hurt to sneak away and go running in the trees?

"The third full when she ran, her husband found her. He followed her footprints in the snow and watched from downwind as she shifted back. He had such betrayal in his face, it broke her voice.

"He had only his knife with him, but he lifted it so it caught the Lady's light. 'I have no doubt one such as you can run long before I reach you,' he said. 'So run.' Tears streamed down his face, and she ran.

"She ran until she collapsed with grief. What of her son? She had to say good-bye to him, at least. She circled back. Surely she could slip into the house undetected in the darkness, see her son one last time. Or even take him with her. He wasn't Were, but he was her son, and her pack would understand that.

"But another darkness found her first. She looked back and discovered Death following patiently at her heels. She knew what that meant. 'I've made my decision,' she told him. 'You cannot dissuade me by looming there. I would give my life for my son.'

"'And what would your son do with your life? He cannot use it. He does not want it. The only thing he wants is a mother who is not dead,' Death said.

"The woman growled. 'That is not what I mean! I would do anything for him. Anything and everything in the world, until there's nothing left of me.'

"'I know,' Death said and stalked her in silence for a while. 'And if you think that is the way you must raise a child, you should give thanks the Lady never gave you two.'"

Silver let silence settle over them both and turned over small pebbles near her hip with her fingertips. One was so unevenly shaped it could not balance and it rolled back over.

Portland raised her head completely, and Silver felt the intensity of her gaze like the heat of the sunlight. "What happened to her?"

Silver rolled the stubborn pebble back and held it there, wobbling on its tip. "She went back, of course. And the other humans her husband had told killed her."

Portland used her fingers to comb her hair into some sort of order and settle it behind her shoulders. "It's easy to say it's not healthy to subsume yourself for your child, but letting yourself be completely driven by your own wishes is selfishness. Where's the line?"

"That time, the line was when the woman tried to do something so against her fundamental nature she couldn't sustain it." Silver moved to kneel in front of Portland and take her chin in a gentle grip. Stories slipped in and taught from underneath, but sometimes advice had to be direct too. "Only you know what your fundamental nature is."

Portland tipped her head enough to get her chin out of Silver's grip, and she looked to the sky, far away. "If *she'd* stayed true to her fundamental nature, she wouldn't have had a child."

Silver huffed in frustration. "Maybe, maybe not. What was based on lies to herself failed. What is based in truth may also fail—sometimes. But what is based on lies is *sure* to. Seek truth and see what happens. The Lady provides more often than you might think."

Portland didn't answer, but that was understandable. She

needed time to think. Silver returned to her seat beside Portland and this time she leaned against the shorter woman. Together, they listened to the background rushing-water sound of all the humans around them.

"Alli—Sacramento—told me about what she said to you, about being unable to understand because you can't have cubs," Portland said at length. "I'm sorry, Roano—"

Silver murmured a forestalling syllable. This wasn't a conversation to have between alpha and sub-alpha, if they must have it. She supposed it was only fair that they did.

"Silver," Portland finished. "You're usually so at peace with—" She sat up to touch Silver's useless arm, then settled back again. "I think all of us forget."

Silver smiled thinly at the sky. "I need to listen to my own stories. That woman's son was no less her son because she had not carried him in her own body. I'd have a daughter, if only she wanted me." And was that pure selfishness? Silver wondered. Wanting a daughter for herself, rather than wanting Felicia to have a mother only if she wanted it?

Portland huffed a ragged laugh. "I think she'll be an alpha someday. You probably can't remember what it was like growing up, but I remember when I was just reaching my adult dominance. You want something so badly, but you don't understand that it's responsibility and respect you want, or how to earn it. You just *want,* and you keep doing stupid shit, which of course gets you the opposite of more responsibility and respect."

"I think my brother . . . channeled me," Silver said. The memories hovered near the point of causing pain, but she found if she spoke without thinking, the words came anyway. "He got into a lot of trouble when I was younger, but by the time I got restless, he kept suggesting things for me to do."

"Tom could be a good influence on her," Portland suggested.

Silver gave a bark of a laugh. "If she doesn't bowl him right over with the force of her personality. Besides, they're fighting right now. Lady knows exactly why." She rubbed at her temple. Maybe she should be pressing Tom for details instead of Felicia.

"Kids." Portland laughed softly and then looked down at herself and set her hand on her flat stomach.

On an impulse, Silver let her grip on the world everyone else saw slide from her mental fingers. Trees, great and ancient to suit the Lady's world, surrounded her, and the air smelled of the soft brightness of the Lady's light. That brightness concentrated and curled protective tendrils over Portland's belly. Silver set her hand over it too, and the tendrils licked pleasantly at her fingers.

She looked deeper, deeper past the light to the shadows it cast, the mortality of the child. It hardly had a shape of its own, wild or tame, just a spark of life with a spark of wild held within it, as children held their wild selves behind their eyes until it was time for their Lady ceremonies.

"His voice will not be mine soon," Death said, soft. "If you were wondering."

Silver wondered instead why Death was finally telling her what she needed to be able to tell Portland. Usually he avoided such reassurances, but she was not about to argue. "A boy," she told Portland, concentrating again on the tendrils tickling her hand in light of that, as if she could find the sex herself. "Death says he'll be healthy."

Portland half laughed, half gasped in relief, and tears welled in her eyes. She lifted Silver's hand and kissed it, kissed it again, until it had caught a little of the dampness from Portland's cheeks. "Lady, you may be crazy, but I still hope you're right."

"Believe it hard enough, and you'll *make* me right." Death strode into the ancient trees and their shadows, pulling the shining reality of the world with him, leaving Silver with the flatter, more metallic smells of the path she walked between the Lady's world and Dare's, Portland's.

Part of Silver mourned to see it go, but Dare's world held Dare, and her pack, and all those she valued. She stood and offered Portland a hand up. "Let's go try to talk your sister into going home, shall we?"

12

Felicia sniffed her wrists as she walked from where she'd parked her car in the neighborhood by the cupcake shop she'd suggested to Enrique as a place to meet. The perfume was much easier to bear now. She planned to explain it away as meant only for her pack, but she imagined he'd be much more suspicious if it was too strong for any Were to stand wearing.

When he'd suggested—or demanded—the meeting, he'd asked about a bakery, and while she thought it was odd for a shop to specialize so much, she liked the cupcake place's frosting: not too sweet. Not that she planned to pay much attention to the food. The perfume should cover her scent enough that Enrique wouldn't smell her resolve to work against him, and she was almost eager for this meeting. Once she discovered specifically what his plans were, she could start thwarting them.

Enrique met her outside the shop's glass doors, a cupcake

in one hand. He offered it. "I remembered how much you always loved my mother's strawberry jam on your toast."

Felicia's voice tightened momentarily as she accepted the cupcake, vanilla with real strawberry pieces visible in the light pink icing and probably baked into the cake as well. She had loved that jam. She didn't tend to think about that much, or about most of those childhood times. Even three years later she hadn't figured out how to treasure them without them bringing up all the bad things that had made her leave Madrid.

And now Enrique was tainting them further, trying to use them against her. Damn him.

"Don't even try the we-were-cubs-together stuff, cat." Felicia frowned at the cupcake and considered dropping it on the sidewalk. Tantrums wouldn't help, though, and it did smell good. She nibbled the edge.

Enrique snorted and his manner relaxed into something harder and more smug. He held out his arm, inviting her to walk along the sidewalk. He raised his eyebrows as she reluctantly fell into step beside him and he smelled her properly. "It's to keep the others from realizing I'm lying about you." She shoved his shoulder, hard. "So whatever it is you want from me, start talking. Fast." Despite herself, thoughts of jam reminded her of an incident when they were young. It had been apricot jam she'd rubbed into his hair, not strawberry. She wanted to growl. Why? Why did Enrique have to turn out this way, someone who would use their shared past against her?

Enrique hooked a thumb into the top of the hip pocket that showed the shape of his phone, as if she needed the reminder of what he was blackmailing her with. He switched to Span-ish, perhaps for the privacy. *"We're going to get Silver arrested and committed."*

Felicia stumbled a step over a tree-root crack in the side-walk as the implications spread across her mind. She could see that working, all too well. Silver was crazy enough in Were terms; to a human she'd seem absolutely off the deep end. *"And then my father would be so tied up with wresting her out of the clutches of the human psychiatric and justice systems . . ."* Enrique had said his plan wouldn't hurt anyone. Felicia sup-posed this wouldn't, in the narrowest sense, but she could also imagine the emotional toll on everyone. And what if her fa-ther couldn't get Silver out of the system?

Enrique must have seen some of that on her face, if not in her scent, because he exhaled slowly and smelled almost like sympathy. *"Madrid wishes her no particular harm. She's just the best way to get a mass murderer out of power."*

"Don't," Felicia said, sharp. She didn't want to hear his jus-tifications. She was sure Madrid had killed plenty of people in his time, and he didn't regret the deaths the way her father did. *"What's your cunning plan to get her arrested, then?"*

"Madrid left that to my discretion. We"—Enrique smiled over the word, emphasizing it as a correction—*"are going to figure that out now."* He stole a fingerful of frosting from her cupcake and licked it off with a smack.

Felicia imagined smashing the thing into his face, but in-stead she handed it over. She wasn't that hungry, so he could have it if he wanted. He shrugged and demolished the rest in a couple bites. *"If we could kill a human, they'd arrest her in a snap,"* he said, tone low as he thought out loud.

Felicia couldn't stop a rolling growl from escaping. The little pussy claimed to be taking a murderer out of power but would casually discuss murdering humans to accomplish it. Like humans were worth nothing, like they weren't also thinking beings. Maybe before she knew Susan, Felicia would have dismissed humans as being bland and uninteresting, but she'd never have considered them so inconsequential that she'd kill one because it was convenient.

Enrique laughed at her growl, and Felicia wrestled it under control. There were humans around. At least she had an obvious counter for this plan. *"They'd be able to tell she didn't do it. Don't you watch TV? They have computers to sniff for them. No matter how careful you were, you'd leave behind a hair, or a fingerprint, or something, and they'd find you instead."*

Enrique's laughter faded. *"A kidnapping, then. The humans constantly seem to be all bristled up over some stolen child or other. We could steal one and hand it to her."*

"And how do we get her arrested before she retraces the trail and hands it back? Silver's not stupid, Enrique. I can't think of any reason for me to have a human child that she'd believe. Besides, if it's too old, it'll tell the cops about the first person who took it." Felicia started to get into the rhythm of it. Enrique proposed an idea, and she found something wrong with it. She could continue this indefinitely.

Enrique's expression darkened, and he took out his phone and tossed it idly from hand to hand. Felicia pressed her lips shut. Fine. No more tearing down his ideas, then. But there was no way he could coerce her into giving him better ones. Even a purse dog should realize that.

"Territory trespass," Enrique said at length, after sliding the

phone away. It sounded like he was going down a list of Were crimes in his mind, trying to match them to the human equivalents. *"The humans have that, and if she has trouble seeing new places, she wouldn't see the markings."*

Silence fell, and Felicia managed to enjoy the scent of Enrique's mounting frustration. Finally he looked over at her, and she raised her eyebrows. Oh, did he want her opinion now? *"Sure, she'll be in their territory, but she'll be looking confused and fragile, not threatening. She doesn't pitch a fit when she's upset about being dragged somewhere new she doesn't understand, she goes quiet. The whole pack went to a Sounders game once, and she sort of hid against Papa and didn't say anything."*

Enrique waved a dismissive hand. *"Not a sports game. Somewhere private. A human's home. They would call the police if they found a stranger there, no matter how the stranger was acting."* A grin grew as he warmed to the idea. *"If you lay a scent trail for her to follow inside, the humans won't even know it's there. They'll call the police and she'll be too crazy to explain herself."*

Felicia kept up her casual ambling steps down the sidewalk, though something inside of her stilled like at a flashed glimpse of some prey. As far as Enrique knew, Silver would be too crazy to explain herself. But Felicia knew better. She knew Silver could be perfectly sane when she needed to be, and she hadn't let that slip to Enrique yet. Sane explanations wouldn't get her out of an accusation of murder or kidnapping, but they might get her out of having wandered into someone's home.

But Felicia didn't want Enrique to see her jump at the idea. *"Lady, Enrique. You should leave Silver alone. All of this—it's so prey-stupid.*" Hopefully that sounded too heated, like she was retreating in the face of an idea that sounded to her like it would work.

Enrique smiled like he'd taken it that way. He stopped them on the path, under the drooping branches of one of the sidewalk-buckling trees. He turned Felicia to face him, hands on her shoulders. "She won't get hurt," he said again, trying to be gentle. "Look, I hate that I had to force you into this. I really do just want you come home, when our mission for Madrid is done, so things can be how they were." He smoothed a lock of hair behind her ear and Felicia had a split second of intuition that froze her. Surely he wasn't going to—

He kissed her. Her body tried to react once more, but the rest of her emotions washed right over that. She wrenched away. "Damn you," she said, panting, because rage made her want to snarl. "Don't be like Madrid, who tells himself he cares for people even as he manipulates them, hurts them, to accomplish his goals. Threaten me, threaten my relationship with my pack, but don't try to tell yourself or me that you care for me while you're doing it."

Enrique's face had gone a little blank in shock, and Felicia stared at him as she fell silent. He didn't try to touch her again, and gradually her rage ebbed. Did he really care for her, or was all this just another way to control her? She'd decided Madrid had cared for her, despite what he'd done, but that was after three years to think. She didn't know what to think about Enrique now, and the Lady as her witness, she didn't *care* why he was doing it, just that he was.

"Fine." Enrique shrugged. He sidestepped downwind, so she couldn't read his scent. Felicia's stomach wavered with

nausea. Had she gone too far? Would he go and show everyone the forged e-mails now? She mentally cursed herself.
Speaking her mind for a few moments wasn't worth getting
kicked out of the pack forever.

"I'll get a rental car and scout for the right place, then call
you to lay the trail," Enrique said and turned back toward the
shop and whatever bus stop he'd presumably arrived at.
"You're in this deep, Felicia. Remember that."

"I know." Felicia watched him walk away. A surge of relief
that he wasn't going to use the e-mails lasted maybe a second
before she remembered that she'd still have to make sure that
things went according to her plan, and Silver didn't get arrested. Worry settled heavily around her voice.

But deep was where you had to be to do any sabotage.

Silver heard running, bouncing footsteps from halfway across
the den. Tom, with good news, she presumed from the gait.
The rest of the afternoon had been quiet, all the guests
chased out of the den for the moment. Even Felicia had disappeared off somewhere, smelling of flowers that had been
lightly abused rather than tortured. Silver supposed she
should have demanded the young woman show progress
finding work before she let her go, but having her out of the
way was easier at the moment. Death looked bored, as much
as he allowed himself to appear anything so undignified. He
lay across her feet, muzzle down on his paws, only his eyes
moving to follow any action.

Tom bounded into the room. "It's Dare!"

Death laughed and rose smoothly to avoid being jostled off when Silver shoved to her feet. She smiled even though her mate couldn't see it. "Dare?"

"Silver?" Dare's voice came indistinctly, clearly from very far away indeed. Silver frowned to cut through the intervening fuzz of noise. She wished his voice was rich, rich enough she could close her eyes and wrap it around her.

But even indistinct it was much better than nothing. "Lady, it's good to talk to you," she said, laughing awkwardly. She became aware of Tom hovering, unsure whether to go. She gestured him to stay and removed herself instead, striding toward their bedroom.

"And you. I've missed you, Silver. How are things there? Is Felicia behaving herself?" Dare's tone turned wry at the end.

"A better question would be, can you control her all by yourself?" Death said, matching and effortlessly exceeding her pace.

Silver gritted her teeth as she mentally chewed over her answer. She'd told Dare she could handle Felicia, and now he asked to speak to his daughter at the worst possible moment, when all Silver had was questions: about the roamer, about the abused flowers.

And she didn't want to ask for his help, she realized. She wanted to deal with this herself. Even if she told him about the problem, what could he do? He couldn't smell Felicia and answer the mysteries from so far away. Better to avoid the question and talk about one of their other problems. "That's not what's worrying me at the moment. Tom said he could leave messages that you'd hear. Did you get any of those?"

On reaching their bedroom, Silver burrowed into their

shared bed, though Dare's scent had faded over her nights there alone. She pulled the bedding over her and curled around Dare's voice from far away, to help hold back the growl when she thought of Craig.

"No, I—" Dare said several things that Silver didn't follow, but she waited, and he trailed off and started again automatically. "I had to borrow . . . a place to call from. That's why it's taken so long, to find somewhere that won't have three-quarters of the humans in the town hanging around to listen. And why I didn't get the messages."

"Well." Silver exhaled a laugh as considering Dare's situation in light of her own sparked a flash of humor. Not only did everyone have an opinion, they were always desperate to listen in to discover what they should offer an opinion about. She told Dare about the events, beginning with Craig's petition, though she stepped carefully around the parts where Felicia intruded. She couldn't see how to include those without the thread leading to the whole tangled mass.

"Lady above," Dare said as she wound to a close. "If I thought anyone would pay any attention, I'd make a rule about playing chase with betas." He fell silent, and Silver imagined him pinching the bridge of his nose as he did when organizing his thoughts, like the pressure would help push things into line.

Dare blew out a frustrated breath. "And it doesn't look like I'll be home soon. The human woman, she's very young, and she can't afford to raise the baby on her own. I told her I was the child's uncle, and I got her to agree to adopt it in the family. She wants to maintain contact, though, so that means keeping it in Alaska. What's taking so long is knocking heads together until a mated pair agrees to move into a town and stay in human most of the time. I think I'll succeed in the end, but it takes time."

"I'll manage here," Silver said, making her tone slightly more firm that she actually felt. But laying it all out had made her realize that while she didn't have things under control yet, she at least had a direction for her efforts. The Were baby in Alaska was just as important as Portland's, anyway. She'd deal with this to leave Dare free for that. "If you have any tricks for stopping people from questioning your decisions, I'd love to hear them, though."

"All my voice is with your decision, incidentally," Dare said, the rumble of warmth returning to his tone. "I don't want to let that go unsaid. As for dealing with the questions, I think I can actually help with that. The secret is to listen—attentively, seriously—while they whine, for however long they need to whine. Agree whole voiced with every point they make that doesn't directly contradict one of yours, and then remind them reluctantly that however good their points, the other side unfortunately outweighed them. It's exhausting and you'll wonder how people can be so stupid, but they want to be listened to, and they want to be understood, even if you don't rule their way in the end. Let people wear themselves out whining, and then most will go home happy."

Dare sighed. "Only most, however. I'd watch Charleston on something like this, for instance. And Billings."

Silver smiled. "I think I took care of him, at least for the moment. I asked him who was alpha to the Lady."

Dare laughed richly enough to fill the small space she'd cupped around their voices. "Well done. You might remind some others of that as well. I'll yell at Charleston and whoever else I can get hold of before I have to leave here. First, though, is Felicia there?"

Death snorted, the sound muffled by the bedding between them, and Silver winced. She couldn't tell properly without scent, but Dare did not sound entirely convinced that Felicia hadn't been causing trouble. "She's not home," she said. "I'm sorry."

Dare made an acknowledging noise, then fell silent. As if summoned by her earlier thoughts, an errant air current brought a hint of Felicia's flowers. The young woman had killed so many of them, their stench lingered in the den even without her, apparently.

The silence stretched until Silver started to worry. Was he annoyed, did he sense she was hiding something? Or with Dare so far away, had something had come between them, so he could no longer hear her voice? "Dare?"

"I'm here." Dare's voice rumbled a little lower with distraction. "John was asking about talking to his wife, when we're done here." His tone sharpened. "You know, since we're both trapped here with no one much else in human to talk to, John mentioned something. He said it wasn't 'Dare' you asked for after Tom was hurt."

"No, I suppose it wasn't." Silver waited for the worry about being found out to catch at her voice, but with more important things to hide now, trying to save Dare from worry about her overextending herself seemed foolish. "Tom was hurt. Death helped me remember so I could do what I had to."

Silver heard in the tone of Dare's breath that he wanted to apologize for what she'd had to do, but she was glad he refrained.

It was in the past, Tom was all right, and she was all right. "I didn't know you could call your old name and your memories back completely again," he said instead.

"Neither did I." Silver trod too close to the memories, even just remembering having them, and her chest constricted. She had to cough to get her next breath in. "I can't—just because I did it a second time doesn't mean I'll be able to get her back for good or even do it ever again. What if the next time I lose myself completely? Don't ask me to push for it, please." Her voice whined at the end.

"Shhhh, no, love, no. Never." Dare kept murmuring nothing in particular until Silver could breathe properly again, and the memories no longer hovered, waiting to stoop and rend her with their talons. "I'll do anything to make sure you don't have to."

Silver scrubbed at the side of her face not resting against the bed. She didn't want to talk about this anymore. "So what's it like up there? Are you ready to move out and spend your life in wolf?"

Dare growled, low and amused. "I have never been so Lady-darkened bored in my entire life. You can't talk to anyone properly. If you say screw it and go back to human for a while, you're still outside, so it's too damned cold, even for the short time to get dressed. I hate to think what it's like in winter."

"I'm glad you only miss my *conversation*," Silver said, the innuendo coming out even more outrageously with her relief that he was running with the change of subject.

"Oh, I've had plenty of time to make plans for when I get back." Dare told her about them, in detail. Silver laughed and burrowed deeper, as if she could save up his voice for later.

13

Felicia arrived back at the house after the meeting with Enrique to the news that her father had called, and Silver was still on the phone with him. She jogged halfway up the stairs before she thought it through. Did she actually even want to talk to her father? She missed him with a strength that annoyed her to realize, but what about everything she couldn't talk about? Wouldn't it be better to avoid talking to him?

By that time, Felicia's slower steps had carried her to the open master bedroom door. Silver didn't always remember to shut doors. Silver and her father's voices carried, a little muffled like she was under the covers, but Felicia tried not to let the words resolve into meaning. She wasn't here to eavesdrop.

Of course, that was before she heard her own name. After that, she couldn't help but hear the actual words. She just couldn't. And when Silver said she wasn't home, Felicia stopped her hand just before knocking against the doorframe. That was a perfect excuse not to speak to her father, and she really shouldn't ruin it. If she didn't want to talk to her father, which she still wasn't sure about.

And then they started talking about what Silver had done at the vet's office. Felicia froze as all thoughts of interrupting disappeared. Silver couldn't do that again . . . ?

And then before she'd gathered her wits, the conversation turned to things she was desperate not to hear. Felicia put her fingers in her ears and fled. Any longer and she'd have to smash her forehead against the wall until the parts of her brain with the mental images were destroyed.

She needed space to think. If Silver couldn't summon sanity again, that changed everything.

Felicia thumped down the stairs and hesitated at the bottom. Privacy was never assured in a pack house. Or around it, for that matter, but her chances of space to think outside were at least better. She headed for the front door. She could use airing out the car as her excuse. Since it was a pack car, to be polite she'd meant to return later and check the perfume had dissipated anyway.

Felicia opened the car door and collapsed to sit sideways on the passenger seat, one foot propped on the curb. The more she thought about it, the more what she'd heard drew over her like clouds covering the Lady's face, stealing her voice.

Silver might actually get arrested, might actually get locked up for being crazy. She'd been so Lady-damned pleased with herself for nudging Enrique into that plan, and now it seemed it would actually work.

But she'd found out before they'd put the plan into action. She clung to that glimmer of the Lady's light. She could still do something about it.

Felicia shoved to her feet, slammed the door, and circled the car to the driver's side. She needed to call Enrique immediately and at least try to stall him somehow. That needed absolutely assured privacy. She drove across the closest arterial to park along a side street the pack would have no reason to travel or glance down. She opened her address book to Enrique's entry but stopped herself before she connected the call. He couldn't get Silver arrested in the next two minutes. He was relying on Felicia's help anyway. Better she plan out what she was going to say, and not sound breathless and panicked.

When she had it straight in her mind, she dialed his number. When he answered, his greeting sounded suspicious. "Has something happened?"

"No." Felicia licked her lips and closed her eyes to aid her composure. She wanted to sound absolutely nonchalant about this. "I've been thinking about your plan. Isn't it too risky for the Were as a whole to have her talking to the police? When she's babbling, who knows what she might say that would get someone thinking."

Enrique snorted a laugh. "Felicia, I thought better of you. Your white tail is showing." Like a rabbit or deer as it ran away, he meant. "That's a pitiful excuse. No. We go ahead with the plan, or I show your pack the proof of where your loyalties really lay."

"Lie," Felicia corrected without thinking, and then wanted to release a hysterical giggle. Lady. It all came back to those stupid e-mails. Why did Madrid have to be so good at forgery, so they were so very believable? Why did she have to be so stupid as to lie for and get drunk with someone she couldn't trust?

"Do you want me to do that?" Enrique gave Felicia several beats of silence, and when she didn't answer, she heard his smile in his voice. "That's what I thought.

Felicia ended the call, tossed the phone on the seat beside her, and clenched her hands on the steering wheel to stop herself shaking. She shouldn't have called him. She should have known she wouldn't change his mind, and now she'd verified for him how good his hold was on her.

Fine. Felicia slapped her hands on the sides of the steering wheel, repeated the word out loud. He had a hold on her, but she was still working against him. Felicia took a few deep breaths to try to think logically. She needed delaying tactics, not direct opposition, which would send Enrique to the pack with his "proof."

They had to get Silver to go into the house where she'd be trespassing, and it would have to be Felicia who led her there. Silver would never follow a stranger anywhere. Felicia could lead Silver to the wrong place, somewhere she'd be stopped before she even got inside, but that would also be too obvious.

It came to her like frightened and confused prey bolting the right direction directly into your jaws. She could get herself grounded. All she'd have to do is mouth off a little. Then she wouldn't be able to lead Silver anywhere.

But what would piss Silver off, without getting Felicia kicked out of the house or the pack completely? She knew her father's buttons intimately, but Silver's anger was usually deep and hidden and creepy, not something Felicia could chart easily.

Felicia hiccupped with laughter as a crazy idea occurred to her. Why not a pet? Bringing home something weak and prey-like that no one was supposed to eat was dumb enough to piss off any Were. Plus, it seemed like just the kind of thing she might have done when she was younger to prove that she could do whatever she wanted.

Felicia started the car and pulled away, anxious to put her counter to Enrique in motion as soon as possible. She knew where the animal shelter was, she'd passed it often enough when driving around.

When she arrived at the shelter and pushed in the front doors, the vet's office came uncomfortably to mind. The shelter had the same kind of linoleum and the same smell of cleaners and animals packed close together. Felicia bit her lip and tilted her chin up. That didn't matter. She was doing this. She went right up to the counter and told the shelter employee, a woman with gray in her enthusiastically curling hair, that she wanted to adopt.

Of course, when the woman asked what kind of animal Felicia wanted, she had to think fast. Not a dog. That was just weird. They looked too much like people, but stupid, but still people . . . Apparently the shelter had rabbits too, which Felicia also immediately discounted. *She'd* want to eat one if she brought it home, never mind the rest of the pack. But a cat seemed right. The gray-haired woman smiled and gestured her through the doorway beside the counter. She met Felicia on the other side to accompany her.

Felicia had known from the smell that the animals were immediately behind the door, but she hadn't realized she'd have to walk through the dogs to get to the cats. Both sides of the hall had floor-to-ceiling chain link, with the fenced-off area divided into individual runs for a dozen or more dogs. Felicia didn't have time to count because the moment they caught her scent, they all simultaneously launched themselves at the fence. Some were wagging their asses off, ready to play, some wanted to challenge her—she supposed she should be grateful that none of the males were intact, to want to mate with her—but they all barked.

The employee put her hands over her ears and stared around her. "They don't usually do this, except for new animals, I don't understand—" She had to almost shout to be heard.

Felicia held her hands open. "I did cook bacon earlier today—" She kept her body language as unthreatening as she could without a tail or ears she could move, but the barking just went on and on.

"*Shut up!*" she finally shouted, and followed it with a bark of her own, channeling her father at his most alpha. She was the high-ranked one here, and they would listen to her, by the Lady. The dogs shut up. She breathed a sigh of relief in the blessed silence afterward.

Of course, then the employee was staring at her. "I saw it on one of those pet psychic shows," Felicia said hurriedly. "You have to sound like them so they understand you, you know?" She moved on to the next door, the employee trailing uncertainly behind. The last dog on the right, a barrel-chested Lab mix, wagged his tail and grinned at her, as if to say, "Sorry about those noisy morons. Nice to meet you." Felicia laughed.

The cats had a room of their own, two walls filled with smaller built-in cages, stacked four high. The cats were much quieter about their disapproval, but she could smell the stink of it when she entered. Only one hissed at her, but several more pressed themselves into the back of their cages.

The employee faded to the background, rattling around

with empty food dishes in a sink at the back. Felicia bent in front of the bottom cages one after the other. You saw pictures of kittens cuddling with dogs all the time. One of these would accept her, right? Especially a young one without any bad experiences with dogs yet.

On the second row up, a young cat blinked at her from its flop right against the cage bars and then yawned, showing teeny pointed teeth. It was older than Felicia had thought of getting, but it was still small and leggy in a way that told her it wasn't done growing yet.

Indifference seemed promising, given the other cats' reactions. Felicia crouched to put her face level with that cage. The cat was somewhat fluffy, with little fur feathers on its ears and between its toes, but the color was what caught her attention. The cat had stripes, but not in the stark light and dark gray Felicia expected. Its coat had a smoky, almost purplish cast, the stripes darker bands of the same shade. She hadn't seen a cat colored like that before, not that she'd ever particularly paid attention to cats. Smart felines stayed away from Were houses.

The association with smoke made Felicia think of what Silver had called her when Tom was hurt. That seemed as close to a sign as you ever got in this world, so she stood. "This one," she told the employee.

By the time Felicia made it out of the building with her cardboard carrier, she never wanted to see, never mind fill in, another form again. She'd had to lie to the woman in answer to all the questions about her "readiness" to adopt, and whether the kitten would suit her household and lifestyle. In the end she'd resorted to looking the woman in the eye and acting high ranked. It was a rare human who didn't accept a Were's word with that backing.

And it had cost more than she'd thought too. With Enrique around, she'd completely forgotten how the neglected job search meant no income until she got a job or her father got home and could be talked into extending her allowance a little.

She set the box on the passenger seat, climbed in, and opened the top just enough for little feathered ears and then a little fluffy head to pop up. "I'm sorry in advance," she told the cat seriously. It sniffed in all directions and then focused on the fingers she offered. "But it'll only be a few weeks, and then I'll give you back. Think of it like a vacation, huh?"

The cat scraped its cheek along her fingers and then gathered itself to spring out of the carrier. Felicia hurriedly closed the box and made sure the cardboard tabs were seated securely. Hopefully the cat wouldn't be too traumatized at the end of two weeks, but it seemed so mellow she was cautiously hopeful.

When she arrived at the house, Felicia didn't even make it to the stairs before Tom thumped in, eyebrows high behind his shaggy bangs. "What in the Lady's name—?"

The cat changed position suddenly, throwing off the balance of the box and forcing Felicia to grab the handle with both hands. "It's a cat. You're aware of the species, I assume."

Tom came close as if to take the box and open it, but Felicia twisted to keep it out of reach. "But . . . why?"

He seemed honestly confused, not accusing, so Felicia bit back a retort. "I liked it," she said and tried to detour around him. If she could just get it to her room without everyone gawking—but people were starting to wander up already, as the scent of the new animal drifted around the house.

Silver didn't bother with wandering or otherwise disguising her entrance. She strode straight into the front hall and gestured for Felicia to open the box for her.

"Roanoke," Felicia said, and set the box on the floor. Her residual perfume and the cat smell made it hard to read Silver when she wanted to know every nuance of the woman's emotions. She wanted Silver to be angry, but not *too* angry. Nervousness made her smash the tabs as she opened the box.

The cat led with its nose as it appeared above the rim. "Why is this here?" Silver asked, her own chin tipped a little as she sniffed too. "You don't intend it to be a toy, do you?" She fixed a piercing look on Felicia.

Felicia shook her head emphatically. Were who would enjoy hunting something bred to be too trusting to run away at first were disgusting. "No, the shelter had an event. I saw it and I liked it. For a pet, not a toy." The part about the cat not being prey was true at least. For the rest, including the nonexistent event, she was lucky for the perfume.

Silver crouched to look the cat in the eyes. It flicked its ears idly and said *mrp*, which didn't sound anything like what Felicia thought meows were supposed to be. "And you thought it would be a good idea to have a pet in a pack house?" Her face was neutral, but her tone was cutting.

"I'll keep it out of trouble." Of course, the moment Felicia said that, the cat grew bored with just looking around. It jumped right up over the high box side and streaked for the living room.

Silver snagged it by the scruff as it passed and held it far enough out to avoid claw swipes from all four paws. "See that you do." She straightened, dropped the animal into Felicia's arms, and continued deeper into the house. The cat squirmed and scored Felicia along her upper arm and collarbone before she got it into a position where she could hold its paws down.

Tom came over and set his hand over the cat's whole head like he didn't quite see how to scratch behind ears so diminutive. The cat made the *mrp* sound again. "Are you *trying* to piss off Roanoke Silver?"

"Silver can deal." Felicia escaped upstairs before she could see Tom's shock. She hadn't thought this would be so hard. She hadn't really expected that Silver would set eyes on the cat and ground her instantly, but if faking this attitude was hard now, how hard would it be to keep it up long enough to get Silver to that point? She clenched her jaw as she lugged the cat into her room and shut the door. It didn't matter. It was her fault she was in this situation, so she would do whatever was necessary to get out of it.

14

Felicia did have to give the stupid cat this: she didn't have any time left to brood, she was run so ragged trying to keep up with it. She left it locked in her room while she went and bought its litter and food, and returned home to find it yowling continuously at her door. "Poisonous" hardly did justice to the looks she gathered from the rest of the pack.

While she set up the litter box, the cat jumped from the bed to her dresser and nearly missed, knocking off everything it could reach as it scrabbled for purchase and scratched the wood. It lulled her into a false sense of security by hiding under the bed for a while, so that the next time she left, it streaked through the door and disappeared into the house.

Felicia tracked it by the cursing and finally ran it to ground in the nursery, where it had stopped to sniff at Edmond, who was on the floor enthusiastically running over his farm animals with his tractor. "Hello, kitty," he said and made a wide-armed hugging grab for it, as he would his puppy.

The cat apparently objected greatly to being hugged. Before Felicia realized what was happening, Edmond *screamed* and the cat squirmed away, leaving blood from a quickly healed scratch along his arm. Edmond stomped after it, murder in his eyes, trying to grab little handfuls of fur to yank. "Mean Lunch!"

Felicia caught the cat and lifted it out of his reach. "Don't touch, Edmond!" She doubted he could hear her over the sound of his screaming. When she didn't hand him the cat for his revenge, he beat his fists on her knees.

"Edmond!" Susan arrived and scooped up her howling son much as Felicia had done the cat. She examined him and smeared the blood with her thumb to check no wound remained beneath it. Only then did she take in the rest of the situation.

Felicia swallowed. Susan was someone she liked too much to want to piss off as collateral damage. "I'm sorry, he just—"

"I see that," Susan said with a quiet laugh. Felicia wondered if, as a human, she understood cats better. Maybe she would have predicted this would happen. She adjusted her hold on Edmond to speak to him. "Cats don't like to be squeezed, sweetie. You have pat them, okay? If they want to be patted. This cat is new, so it's probably scared, so it doesn't want to be patted right now."

"I wanted to hug Lunch," Edmond whined and pressed his head against his mother's chest.

Felicia choked, but Susan just rolled her eyes. "Who told you it was named that?"

"Pack Uncle Pierce," Edmond muttered after a long pause where he apparently had to decide whether he wanted to answer.

Felicia was unsurprised. It wasn't that the others weren't all thinking it, it was that Pierce had the edged sense of humor that would make him actually say it. The cat had been actively resisting her since she picked it up, but when she adjusted her grip, it finally relaxed, content to be held. Felicia looked down at it, frowning. Maybe this was the way cats were supposed to be held, one hand under their back legs, one hand under their upper body, and it liked that.

"The cat's not named Lunch. It's named—"

Susan looked at Felicia, but Felicia was more concerned with Silver's appearance in the doorway, so the silence stretched long and awkward. She'd thought of calling it Smoke, but it seemed weird to say that now with Silver standing right there.

"Morsel," Silver said, deadpan.

"Morrie," Susan told her son. "But you can't touch it while it's still scared, okay? It's going to go away now." She gave Felicia a pointed look, and she took the hint.

Silver stepped aside to allow her out of the nursery but blocked her way farther down the hall. "Strange definition of keeping out of trouble you have. I don't think you're ready for this responsibility, Felicia."

Felicia didn't take a deep breath, because that would show, but she took a firmer grip on the cat and prepared herself internally. This seemed like a good opening. Maybe she wouldn't have to keep this up too long after all.

Lady grant her luck. "Are you sure you don't want to check with my father on that?"

Silver went very still. "I am your alpha."

"An alpha who can't even drive. Or make her own phone calls. Or use a credit card. Or hold down a job like I'm supposed to do. Strange definition of an alpha." Felicia prayed as she said it. Lady forgive her.

She'd thought Silver had been still before, but that was nothing compared to now. "You have one chance to apologize, and I'll pretend I didn't hear that."

Felicia desperately wanted to run, and her tension transmitted to the cat, which started to squirm again. "I'm sorry, Roanoke, for saying what's true."

Silver backhanded her. The force made Felicia stagger into the wall behind her, and the cat springboarded off her chest, knocking her farther off-balance. She caught herself on the wall and pressed a hand against her cheek, tears springing up purely from the pain, though that was fading quickly enough.

"Leave this den. You may remain in the territory until your father has had a chance to speak to you about your actions, as I'm sure he will. Yes, and I'm perfectly aware of your opinion." Silver snapped the last to the air at her side and stalked out, leaving Felicia staring in her wake. Where . . . where could she even go? She'd known this was a possibility, but she supposed she'd never really believed Silver would go that far. Felicia hadn't even considered what she would do if it Silver kicked her out. The tears from the blow stung her eyes.

She should get her stuff, Felicia told herself sternly, after several more moments of blank staring. Everything in a pack house had an audience, and she couldn't just stand here. Telling herself that this couldn't be happening wouldn't make that true. She pushed off the wall and made it as far as her room, where she shut the door too hard.

She folded to the floor beside her bed and dropped her head against the side. The wood inside the box spring pressed uncomfortably into her forehead. Lady, what had she done? She didn't want to be kicked out. She'd meant to piss Silver off, not enrage her. Obviously she'd chosen the wrong thing to say for that.

Or maybe she'd accomplished exactly what she needed to. Silver wouldn't follow her anywhere now. Enrique's plan was down and bleeding out. Felicia wished it felt more like a success.

Felicia looked around her room from the floor, trying to see the familiar clutter properly. What should she even take? When she'd walked away from the Madrid pack, she'd done it with nothing but what she was wearing. Reminded, she pushed herself to her feet and got Blanca from where she was flopped on the windowsill, watching the sky or possibly checking the upper frame for mildew. She stuffed her at the bottom of her school backpack and added her laptop and some clothes.

And what else? Felicia's mind felt too foggy to think. She sat down on the bed. Someone knocked on her door and she jumped and clutched her bag. Didn't she get time to pack? "Yes?" It came out wavering and she cursed herself.

Tom entered, the cat slung casually with its belly along one arm. It looked ridiculously comfortable. "I found her hiding under the couch." He closed the door carefully behind himself.

"Thanks." Felicia looked at the pack in her arms so he couldn't read her face. "I'll take it back to the shelter when I go."

"I don't know. She's kind of cute." Tom ruffled the cat's ears more successfully this time and it rumbled a quiet purr for a few seconds. "You could take her with you where you're going."

He set the cat on the floor, and it started sniffing along the carpet like it hadn't covered every square inch when it first arrived. He sat down on the bed beside her. "If you have somewhere to go."

Felicia tightened her arms over her pack and didn't answer. It struck her like a first shift—inevitable and unavoidable, but shocking as your whole perspective changed—that she wanted to confide everything to Tom more than anyone. Not just to play chase with him, but pour out her problems and have him listen and nod seriously and then make some dorky joke to cheer her up. She could never remember feeling that way about someone before.

If she told him, would he believe her? She wanted to think that he would, but what about the way she'd danced with Enrique in front of him? Would he decide that she was so into Enrique that she'd chosen to work with him without being blackmailed? Could she make him understand how a shared childhood was so strong, it had made her willfully blind to who Enrique the adult really was until it was too late?

Tom put a hand on her back. "What's wrong, Felicia? None of this is like you at all, and it all started when that cat of a roamer got here."

Felicia swallowed against moisture from tears at the back of her throat. "No, it didn't. It started when you got hurt, and I realized I need to grow up."

She forced herself to move away from him and stand. She didn't usually mind how small her room was, because that meant she got it to herself, but with Tom right there when she wanted to throw herself on him, and the cat getting underfoot, she wished now that it was bigger than a closet. "Maybe this will be good for me, getting out on my own. Roaming, like you said I should do."

"I didn't mean you should get yourself kicked out of the house to do it." Tom's humor came out a little twisted.

Felicia stopped by her desk and surveyed her collection of DVDs stuffed among the books. She didn't need any of them, but she picked up *Sense and Sensibility* anyway out of pure nostalgia. How humans managed rank in historical stories always interested her, and this particular one had a Spanish subtitle track she'd turned on whenever she was tired or homesick when she'd first come to stay with her father. She stuffed it into her backpack.

"You'll want to raid the pantry too," Tom said from the bed. He tapped his toe, and the cat lashed its tail and launched itself in for the kill. "Even if you're eating crap from fast-food places all the time, your money disappears like that." He snapped his fingers.

"Good idea." Felicia looked around. Even if she'd forgotten something, she needed to go now, or she'd blurt something out or start crying. But there was still the cat. She grabbed it, but it squirmed right out of her hands again.

Tom scooped up the cat and it relaxed for him. He lowered it into its box so quickly it didn't have time to brace its legs before he closed the lid. It thrashed around angrily inside, though. "Here." It took Felicia a moment to stop focusing on the box and worrying about an escape to notice that the cat wasn't what he was offering. He extended his hand, a key on the palm. "Take my truck. You can sleep in the back, with the canopy it's pretty comfortable. Just remember to move it frequently."

"Tom, no." Felicia shoved his hand back. He moved with

the push easily enough but held his hand right back out again. So like Tom.

"I'm not sure the direction you're choosing to 'grow up' is the right one, but that's not for me to say. Just figure yourself out, and we'll be here when you're done, okay?" He put the key into her unresisting hand and let himself out, leaving with her an unexpected gift, a box full of yowling cat, and the heavy weight of guilt.

15

"Ask her father for help, she says. When I'd just finished hiding her troublemaking from him." Silver reached the bed and turned. Not nearly enough space in this room to pace. She was keeping her voice down to avoid sharing her rage with the pack, but she had plenty of intensity to shove into the tone. Death watched her, his expression mocking as he listened. She knew she should shut up, her justifications were just amusing him more, but it was all too much at the moment.

"I told you I thought she was smart, but where is that intelligence now? How does she go from tactfully stopping a fight to picking one for no reason? I told her father I'd deal with her, but how am I supposed to deal with *that*?" Silver pointed out into the den. Death didn't answer. "She covers her scent, she brings prey home and sets it loose, she all but snarls in the face of her alpha!"

Death finally moved to prowl around her, closer and closer. "And she taunts you with your weaknesses. Why are we backsliding, hm? You know your weaknesses, you'd found a peace with them, a confidence that did not need the approval of whining children."

Silver released a breath, and with it the intensity of her rage fled. "Go away," she muttered to Death, for all the good it would do. His words were like tendrils of smoke filling her that she couldn't unbreathe. She had found peace with the fact that she didn't see the way the others do. But this time, Felicia had said it. Why was that different? Why did that cut her so deeply?

"She's not your daughter, Silver. You didn't bear her, you didn't raise her." Death used Silver's mother's voice this time, but subtly wrong.

There was a test there. Death wanted her to find something, not take his words at face value. Silver narrowed her eyes at him, as if she could see wisps of remembered words. "My mother never sounded like that. She . . ." It came to Silver in a rush. "She spoke with love. Not—" Silver had to search for the right word. "Calculation. 'What have I done to *earn* the right to call her daughter?' is the wrong question. Love is offered, not earned."

Death flicked his ears once. "When an offer is not accepted, that does not make it worthless, ash in the wind." His usual voice now, soft.

"But it does lend her words an unintended weight." Silver scraped her hair out of her face. Breaths came more easily as the tightest squeeze of her emotions eased. She examined her actions. She'd gone too far, Felicia's words coming when she was still raw after hiding her lack of progress from Dare. She could not let disrespect to her position as an alpha go unanswered, but neither was it right to punish any young person too harshly for ill-considered words.

So now she needed to fix it. Silver turned from Death to the door and gathered herself, tucking her bad hand into her pocket and arranging her expression into something an alpha would wear. "I need to work this through with someone more helpful than you listening, I think." She knew how to be an alpha to adults well enough, but an alpha also left much of the day-to-day disciplining of cubs to their parents. She could use the perspective of someone with cubs of his own.

She went in search of Tom to help her bring Boston within range of her voice, but she ran into Pierce first. He dipped his head in greeting, one carefully casual lock of hair escaping down over his forehead. He clearly wanted something, so Silver stopped and nodded back in acknowledgment.

"Do you want us to make sure that Felicia can't sneak back in? With the young ones, half the time they get hungry and try to get in just long enough to raid for some food . . ." Pierce's tone was perfectly respectful, but Silver could guess by the way he phrased the question how he hoped she'd respond.

"Definitely not." Silver grimaced. "I'll be trying to . . . repair matters with her directly, but until then there's no reason to put any particular strength of enforcement behind my orders." She watched his face for his reaction, and when he relaxed she did the same.

Pierce had been beta to John as alpha, years ago, so he should understand the problems of leadership more than some. On impulse, Silver confided in him. "I do know that I overreacted."

Pierce offered her a sympathetic shrug. "We all have our

sore spots. Don't forget, we've all lived with Felicia these past years too. She never does anything by halves. Besides, better the alpha concern herself with petitions than sulking teens."

"Yes." Silver pulled her thoughts away from Felicia. She'd tried to keep the business with Portland away from her pack's attention, but of course by now they'd probably heard the whole story from every other sub-pack Craig had spread it to. "Dealing with that petition will probably be a matter of keeping order while everyone calms down, at this point."

"That's optimistic," Death said and slipped past both of their feet. Apparently the quiet business of reassuring her home pack was too boring for him. No less important for Silver to do, however.

Pierce rubbed his upper arm, gaze going abstracted. "I can understand the emotional reactions, but it still shouldn't have come to a petition in the first place. It should have stayed between the parents."

Silver pictured Portland and Craig, the entangling scraps of their former intimacy littering the space between them. Perhaps it was no wonder their problems had exploded outward to all the sub-packs. "If only they'd agreed."

"If you trust your alpha enough to follow her, you should trust her enough to take her word that she has her emotions under control." Pierce snorted, perhaps at the situation, perhaps at himself. "Anyway, I'm keeping you. I'll pass the word to the others about Felicia."

Silver didn't voice her thank-you for his support, but when Pierce turned away, she stepped over and squeezed the back of his neck. He paused, smelling reassured, until she took her hand away, then continued on his way.

After finding Tom and gaining her distant connection to Boston, Silver let herself out of the den. The trees and bushes surrounding it were too polite by half, but it gave her a better chance of privacy. The sun was low, but the warmth of the day lingered in the air. Death was waiting for her.

"Roanoke Silver?" Where Dare's voice had been shredded by the distance, Boston's came as warm as if she was standing beside him. She could imagine his gentle look of surprise and then a pleased smile, wrinkles at the corners of his eyes creasing the delicious brown of his skin. He'd been Dare's alpha, when Dare was a young man, and he'd often offered the wisdom of his century of life to both of them. Even more important to her current situation, he had children, grandchildren, even great-grandchildren aplenty.

"Boston." Having gotten this far, Silver abruptly found herself without the right words. "I need—" She hesitated, fearing to sound weak, but her voice knew better than her mind that she didn't need to fear that with Boston. "A new perspective. This isn't something I've ever dealt with before and I'm reacting too emotionally—"

"Breathe," Boston said on the note of a laugh, and only then did Silver realize how fast she'd been speaking. "Does this concern the matter of our pregnant sub-alpha?"

"No." Silver corrected her own answer a moment later. "Only because of what it made me realize. It's Felicia." Silver briefly sketched out how Felicia had been acting lately—the scent, the cat, and then her insults. Those, Silver didn't trust herself to summarize without worsening them, so she repeated them as best she could remember.

"Ah, well. I suppose Dare's daughter wouldn't hit her roaming period quietly." Boston chuckled. "Dare arrived in my pack at the end of his, but we'd all heard about his departure from his birth pack. Heavy objects thrown at several heads, if I recall correctly."

Silver couldn't help but laugh. Dare had mentioned before how much of a "little shit" he'd been when young, but he'd never volunteered details. She sobered quickly. "It's something to do with that roamer, I know it." She wanted to scrape the ever-escaping wisps of hair out of her face, but her hand was full. "But I can't get her to tell me what, and it's no good asking the same question over and over when she's decided not to answer."

Boston made a sympathetic noise. "So what did you do, when she said those things?"

"I threw her out of the house." Silver winced. "Too much, I know. But she was deeply disrespectful to her alpha. That could get an adult thrown out of her pack entirely."

Boston sighed, making the sound a commiseration. "That's one of the difficult parts of parenting. Deciding what punishment will teach them, not what they might 'deserve' or might make you feel better."

"If I'm a parent," Silver said. She paced a step in one direction, then another.

"Do you want to be?"

"Yes." Silver said it softly, like maybe the breeze could carry it up into the sky as a kind of prayer to the Lady. "Portland has made me realize . . . well. Yes." She gritted her teeth. "But what's done is done. Now I have to figure out what to do next. Removing the punishment entirely would show too much weakness. But if I could soften it . . . perhaps to what a young Were on the edge of roaming would normally expect." She laughed raggedly. "If I had enough experience with roamers to know what that was."

"Grounding, perhaps," Boston said on a low rumble. "After a night on her own, you could offer to let her return to grounding instead. It is more . . . a child's punishment, I suppose you could say. Taking away a child's access to things she enjoys. Less serious than threatening an adult's relationship with her pack. She was childish, the punishment can remind her of that. But do what you feel is best." He paused a beat and then cleared his throat. "While I have you, Roanoke, I thought perhaps we could discuss some of the things people have been saying in my presence about the Portland situation."

"Good idea." Silver folded to sit cross-legged on the ground. Death settled himself beside her and she spared her good hand briefly to set the bad on his back. When she flexed her fingers, they scritched into his fur. Best to be comfortable since they'd likely be there for a while.

For the first few blocks driving away from the pack house, Felicia concentrated on getting all the mirrors adjusted right, but after that her thoughts chased their own tails. If her father had been there, would he have supported Silver, or stopped her from kicking Felicia out? If she'd been similarly disrespectful to him, she didn't think he'd have kicked her out. When she first moved back from Spain, they'd tangled plenty of times, resulting in various punishments, but nothing like this.

Maybe that was because he was her father, though. Felicia stomped on the accelerator and the pickup's engine reluctantly growled up to enough speed to beat a yellow light. Maybe if Silver had been her mother, she would have done something different.

Of course, Silver was Lady-damned close to being her stepmother. Whatever she'd said to Tom, so long ago it seemed now, Felicia had to admit that to herself. But a stepmother was still different from a mother unless Silver tried to act that way. She'd always left Felicia to her father when Felicia got in trouble, until now.

And Felicia had no idea if she even wanted Silver to try to act like a mother. Felicia couldn't—she didn't know—the more she tried to grapple with the idea, the more it slipped from her grip. She'd lost her real mother so long ago, and she remembered so little—how did she know that Blanca had lost her mother's scent, rather than Felicia forgetting what that scent was?—that it wasn't like Silver would crowd out the memories of her. But even if she didn't remember her, Felicia knew she'd had a mother, a mother who loved her, and she didn't want Silver changing that. And why did she need someone in the role of mother, anyway? She was practically an adult herself.

That was much, much more than Felicia wanted to deal with right now, though. Right now, she wanted to find somewhere to park, eat dinner, watch her movie on her laptop before the battery ran out, and then maybe try to sleep.

She found a grocery store with plenty of empty spaces, parked at the edge, and came around to the truck's canopy-covered bed to stretch out while she ate. The temperature outside was on the chilly side of pleasant as the breeze gained ground after dark, but the enclosed space was still stuffy from trapped sun's heat. She slid a side window open wide enough for air but too narrow for a cat.

She opened the cat's box, but it hid for a while before creeping out. It scuffled around in its litter and then came over to sniff Felicia's knee. She eyed it. "You better not want to walk on me with those paws now."

It curled into a circle, apparently ignoring her. When she finished eating, she stroked the fur of its flank as she would someone in wolf. It purred. Felicia supposed that was all right, then.

Enrique texted about ten minutes into the movie. Felicia stared at the words until her phone got bored and the screen went dark. He'd found a location, and he wanted to know when she could meet him there. She hadn't expected he'd find a place so soon.

She shook herself. She had a good reason now that she couldn't go through with the plan, she reminded herself. She texted him the location of the lot and told him to meet there instead. Better to tell him in person.

A rental car pulled up beside her truck twenty minutes later. Felicia's lips thinned as she bundled the cat back into its box. She didn't want it streaking off for freedom when she opened the tailgate. Then some predator really might eat it. She didn't have Tom's finesse, so she got half a dozen scratches for her trouble.

Felicia opened the tailgate and sat on it in the darkness, feet dangling, and waited for Enrique to come to her. The light here was an odd meeting of contrasts, a wash of orange from the light over the adjoining street, and a stronger wash of blue from the parking lot's light. Both threw Enrique's frown into relief as he strode over. Felicia avoided his eyes by licking away the residual blood from her healed scratches.

"What now?" He set his hand flat on the gate and leaned into the bed to look inside. Maybe he expected another Were, but the only thing there was the box jerking with the movements of the unseen cat. He straightened and raised his eyebrows at her for the blood. "Why are you here?"

Felicia shrugged, then winced when the cat lunged so violently the box tipped over. "It's some stray that made the mistake of crossing our yard. The kids were tormenting it, so I took it with me. It's kind of cute, in a dumb way."

Enrique eyed her but seemed to accept that. He waited, letting silence reiterate his question.

"I fucked up." Felicia kept her head down and tried to look panicked about him showing the e-mails to her pack because of her mistake. She *was* worried about that, and hopefully the perfume should cover anything else. "Silver was just . . . stepping on my tail again, so I mouthed off, and now she's kicked me out of the house."

Rather than a frustrated growl or cursing, Felicia got more silence. She lifted her head to check his reaction. He was smiling. He gave an explosive "ha!" of satisfaction and thumped his hands on the gate on either side of her knees. "It's perfect! You're a genius."

Felicia stared at him. She . . . what? She'd expected anger, hoped that he wouldn't be smart enough to realize she'd done it on purpose, but . . . celebration? "I am?"

"Of course. If you wanted to step outside the normal daily

routine to take Silver somewhere unusual alone, you'd have to come up with a plausible reason. But now, if you call and arrange to meet somewhere to apologize, she won't think twice about coming alone if you ask. I found a place and watched what time the owner came home. You can arrange to have Silver arrive around that time tomorrow to be found." Enrique grinned at her.

Felicia took a deep breath so she didn't scream. Lady, she tried to fix things and just made them worse. What now?

Enrique climbed up to sit on the gate beside her. "Stop moping. If you're so set on staying here, you can go back to the pack house in the chaos after we succeed and no one will even notice."

Felicia made a noise of agreement to make it seem like she was actually paying attention. She could break with him now, let him do his worst and show the e-mails to the pack. Maybe her father would believe her side when he got back. And maybe he'd be able to convince everyone else.

Or maybe she'd get kicked out of the pack for good, or maybe everyone would go around muttering about Europeans behind her back for the rest of her life. Maybe Tom wouldn't speak to her again. And either way, she'd definitely have hurt Silver, and hurt her father by doing it. Felicia finally realized that to her, hurting Silver was bad enough. Silver had been kind to her, kind when she'd been defiant and scared and hardly trusted even her father.

Felicia yanked herself out of all the maybes. Silver hadn't said she *couldn't* be sane for a while again, just that it would be difficult and risky. Even if she was just her normal self, how bad could she really be? Humans acted plenty crazy all the time and didn't get themselves locked up in institutions. And with the financial support of all of Roanoke behind him, it wasn't like her father couldn't hire the very best lawyers. How serious was trespassing, anyway? It wasn't like framing Silver for murder.

"I'm sure it will all work out, and then you can go home the victorious alpha," Felicia said, throttling down her irony until it escaped near the end.

Enrique laughed, her sharpness rolling off him. "I want to move up in the pack, like every Were." He looked up into the soft overcast of the sky, lit at the horizon by the city's light pollution. "Madrid will see I'm the one to help lead us out of this mess."

Felicia looked up at the sky too. Lady damn Enrique anyway, but she found she still wanted to *understand* somehow, even though she knew that was stupid. "Why do you care what Madrid thinks? If it's so bad at home, why even go back?"

Enrique looked over at her in surprise, ran fingers through his black locks while he found words. "Because Madrid's my alpha."

Felicia turned sideways and tucked one leg up so she was facing Enrique. "But he sent you here, at no small risk. If Papa got home unexpectedly, or anyone else figured out who you were, or if I'd turned you in, you'd have gotten a hell of a beating." She lifted a hand to forestall Enrique. "And I know it's an alpha's job to risk his Were sometimes, but for *what*? For petty revenge? What does it matter what North Americans are doing when, as you say, Madrid's fight is at home? He's using his position to make you do things for his own selfish goals."

Enrique's stubborn expression made Felicia want to snap

her teeth at him. She bet he hadn't processed a single word of that. She'd known that before she said it, and here she'd proved herself right, and she still wanted to punch something.

"Not all of us can leave everything that makes us who we are so easily, Felicia." Enrique made her name as flat and American as possible, drawing out a *sh* in the middle.

Felicia did snap her teeth at him then. "I suppose that's all you'll ever be, then, Enrique. Spanish."

Enrique sighed and looked away. "You say like it's an insult, but it's not."

Felicia scooted to sit straight, legs over the edge again. Silence stretched painfully—briefly broken by an experimental yowl from Morsel—until Felicia got so tired she couldn't sustain the frustration and let the silence become resigned instead.

"I do care about you, Felicia." Enrique looked away as he said it. Maybe he was picturing her as a child with jammy fingers, the same as she did him sometimes. A shame those memories hadn't stopped him from blackmailing her in the first place.

Felicia couldn't muster her earlier anger this time. Everything was too snarled and fucked up. "Shut up." She sent a brief prayer to the Lady that she'd made the right decision in not breaking with Enrique. Now she needed privacy to plot new ways to sabotage the plan. She thought hard about how tired she was, and a yawn came almost naturally. "Go on, get out." She shoved Enrique's shoulder until he jumped off the gate.

"My hotel's only about ten minutes away. You should follow me back." Enrique pointed in the vague direction of the highway.

"Oh, I didn't know him until he showed up the other day, but now I'm staying in his room." Felicia made her voice sing-song for the imaginary conversation. She glared at Enrique and went back to her normal tone. "They'll totally believe that. Besides, hotels don't take cats."

Enrique leaned in to pointedly sniff the side of the truck, though of course he must have gotten a good idea of the scent when inside. "So you'd rather sleep in your boyfriend's truck? I suppose that makes sense. Is your boyfriend going to be joining you?"

Felicia bit back a correction about Tom not being her boy-friend, but only barely. Enrique was baiting her, but he knew enough to bait effectively. "I refuse to believe you're worried about competition."

Enrique snorted. "Maybe if I *could* seduce you, you'd come to your senses and come home, but no. You're too damn . . . infuriating, same as you were as a child."

Felicia kicked out, missing him by a mile. She smiled, though it felt hollow underneath. It would be nice to fall into this teas-ing again, but she knew better.

"Is he the reason you're so loyal to North America?" Enrique was abruptly serious. When Felicia frowned at him, he slapped the side of the truck to make it clear he meant Tom. "First love is all very nice and all, but you can't be a puppy about it."

Felicia opened her mouth for the automatic denial of that too but stopped for a different reason. Did she love Tom? She'd put her emotions aside after their earlier conversation, but now she couldn't avoid them. She didn't know. Was she too young to know?

But that was still not something she could deal with right now. She wouldn't have anything at all with Tom if Silver was arrested or she was kicked out of the pack completely. She pointed. "Go," she ordered Enrique. He held up his hands, grinning, and went.

When his car turned out of the parking lot, Felicia shut herself up under the canopy again and got Morsel out. She hugged the cat, tight, until it stopped squirming and relaxed. Felicia waited, and eventually Morsel went back to sleep. The twitch of an ear here and there brushed its ear feathers against Felicia's skin and tickled. She imagined curling up with Tom instead.

Then Felicia put him out of her mind and concentrated on what she had to do to make sure Silver stayed safe. One step at a time.

16

Felicia walked by the house Enrique had chosen several times as the afternoon mellowed into evening, fingering the cheap winter gloves in the pocket of her windbreaker. She'd had to get them at a thrift store this morning since none of the regular stores stocked them in the summer. Used things always smelled so weird. She didn't plan to get far enough to use them, but if things kept going wrong, she didn't want the police using her fingerprints to catch her.

When she turned the last corner, she could see Enrique's car. He sat inside, apparently texting but really keeping an eye on things. This circuit, he looked up and nodded encouragingly. Felicia squashed an impulse to snarl at him and kept up her meander. She'd laid a childishly easy trail to here from Silver's favorite park, and Enrique had timed her for that, but he had only the estimate she'd given him of the time from pack house to park. She hadn't been able to underestimate much without it seeming outlandish, but if traffic was good, maybe the owner of this house would arrive before Silver. Especially if—Felicia didn't look at her phone clock, because Enrique would notice—she kept stalling and didn't call Silver until too late.

Enrique started his engine, pulled alongside her, and rolled down the passenger window. "You better call her now if we want her here in time for the owner to walk in on her." He leaned to see her better, hand on the shoulder of the passenger seat.

Felicia took her out phone, but paused when he didn't keep driving. "You'll get your scent all over the trail and she'll know something's up." She made shooing motions while she tried not to panic internally. Plan J or K or whatever Lady-damned letter she was up to by now was to fake a call and half a conversation, after which she'd claim Silver hadn't been home, but if Enrique was right there, he'd be able to hear the other half of the conversation perfectly well.

"I'm in the car. And your perfume covers everything." Enrique raised his eyebrows at her. Felicia could read his implications: if she was worried about him hanging around, she should make the call faster. He lowered his voice and switched to Spanish. *"Or I could call for you. Remind everyone about the European in their midst and everything she's been helping me plan."*

Felicia swallowed her snarl and called Tom's cell rather than the house phone. Maybe he'd be annoyed with her and wouldn't answer. Or maybe he would refuse to let her talk to Silver. Felicia didn't think either was very likely, but she was snapping her teeth at guard hairs at this point.

He answered after two rings. "Are you all right?"

Felicia clenched her jaw to avoid blurting out an honest answer to his question. Enrique watched her from the car, expression neutral now. "I'm fine. I've been doing a lot of thinking today, though. Can I talk to Silver? I want to apologize to her properly."

She held her breath in pathetic hope, but after a pause, she heard him relaying that to Silver, tinny at the edge of the phone microphone's pickup. Then the phone conveyed noises from bumps and jostles as it transferred hands.

"Felicia?" Silver always sounded confused on the phone, like she was on the other end peering into corners to find someone who wasn't there.

"Roanoke." Felicia closed her eyes. Lady forgive her. "I need to apologize. What I said was . . . well. But I hoped maybe we could talk in person? I'm not asking permission to come back to the house, but if you follow my trail from that park you like, you'll find where I'm staying. I know I don't really deserve the consideration, but it's so hard to speak at a distance like this . . ."

"True enough." Silver was silent for a few moments, then: "I'll meet you there."

Felicia hung up before Tom could come back on the line and held the phone to her chest for a few moments, cursing mentally. Why couldn't something go wrong now that it would *help* her? She gave Enrique a sharp nod and he pulled away, going back to his earlier station with a good view of the house.

Time to let herself in, since she couldn't think of a way out of that either with him watching. Felicia strolled up the curving driveway of their target house like she had every reason to be there. At the garage, she ducked along the side of the build-

ing, shaded by several tall evergreens that took up the space to
the property line. She paused to pull on her gloves and then
tugged the yard waste bin over to provide a step up to the roof.
The gutter creaked worryingly when it took her weight, but
she pulled herself up quickly and it didn't break.

The house had two levels of pitch, one shallow before the
second-floor windows, and one steeper above that. Felicia
inched along the pitch toward a window that had been left
half open to allow air flow in the summer warmth. This was
the dangerous part, as the evergreens on the property would
disguise her from most angles, but not straight on. Anyone
walking along the sidewalk or driving past and pausing at the
driveway would see her. Getting arrested herself might defeat
the plan to ensnare Silver, but Felicia didn't think she could
talk her way out of breaking and entering the same way Silver
might be able to talk her way out of wandering in.

Fortunately, the neighborhood was quiet, most people still
at work, and Felicia worked quickly. She slit the screen with
her pocket knife and took hold of the window. She'd worried
about having to snap a lock with werewolf strength and the
noise that would make, but the window slid smoothly up. She
supposed they didn't think that would-be burglars would
bother climbing up here.

She climbed in, closed the window to its earlier position,
and finally allowed herself to breathe. The room looked like a
home office: a plush ergonomic chair stood in front of a desk
that took up most of one wall and held the computer and
printer and assorted mess. The rest of the space was filled with
houseplants, tall in pots or short on tables, like a minijungle.

Felicia slipped between them without touching a leaf,

conscious of not disturbing these poor people's lives more than necessary as well as giving them nothing else to accuse Silver of. And leaving no evidence of herself for the police to find.

Downstairs, she dodged a few more scattered plants and studied the front door. Just a dead bolt, nothing she could pull closed while Enrique watched and have it lock without the key. Lady damn it. Felicia's voice was twisted up tight in her throat. She didn't want to linger in the house any longer than she had to, certainly not long enough to come up with another idea.

She unlocked the dead bolt and let herself out, once again like she had every right to be here. So far, no one seemed to have noticed, though of course someone could have seen her climbing around and called the police and they just hadn't gotten close enough for her to hear the sirens yet.

At the bottom of the driveway, she took out her perfume bottle and gave a good spritz in the direction of her ankles, as Enrique was undoubtedly watching for her to do. There would be two paths for Silver to find, one leading her to the side of the garage, so Enrique had wanted to be very sure that the one he needed Silver to take stank so much there was no question of following the other.

She walked reluctantly up to the house, stepped inside, and then let herself out for a last time, walking precisely over her trail. Coming or going, it didn't matter, now the scent was double strength.

She walked back along her trail from the park far enough she judged the perfume had dissipated a little, and then abandoned her gloves to rub wood chips from someone's garden over the bottom of her jeans to cover the last of the scent. She left the gloves buried in the wood chips and found herself a spot to watch, well away from Enrique. From her position she couldn't see the house or the path Silver would be taking, in case Silver noticed her in turn, but she could see the main road, if the police were to arrive. Lady grant that if Silver got here, she would be able to sweet-talk the homeowners, and no police would be called in the first place.

Felicia leaned her ass on a fire hydrant and took out her phone to flip through menus at random and type occasionally like she was texting the ride she was waiting for. After all her plans, it seemed she was down to praying.

Felicia may have said she wanted to apologize, but Silver still smelled abused flowers along her trail. Death put his nose to the ground when she hesitated, and she snorted and jogged a few steps to get ahead of him. She was aware a human could follow this trail. He didn't need to put his nose down for any trail, however difficult, anyway.

What she didn't know was whether Felicia had been sincere. Silver supposed it didn't matter either way. Hadn't she already planned to let the young woman come back to a lesser punishment?

"A coward's way, to apologize alone, so others cannot hear," Death said. He stopped, head coming up in interest. Felicia's trail led into one of the humans' dens. "If you think that an apology is what she actually wants to offer."

This time, Silver hesitated for much longer. Why would

Felicia be in a human's den? But she'd been learning with other humans of her own age recently enough. Maybe she'd had a friendship with one and turned to her when shelter was needed.

Still, Silver would be stepping onto someone else's territory, probably that of the human friend's parents. Best to be polite. She rapped her knuckles against the door and waited. No one came. Without Were ears, had they failed to hear her at the back of their den? She entered slowly, cautious. "Hello?" she called.

The den echoed back, empty. Things were growing everywhere, and Silver scrubbed at her eyes. Lady damn it! Was her anger at Felicia making her stop seeing clearly? Plants didn't grow inside of dens, even she knew that.

She'd lost the thread of Felicia's scent in the confusion, and she ventured deeper into the den in search of it. She smelled two humans, a man and a woman, but she would have said they were older. Where were Felicia and her friend?

"Watch yourself," Death said, and Silver turned hurriedly to find the source of the threat. The man she'd smelled had entered behind her. He had black hair peppered with gray, and though he wasn't tall, he stood very straight, all but shouting his rank.

Silver opened her mouth for a greeting, polite as she'd resolved earlier, but the man didn't give her time to speak. He dropped what he was carrying, leaving his hands loose and ready, threatening. "Who the hell are you? How did you get in here? I'm calling—"

Silver tried not to breathe too fast as his words slipped away from her in a familiar manner. First the plants inside, and now this. She had to hang on, think through the poison's effects on her mind. The man spoke to whoever he had named before, telling them to come quickly, and Silver looked around her. The man stank of anger, and she doubted any allies he called would wish to discuss things rationally.

Time to leave, and quickly. The man blocked the entrance, but dens never had only one way out. Silver turned and ran, deeper into the plants. Somewhere. She'd smell fresh air and find her escape.

With each step she took, the growth around her increased, grasping, gnarled roots catching at her toes, slim braches reaching for her hair. Silver snarled at them. She didn't fear plants, even inside a den, but too late she realized that was not their purpose. No paths lay before her, no trails suggested themselves to her nose, only leaves and more leaves.

She whirled, tried a different direction, stumbled, tried another. A maze could hold her only if she let it. She thrust straight through the nearest patch of branches only to smack into the unyielding trunk beneath. The man's anger did not need to traverse his maze to reach her, his words sliced right through. "Stop! Stop where you are!"

"Hurry, hurry," Death mocked. Silver gritted her teeth and stopped. Thrashing in the maze served nothing. She'd wasted far too much time as it was. If she couldn't run, she would have to show her belly to the man, emphasize her weakness until he thought her too much trouble to punish for her trespass on his territory.

She held her good hand open and wide beside her, unthreatening. "I'm looking for Felicia. Is she not here?"

"No, she's not. I've called the—" The same word again. His

allies. "How did you get in?" The man could not snarl as well as a Were could, but he certainly tried.

Silver suspected "I walked in" would not satisfy him, so she hunted desperately for more precise words. Her heart beat too fast, drowning out her voice. The den entrance had not been blocked or guarded. But humans would not say it that way. They'd say—

A root caressed the man's boot, the maze acting like a favored pet fawning over its master, then struck at Silver like a snake. Not a snake, a root, but Silver had been too much hurt by snakes in the past, when they writhed and bit at her bad arm. She stumbled back with a shriek. No, no, just a root. No poison to enter her blood.

She needed to keep control of herself. Whatever this man's defenses, they were not things of snakes, of poison. But no matter what Silver did, the plants still swarmed around her, and the roots curled and wound across the ground. She needed another set of eyes, untainted, but she had only Death. "Death," she begged, "you have to help me. What's real?"

Death placed himself beside the human man, putting the man's regal manner to shame with a stance of real power. "He thinks you asked him." He tipped his head to look at the man's expression, congealing to fearful disgust, and his laugh sliced at her. "But perhaps he does not wish to answer. Perhaps he does not understand why you asked. Few but the most weak and the dangerous must ask what is real."

"No!" Silver shouted it at the man, at Death, forgetting that she was supposed to be weak. But she didn't want to be this weak. Not real weakness, unfeigned. She drew in a breath of the man's scent, and it held all she feared. He was older but still considered himself more than strong enough to physically control a woman such as her. His fear was subtle, perhaps even unrealized, fear of something so strange, so wild, you could not predict its movements. Crazy. Crazy things could hurt you badly even when you were strong.

There would be no reasoning with the man, if that was his fear. Any words would be seen as a ploy, a distraction before some more unpredictable action. Silver saw little choice left but to run.

Out, out this time, she didn't care if the man grabbed at her. It was worth the risk. She slammed past him and he got no grip. The branches tossed violently, nonexistent wind whistling among them to make a high, wailing sound that grew louder and louder. They were angry at her escape, perhaps. Silver took it as a good sign and did not stop.

The wailing ceased as she burst through the den's entrance. Silver did not pause, because the plants were outside the den as well, grown to jungle heights beyond the confines of the structure. One path was empty of them, one path to freedom without the roots striking at her, holding her here.

Silver released a sobbed breath. Two humans tromped up that path, heavy footed. One was more broad shouldered, the other dark skinned, but they both had a similarity of movement. Enforcers. If she ran now, they would run after, run her down. She had not the speed to escape such as these, and she knew it.

"Please," she begged them. She feinted one direction, in case they did not know the plants' malice for her and would believe she'd run that way. Both moved to stand loose, ready to chase.

"Ma'am. You need to stay where you are." The one of broad

shoulders had a true enforcer's voice: pure power without decision. His authority lay in carrying out another's orders, making him implacable, mind never to be changed.

Silver stayed. The chief enforcer bound her wrists behind her with hard metal, but not silver. He must have noticed the way her bad arm hung dead, but he merely pulled it firmly into the binding himself. "You have the right to remain silent," he said, and something more, but Silver missed it in wondering what he could possibly mean by the first part. Of course she could always choose to stay silent. In this situation, she planned to at least try to explain herself first—just because they were enforcers didn't mean they couldn't understand logic or reason. Did humans feel they must always answer any question an enforcer asked?

He touched her all over, searching for weapons, Silver supposed. He found her talisman and took it away. Silver watched tightly as the enforcer examined the small square. Dare had given it to her so she could show that she was herself, or was such a person as humans could understand. Would it calm the enforcer? He liked it enough to hand it to his partner, who spoke at a distance to someone about it, saying her old name several times.

Silver rolled her shoulders, hating the way her bad arm dragged at the binding. Had they told her to remain silent because they planned to ask her no questions? She tried to read the chief enforcer's scent, and failing that, his manner. When she looked closer, shadows lurked on his arms, shadows as Silver was used to seeing on people in great pain. They moved sluggishly, and Silver was glad they hadn't noticed her when he searched her.

Then one separated from the skin of his hand and reached out for her, as if it had heard her thought and planned to make up for the oversight. Silver flinched away, she couldn't help herself. This was worse than any snake, this was the evil snakes carried with their poison. And yet she saw none of that evil in the enforcer's eyes. How could that be?

Another shadow peeled away from the human and drifted toward her with malevolent interest. They weren't *his* pain, *his* evil, Silver realized. They belonged to others and had come to rest on him like a scent. What pain must surround him for it to adhere so? She risked a glance at his partner and found he bore a burden of shadows too, now she knew to look.

"Ma'am. Calm down. Tell us what you're doing here." The chief enforcer frowned at her. His partner went to speak with the den owner. Silver caught his wide, angry gestures from the corner of her eye.

"My—" Silver wanted to say "mate's daughter," but of course she shouldn't say "mate" in front of the humans. She knew plenty of other words, but she couldn't *think* with the weight of the hovering shadows. "My lover's daughter, she—"

More shadows drifted for her, and Silver jerked away from them. What would happen if they attached themselves to one as poisoned as she already was? Would they drain her dry? But she needed to explain herself. She had not meant the human harm. "She told me to meet her here, but she's not here . . ."

A shadow slashed at her face and Silver cried out. "You have too many shadows, I'm just the kind of easy prey they like. Please, just let me go. I meant no harm, I hurt no one."

The enforcers kept their distrust mostly hidden, but Silver saw its growth in the ugly purple-green bruise hue deepening in the shadows. The same fear the den owner had shown, of her unpredictability. "Shadows," the chief enforcer repeated. He touched her shoulder, perhaps to remind her she was bound, in their power.

The shadows boiled and surged gleefully up her arm, taking the old scars as river channels, questing for her blood, her bone. "No," Silver begged. "Death, please. Chase them away." Death did nothing of the sort, and the enforcer's grip tightened.

He asked her again why she was here, what she'd been doing inside the human's den, but she couldn't find any words to answer. She'd chosen silence after all, she supposed. She panted, knowing she was doing it, but she couldn't stop. He wouldn't release his grip, not now she looked ready to run from him, and the shadows swarmed over her skin. It was all she could do not to sob. "You have too many shadows! Stop touching me!"

"Merely hearing they exist has not banished anyone's shadows yet," Death said in her brother's voice, gentle now. "Hold yourself together and they will find few cracks to enter."

Silver gritted her teeth on any further outbursts. Death would not take her, she was sure of that, and any taint the shadows left behind could be exorcised later. Hadn't Dare helped her remove the poison the snakes left in her arm, once upon a time? She would survive this.

Finally the enforcer guided her away from the den. He was taking her somewhere, and Silver smashed down the thought that the somewhere might be the source of the shadows until the accompanying panic made her heart race no more than it already was. No cracks. She would allow no cracks for the shadows.

17

Felicia had to jolt her brain back onto the trail of another plan when the police led Silver away. She'd snuck in closer, hiding behind the crowd that gathered when Silver came outside and caused a scene with her ramblings. Felicia had heard weirder things from her, but they sounded so alien dropped into the mundane, human world of cops and trespassing laws.

Felicia groped after what to do next. She'd known Silver talking her way out of trouble was a long shot. Felicia should have been thinking of what to do if Silver *was* arrested, but she couldn't—she didn't—and now Silver was, and Felicia fought a rising tide of self-directed anger for her uselessness.

If TV was to be believed, Silver would need a lawyer. Felicia's father had a Were with training back East who did wills and paperwork, but that didn't seem like quite the same thing.

But Susan was human. She'd know how to get a lawyer. Felicia almost dropped the phone in her relief as she fumbled it out. Better call quickly, before Enrique stopped congratulating himself and came over.

"I'm at work, Felicia." Susan's voice when she answered wasn't precisely angry, but it wasn't welcoming either.

"I don't know what Silver just . . . she must have seen something, she was coming to meet me, she took a wrong turn and went into someone's house. I think they called the police, because they showed up, sirens and everything, and arrested her." Felicia allowed her real panic into her voice to make it fast and hopefully confused enough to hide any details that didn't match up.

Something clunked down and then a door slammed, like Susan had shut herself in an office to take the call. "She went—what? What the hell is going on?"

Felicia repeated herself and then listened to silence for several seconds. Susan finally blew out a breath. "She'll need a lawyer. Things are going to be bad enough without her getting any old public defender." Susan paused a beat, like maybe she expected Felicia to contribute, but Felicia didn't want to reveal she'd had time to think about it. She made a helpless noise and Susan continued. "My coworker, her brother is in family law, so he can't help, but hopefully he'll know someone. I'll get the number before I leave. If they don't put her in jail, she'll need someone to pick her up. Where are you? I have to figure out which station they'd take her to." Susan hung up after Felicia gave her the address.

Felicia stuffed the phone away when she spotted Enrique coming toward her, beaming. He didn't seem to notice it. "Perfect! It's like she figured out the worst possible way to act. The only thing better would have been if she'd fought them."

Felicia gritted her teeth and punched his shoulder, hard. "Looking as weak as she does, that would have raised dangerous questions for all of us."

Enrique acknowledged that with a grimace, then shrugged. "Anyway, it's done. Now, we wait and let the human justice system do its job." He grabbed her hand and tugged her back in the direction of his car.

Felicia planted her feet and refused to be tugged. "If I don't show up, all apologies for misleading the alpha and concern for her, they're going to figure I did it on purpose. I want to stay in this pack, remember?"

Enrique growled softly in frustration. "Yes, all right. Good luck." He dropped her hand and strode off for his car.

Felicia hugged herself, momentarily overwhelmed by her situation once more. But she didn't indulge it for very long this time. She wanted to be at the pack house when Silver and Susan arrived. She couldn't go in, but she could park down the street and wait.

When Felicia reached the house, one of the spots on the street in front of the house was open, so she pulled in and watched the road in her rearview mirror. Something thumped in the back, but Felicia couldn't think of anything Morsel could damage, so she left the cat to it. It had food, water, and litter, and the small sliding window was still cracked.

Susan's compact pulled up over two hours later. Felicia stumbled on the long step down out of the truck's cab and arrived at the car as Susan opened the passenger door for Silver.

Silver didn't look good. She was white lipped, and her bad arm dangled free, which Silver never let it do when she could help it. Worse, she wasn't holding herself like an alpha. She clutched a piece of paper and a card to her chest, and once she stepped out of the car, Susan started coaxing them out of her hand.

Susan checked the card—the nondriver ID her father had gotten Silver, Felicia realized—and handed it back. She kept the paper and read it, eyes flicking quickly down the sheet. "Burglary," she said in Felicia's direction, pointedly. "It's got her court date on it. I thought she might have to stay in jail until they set bail tomorrow, but I guess they decided the case wasn't strong enough to need that."

Thus acknowledged, Felicia dared to come closer. She craned her neck, but Susan smoothed the paper with a jerky, frustrated movement and held it too close for Felicia to read. Burglary, wasn't that worse than trespassing? Lady.

"I've got her a rush appointment for tomorrow morning with a lawyer my friend knew." Susan was looking at Felicia when she said it. Felicia didn't understand why Susan was telling her anything, but she realized suddenly that Susan was stressed enough to feel the need to tell *someone,* and Silver wouldn't follow.

"The lawyer can defend her from that, right? Convince them it was a mistake?" Felicia bit her lip. She should have paid more attention to the lawyer TV shows as well as the police ones.

"Well, if it was you," Susan said, spearing Felicia with a look that made her want to flinch, "I'd say that it wouldn't be too big a deal, because I presume she didn't take anything, or touch anything. But I really don't know. How the hell is Silver going to speak in court?"

Silver shook herself as if returning from a great mental distance and put her hand on Susan's arm. "I'll speak when I need to. The shadows will not catch me off guard again." She seemed to rebuild the alpha piece by piece, starting with her shoulders, traveling through her body in both directions, and ending with a tilt of her chin. "After a meal."

"Oh, of course." Susan bustled Silver into the house, leaving Felicia standing on the driveway. She hadn't missed the way Silver's eyes had skipped right over her. Clearly, she was being pointedly ignored, but at least she hadn't been chased off.

Morsel came forward to put her nose to the breeze as Felicia opened the canopy, but she shooed the cat back and managed to get inside without any escapes. She settled in, opened a package of beef jerky, and ate her own dinner.

Afterward, out of sheer frustration with having nothing of substance to do, Felicia decided to start accustoming Morsel to wolf forms. Maybe it didn't matter since she was just going to give that cat back to the shelter, but being friendly with large dogs should make it more adoptable later, shouldn't it? She was doing it a favor.

The cat went all puffy tailed when Felicia disappeared and a big canine appeared in her place, but Felicia flumped down and waited with her head on her paws. Morsel cautiously approached, sniffing, then danced back. A few more rounds of that and it bapped Felicia on the nose with no claws. Felicia surged to her feet and nosed the cat onto its back, where it went after her with all four paws and teeth, delighted by the game.

Felicia had to admit it was at least a little bit fun for her too, like playing with the kids in wolf. When she tired of the game, she curled up in the corner of the truck bed still in wolf. That form was better for sleeping comfortably on hard surfaces anyway. Morsel washed itself for a while and then came to curl against her side.

She dozed until someone knocked against the canopy. People had been coming and going intermittently, so she hadn't particularly noticed someone approaching the truck.

Morsel blinked sleepily at her as she shoved it far enough away to be able to shift back. She pulled on her shirt so she would appear decent to anyone on the road, bundled Morsel into its box, and then opened the canopy while leaving the tailgate up.

Silver waited there, calmly blank faced. Her hair seemed almost to glow in the lowering sun, white drawing in the diffuse light.

Lady. Felicia barely prevented worse curses from making it out of her mouth. "I . . . should get dressed if you want to talk," she said, and Silver nodded silently. She shut the canopy long enough to wiggle into the rest of her clothes, then opened the tailgate and sat on it. Silver leaned her ass on it beside her.

The silence stretched longer and longer, and finally Felicia couldn't take it anymore. "I'm sorry! For earlier, and now this. I didn't mean . . ." Felicia bit her lip. What *had* she meant? To protect her own place in the pack at the expense of someone else? What kind of pack member did that make her?

"Didn't you?" Silver looked up into the sky, though the Lady's face was hidden in another direction at this hour of the evening. "Are you loyal to the Roanoke pack?"

Felicia's head snapped up from where she'd dropped it anticipation of scolding. "Yes," she said, trying to put every ounce of sincerity she'd felt in her life into her eyes to support the word.

"Are you loyal to me as alpha of that pack? Do you mean me harm?"

"Yes. No." Felicia had meant to stick to the simple syllables, but more words came tumbling out after. "When I saw you go in there by mistake, I thought maybe you could talk your way out of it." Perhaps it would be more accurate to say that she'd hoped that, hoped with all her strength. After all, Silver had told Felicia's father that it was hard to be Selene, but not impossible. Right?

"Come here." Silver stepped back to give Felicia room to jump down. When Felicia faced her, Silver took her chin in a grip hard enough to bruise, heal, and then bruise again. Felicia endured it silently, trying not to wince.

Silver's voice lowered, gaining intensity, until it practically vibrated. "I can be what I once was, briefly. But I wish I could make you—make all of you—understand its price. So high a price that perhaps this time I try to pay it, or perhaps the next, perhaps that will be the time I have nothing to pay it with and will lose myself completely. Once, I did it to save Dare's life. When you saw it, I did it for Tom, and to keep the knowledge of all of us from the humans. I would not do it again for anything less, and perhaps I cannot for something more. Do you understand?"

Felicia nodded with a jerk. Lady, she didn't understand where Silver stored that intensity when she wasn't using it. It made her want to shiver.

"What you did was no mistake. This began with the roamer, and I don't know if you're trying to impress him or punish

Tom, but if you meant no harm, you have completely lost the trail of that prey."

Felicia moved slightly, just to redistribute her weight, and Silver jerked her chin hard enough to draw an involuntary cry. She'd been wrong to call Silver creepy to Enrique, she realized. Creepy implied something you didn't quite understand. Silver was Lady-damned *terrifying* at this moment, because she made you understand exactly the things no one wanted to think about.

"And so now we are here. Whatever you *meant,* naïve little girl, this is what has happened. So Susan tells me I will have to pay the price to see your world again, if I can, or the humans will lock me away. So understand this, girl. If I succeed in paying that price, it will be for you. Are your adulthood, your pride, your games with young men worth it? Think on that, and tell me, because I do not know myself." She tossed Felicia's head so it snapped back, then stalked into the house, leaving Felicia panting alone on the driveway.

Terrifying. Because she was also right.

Around 6 A.M., Felicia got tired of changing position in the truck's bed, trying to get a decent night's sleep with a whole different suite of noises constantly waking her up. She gave up and snuck inside to shower and get fresh clothes. Pierce opened his door, looked her over, and went back to bed without saying anything. The others had undoubtedly recognized her scent and gone back to sleep, leaving it to the Were nominally on guard duty to make the ruling.

She didn't steal any breakfast, but she did take a book to read in the truck while the sun edged higher in the sky, chasing away the chill. She kept half an eye the house through the canopy window as she read. If something happened with Silver's case today, she wanted to help.

As Felicia had half expected, Susan ushered Silver outside around midmorning. Susan's suit all but knocked you over and set its boot on your neck, it projected such authority. Silver wore a pair of slacks from one of the female pack members and one of Susan's blouses without a jacket. Felicia topped off Morsel's water from her own bottle, made sure the side window was still slightly cracked, and then jumped down and closed up the truck. She brushed herself off even though the bed was pretty clean and went to join the two other women. She felt underdressed in her jeans, but she hadn't thought to grab anything more formal when she was in the house.

Susan gave her a sharp look. "We have an appointment with the lawyer. We don't want to be late," she said and opened her car's passenger door for Silver.

Felicia dipped her head low, giving respectful signals even if Susan might not read them as precisely as a Were would. "I . . . it's partially my fault she got into this, so I hoped I could come and see if my taking responsibility could help any."

Susan *hmphed*, dubious, but Silver gestured vaguely in the direction of the back of the car. "Let her come. She can help explain, and maybe this will prevent her getting into more trouble while we're gone."

Felicia had to swallow to keep herself from responding to the final barb. She'd gotten what she wanted, she reminded herself.

Susan tested her self-control even more. "If you start making it worse, I'm going to tell you to shut up, and you're going to shut up. Understand?"

Felicia nodded, not trusting herself to answer. The heavy silence persisted through the drive. Felicia assumed Susan had already coached Silver on what their approach would be. At least she hoped Susan and Silver had some kind of approach. They'd have to, wouldn't they? Felicia practiced her own arguments in her head just in case.

The law office took up one floor in a small brick-and-glass office building. There were only two chairs across from the reception desk, so Felicia lurked uncomfortably in the corner in front of a potted plant. Silver shied from the plant and took the chair farthest from it.

"Susan? I'm Rebecca Terrell." The lawyer who let herself out of the inner door and came over to offer her hand was very tall with very pointed toes on her high heels. Having seen Susan use fashion as aggression, Felicia recognized it here as well.

"Thank you for fitting us in on short notice." Susan shook the woman's hand firmly and gestured to Silver. "This is Selene."

Silver shook her hand more awkwardly. "I go by Silver, though."

"Unusual name." Rebecca offered a smile and looked from one to the other. "I'd better warn you, Selene, that if Susan attends our meeting as a nonclient, you've automatically waived your attorney-client privilege."

Susan's expression creased with worry. Felicia didn't blame her. She'd expected that she might not be allowed in, but Silver needed *someone* to translate. But wasn't the client privilege important? It always seemed that way on TV.

"Oh, maybe I'd better—" Susan said.

Silver cut her off with a tight grip on her arm. "That's fine," she said.

Rebecca nodded. She didn't seem overly worried by the decision, at least. "Come on back, then." She threw Felicia a questioning look, probably wondering how she was involved.

"This is her boyfriend's daughter. She was involved in the incident, so we hoped she could help explain what happened." Felicia nodded to the lawyer, but some of Susan's annoyance with her must have transmitted to the other human through her body language, because Rebecca didn't bother to offer her hand. Was that good, because being the naughty teen suited the part Felicia was going to play? Or would it harm her credibility? Felicia couldn't see how to change it either way.

Rebecca showed them back to what was clearly a shared meeting room, not a private office. It had an oval table with half a dozen plush office chairs placed around it, and several shelves with impressive leather-bound books with shiny gold lettering. Felicia wondered if they were actually used, or kept strictly for decoration. She imagined everything was online nowadays.

Silver's attention tracked something along the floor as she sat, but she snapped it back to the lawyer quickly enough. Felicia considered standing again, but she finally took a chair at the opposite end of the table from everyone else.

Susan took out the paper Silver had been clutching yesterday and slid it across the table to Rebecca. The lawyer flicked her eyes over it and nodded, like she'd seen hundreds before.

"On that date, you and I will show up in court, and I'll speak for you. Before then, though, if it was a mistake and you didn't disturb anything, it should be relatively easy to get the charges bumped down to trespass. Criminal trespass in the first degree is a gross misdemeanor. The penalty is up to five thousand dollars in fines and 364 days in jail, but that's almost never given for a first offense. Do you have a criminal record?" Susan shook her head for Silver, and Rebecca continued. "That will help. From your perspective, what happened? Did you know you were trespassing?"

Susan tapped her fingertips on the table. "Here's the tough part. Silver has a neurological language disability. I don't know the exact name, but under stress it can make it hard for her to remember words for complex concepts she wants to convey, and things like addresses, phone numbers, and names."

"And so people assume I'm simple-minded." Silver spoke softly, but with such confidence the eye was immediately drawn to her. "I think they probably thought I was crazy when they gave me that." She tapped the ticket. "Now I'm prepared, I can pay closer attention, but I'm worried about what they might do with that initial impression."

Felicia marveled at how smoothly both of them presented it. It sounded exactly like dozens of human mental problems she'd heard described on the news. Maybe Susan was right, and Felicia adding anything would be more hindrance than help.

Rebecca's eyebrows rose. "Do you have an official diagnosis?"

Susan shook her head. "It's not . . . officially recognized. She worked with someone a while back who helped her treat it, and it's really improved a lot, but I'm afraid that another psychologist might not agree."

Rebecca frowned in thought. "We could use lack of capacity as a defense, if the evaluating psychologist agreed. Competency might still be an issue, however."

Susan voiced the question on Felicia's mind even more succinctly: "What?"

Rebecca laughed lightly. "Basically, competency is whether you're mentally all there enough to understand the trial. Capacity is whether you were mentally all there enough at the time of the crime to actually understand what you were doing and therefore have the intent to commit the crime. So lack of capacity would be a defense, but if the psychologist finds that Silver is still having troubles now, they could put her into treatment until they think she's competent enough for the trial."

Silver's hand tightened until her knuckles went white. "I don't need treatment." Susan reached to take her hand to comfort her, but Silver jerked hers away and sat up straighter. Felicia swallowed. The Were as a whole needed to keep Silver from being dragged into treatment.

Rebecca nodded. "Certainly. The evaluation wouldn't happen immediately, anyway. You'd need to be evaluated by a state psychologist. That could take quite some time, perhaps six months or more. Funds have to become available, and the state's currently very strapped for money."

"No, soon." Silver spoke emphatically. "As soon as Dare can get home."

"Can't we pay, if money's the issue?" Susan sat forward in her chair.

"Well, you could have an evaluation by an expert of your choice at any time you like and submit that to the state." Rebecca nodded to Silver. "Then they can either accept it, or call a competency hearing to decide between that and whatever evidence they get from their own psychologist—and given the funding issue, they're more likely to just cross-examine your expert carefully and then accept that report. If you don't want to wait, that's an option."

Susan nodded, expression tight, but Silver fidgeted. "I'd rather sooner than later, but are you sure it's necessary at all? Can't you just be the one to tell them about my—" Silver struggled for a moment, presumably searching for "neurological language disability," until she gave in and gestured to Susan.

Silver wasn't bad yet, but Felicia couldn't sit here and let her get more and more visibly upset in front of the human who was supposed to be their ally in this fight. "It wasn't like she was actually trespassing, anyway!"

Silver's attention snapped to her, and for a moment Felicia couldn't quite breathe, because she thought Silver was going to denounce her. Then Silver dipped her head and turned to the lawyer. "Felicia asked me to meet her and I thought she was staying with a friend. We'd"—Silver flicked a glance to Felicia and smiled thinly—"argued earlier and she wasn't staying at home for a while. I went in expecting to find her or her friend."

Felicia checked Susan's reaction. She was listening intently, not interfering. Felicia scooted up to the table a little more.

"I'd called her from the park down the street. I guess the door must not have latched and she saw it slightly open or whatever? I guess I wasn't very precise, it's just a tiny little park, and it doesn't have a name, so I told her the streets."

Susan looked like she actually believed that, to Felicia's relief, but of course Silver knew better. Felicia's trail had been unmistakable, as she'd meant it to be. But Silver continued to not denounce her and nodded as the lawyer discussed her approach. Felicia tried to track it all, but it quickly veered into vocabulary even she couldn't follow. The lawyer seemed to know what she was doing. Now all they had to do was make sure Silver didn't do anything any more crazy seeming than she already had.

18

Three days later, the day Silver would have to face the memories, it was all she could do not to pace. They'd gotten word to Dare by calling those who had helped him call last, and everyone else who might have seen Dare, until word passed directly from person to person, not over distances. They arranged it: he'd planned to be home this morning and help her find the memories, if she could, for this afternoon. Three days had seemed not so long to wait, not long enough tangle herself in worry, and then he'd be with her. Wait too long, and the anticipation would make everything worse, she'd been sure of it.

And then came the delays. Tom and Susan explained them again and again in simpler words, but they lacked Dare's ability to understand her world enough to use its terms. Silver didn't need to know why he couldn't return as he had planned, just that he couldn't. But there was still time. Tom and Susan assured her of that.

Death smiled and kept his own counsel.

With an hour to go, Silver read in Tom's scent that even though Dare and her cousin had finally begun traveling, they would not arrive in time. Silver slipped away from Tom's hovering. Susan would undoubtedly have wanted to hover also, but she had been away from her work too much already. Silver had resorted to ordering her to go.

Silver checked the wind outside for Felicia lingering too close to the den, then started walking. The girl and her pet were not in evidence, though Silver suspected she would be back soon enough to insinuate herself into the group visiting the human who would determine Silver's sanity. She didn't know what Felicia was up to, but she did seem to be sincere about helping. Even if that help didn't balance out the trouble she'd caused in the first place.

Lady damn the girl. No matter her protestations now, she'd trapped Silver using her exact weaknesses. Forget finding something to keep her busy, Felicia needed to roam, somewhere far from Silver. She'd tell Dare that when this was all over. Even the thought of a break from dealing with Felicia and her contradictions and her apologies and her lies and her concealed scent lifted a weight that had been thinning Silver's voice.

But all this was stalling, not getting her ready to speak to humans in terms they would understand. If Dare wouldn't be here in time, she would have to find the memories alone. She would find them. She'd done it before, she'd do it again. She had to believe that.

Silver found an open space, manicured but filled with colorful places for children to climb. She leaned her cheek against the cool line of one structure and thought about the memories that she kept pushed deep, the memories that cut, the memories that burned.

But she couldn't bring herself to touch them, having looked at their glittering, smoldering surface. This time, she had no momentum, no sense of running, panting, scooping up the memories as fast as she could, or someone would hurt, would die. Today, she had time to think. Think about the pain in store, and your body froze from sheer self-preservation, no matter how you railed at it to keep going. Silver thought about the memories, and couldn't make herself touch them. What if this time, the pain made her lose herself completely?

"Help me," she begged, seeking out Death where he lounged under the structure, shadows pooled like comfortable bedding around him.

"You have what you need, Selene. If you do not use it, I cannot use it for you." Death flicked his ears, dismissing her.

Silver gritted her teeth and closed her eyes, as if sheer effort would help her. She knew it wouldn't, that fighting such paralysis with strength would lock her metaphorical muscles even more deeply, but she didn't know what else to do.

"Roanoke?" A new voice. Silver's eyes popped open.

Portland's sister ducked her head, diffident, but curiosity shone through in the rest of her body. She must have found Silver's trail before reaching the den, because everyone there knew Silver wanted privacy and would have warned her away.

Silver laughed, jagged. "This is an extremely bad time. Why are you even still here?" She'd hoped that with her ignoring them the past several days, Portland and her beta would have returned home, but everyone seemed determined to linger in her home territory until matters were settled. Silver had known that she'd have to keep nudging the various sub-alphas along the path to calming down, but Craig still acted as if her decision would change.

Eliza opened her mouth but was unable to find her voice for several moments. "I'm sorry. I wanted a chance to speak to you privately, but I can come back at a different time—"

"Speak to me about living your sister's life for her?" Silver knew that was too harsh, even before Death laughed. She tightened her hand around the structure she leaned against and reminded herself of Dare's words. Listen to them whine. "I know you're only concerned for her. But perhaps the trouble is that I don't understand why."

At first, Silver thought her initial answer would keep Eliza from speaking, but the woman's voice bubbled up soon enough, offered an outlet. "It's not just about during the pregnancy." She gestured more widely as she warmed to her subject. "It's the fact that the father's not her mate, and she doesn't seem to want him to be. I hoped when she finally made it to alpha, she'd settle down and stop chasing around, but now she's bringing a child into that . . ."

"With a whole pack to raise it," Silver countered softly, but something about how Eliza said it, so exasperated, sparked a connection.

Ares had said that to her once: "Lady, Selene. Don't you ever want to settle down? I'm all for finding the right person, but you can hold out too long, you know."

And Silver—Selene—had said . . . Silver seized the trail the conversation laid into the core of her memories. Nose down, and follow. Don't think of the pain.

She'd thrown her arms around her brother's neck from behind, hanging her weight from his shoulders, because it annoyed him. "You're right, I'm so incredibly ancient, I'd better settle right away." She jerked on her hands, but he refused to be unbalanced. "I have family. I have a pack. I'll have a mate when I'm ready."

He sighed, and she loosened her grip and swung around to see his face. Warm blue eyes, just a hint of a beard—

—stained with blood from the cut above his eyebrow, not flowing now, because he was dead, too much poison in his veins, one of the last to be injected, should have been strongest as the alpha, but Selene was the one left, the one alive, alive to smell the blood and the silver and the death.

"Ares," Selene whispered. Ares had a mate, Ares had children. A mate who was dead, children who were dead. Selene didn't know how long she'd last this time as herself, whether she'd make it through the psychologist's appointment, but all that time she'd hold her nephew and niece close, even as they choked her with the blood they bled in dying.

"I can't be late," she told Eliza and strode away without further explanation. She and Ares had come to this playground as children, though it had been just a swing set and a slide then, not this grand castle of brightly colored plastic and pipes. Running in the woods was more fun, but they had to learn to pass as human children at school, so they came here and practiced. That memory cut less, let her mind keep moving as she jogged back to the house.

———

Felicia frowned at her phone and switched back and forth between the weather report for Anchorage and the airline's flight-status page. It was summer, for crying out loud. Her father shouldn't be getting delayed by storms. It said he was in the air now, but no matter how many times she redid the math in her head, he wouldn't arrive in time for Silver's appointment. She thought they should cancel—what did it matter, anyway? Things came up. But Silver had seemed pretty sure the longer she waited, the harder acting sane would be. It was up to her and Susan, not Felicia.

Felicia returned the phone to the default clock. She'd need to make an excuse to be at the house again soon. If her father wasn't going to be home, she definitely wanted to go along and do whatever she could to help, even if that wasn't much. She'd parked Tom's truck about a block away this time, but that was a bit far to see people coming out of the house and then show up before they'd already gotten into the car.

She opened the canopy and climbed out, with the gate still up to keep Morsel inside. The first person she saw was Enrique, stalking toward the truck from deeper within the neighborhood. He moved as though he was halfway to shifting through pure anger, graceless on two legs. What now?

He clumped to a stop with his feet braced like he planned to start yelling at her, but then he ran shaking fingers through his hair and said nothing. Felicia pressed her lips together and waited for him to wrestle himself under control to speak. "Madrid is . . . not happy. I reported what's happened, and he seems to think you've been laying me false trails."

Felicia winced, even just imagining what that conversation

must have been like. Madrid could flay you so quietly, so softly, just with words. Of course *he'd* see through her. Lady damn it. She'd begun to hope things might actually work out. "Why in the Lady's name would I do that? You could get me kicked out of my pack in an instant."

Enrique slashed an arm, though there was no whip in his hand. "Because you think you're so smart. Think you can control anyone, like your father. Well, that ends now." His lip lifted, but he didn't voice the snarl. "When is Silver's appointment?"

Felicia pressed her lips together, tight. Now she regretted having told him about the appointment, but when they'd last spoken, it had seemed a good way to reassure him matters were progressing, so he didn't need to interfere. "The appointment time is none of your business. Besides, my father's not going to make it, so they might cancel it anyway."

"No." Enrique grabbed at Felicia's free wrist. He squeezed tight enough to hurt. "You're going to make sure they go forward. You'll go along and do something to set her off again, make sure she's absolutely raving for the psychologist."

Like the tipping point into wolf after a long, hard new moon struggle to shift, seeing Enrique's selfishness triggered something in Felicia. No. Too much. She'd played along with this for fear of Enrique's threat for too long. She was already barred from the house anyway. Better to be kicked out of the pack completely and know she'd kept some honor. She wasn't going to hurt Silver.

Any more than she already had.

"I don't have to do a Lady-damned thing!" She tore her wrist away from his grip. "In fact, I'm going to do everything I can to help Silver get through this."

Enrique snarled audibly this time. "So you're ready for them to find out about how you've been loyal to Madrid all along?"

Felicia pushed forward into Enrique's face. "I'd rather be kicked out of Roanoke than live in Madrid, Enrique. The lowest member of Roanoke has a hundred times the honor of Madrid himself, and you can't make me work against them any longer. Madrid disgusts me, and now you're modeling yourself on him, you disgust me too."

Only worry about her voice carrying to the house kept Felicia from shouting by the end. Enrique stared at her, incomprehension in his face. Felicia tipped her chin up and showed him her teeth in a sharp smile. "So show the pack your clever forgeries. Tell them how I lied for you, how I let you get information out of me. Those were my mistakes, I'll own it. But you can crawl back to Madrid with nothing to show him all on your own."

Enrique reached for her, she could see in his face he planned to shake her savagely, but Felicia didn't let him. She stepped back and knocked away his hands each time he touched her. Bruises rose and faded on both their arms.

Enrique finally jerked away, panting. *"Your honor is worth less than a whisper in the void. Let North America keep you, and may they enjoy you."* He stalked away into the neighborhood, leaving Felicia shaking.

Thoughts of what might happen now tried to crowd into her mind, but Felicia didn't let them. First, she needed to make sure Silver got through this. Then she'd worry about herself.

19

Selene turned a corner onto their street and saw Felicia and the young man of a roamer—Enrique—parting as if after a scuffle, Felicia for the pack house, Enrique in Selene's approximate direction. He saw her before she could think of detouring to avoid him. He smiled, still too oily to be handsome, but the stink of rage hovered around him. He overbowed, extravagant respect wobbling on the edge of mocking. "Roanoke. I hear your mate's daughter arranged you some difficulties. I hope they are quickly resolved." He emphasized "arranged" viciously.

Chile, he'd said. That popped into Selene's mind out of nowhere, drawing a new, sharp meaning with it. She remembered Chile, or at least South American countries in general. The accent there was different from that in Mexico or Puerto Rico.

Or Madrid.

Selene had heard that accent before, or Silver had. In several voices, in fact: Madrid and his beta when they arrived to cause trouble three years ago, and in Felicia herself when she got angry or upset. She'd not call herself an expert, but she was familiar enough to recognize it now. Silver could have too, if not for the fact that Chile and Madrid both were so far outside the web of people she mapped her conception of the world onto. Far was far, and why distinguish direction?

If Enrique was from Madrid, why was he here? Selene mentally cursed herself for missing it before and continued the cursing when she realized she'd gone too long without answering.

"Nothing for you to worry about," she told Enrique, smiling to show her teeth. She strode off without another glance at him.

No time, no time to figure out what Enrique's plans here might be, whether he was involved with Felicia leading her into that human's house. Selene tried to follow even a simple trail of conclusions leading away from her realization and lost it at the first turn. She didn't have the mental strength to do that, and hold on to herself, and hold the memories back, and remember what her story should be for the humans. It would have to wait, she had no choice.

As if to prove her point, thoughts of Enrique's plans brought with them more painful connections. Selene's foot caught on her next step and she stumbled. Enrique couldn't catch this pack off guard the way that monster had, wouldn't even get the chance to torture them the way the other had. But the blood filled her mind anyway.

She made it as far as the car and panted there, palm against the metal, holding back sobs. Sun had warmed the metal, but it was still a grounded sensation, smooth and hard and slightly dusty.

"Silver?" Tom's voice nearly squeaked with his worry as he hurried over from the house. He started to nudge her aside and open her door for her, and Selene smacked him back and opened it herself. She needed that. Door handle, lock, mechanism she could hear lifting the latch. Details of this world.

"I'm going to have to talk enough when we get there," Selene said and punched the radio on the moment he climbed in and inserted the key. She tried to make her voice kind, but she had not enough of that for herself at the moment, none for anyone else. The words on the radio helped her focus: Middle East, mortgage, Internet, Congress. Concepts to wrap her mind around and hold on.

The back door opened and Felicia climbed in silently, slamming it after her. Tom, already twisted in his seat to back up the car, frowned at her. Selene growled until his attention switched back to the road and he pulled them out. "Let her come." When later came, she wanted Felicia very close, to explain what in the Lady's name was going on.

Felicia swallowed audibly. Perhaps Selene's tone worried her. Selene listened to the radio and decided that suited her purposes just fine.

In the psychologist's office, robbed of the radio, Selene tried to focus on details of her surroundings, but the building made it hard. They parked below the high-rise, floor numbers in cheerful colors doing little to distinguish row upon row of concrete columns and low, claustrophobic ceilings. The office itself had glass doors and waiting chairs of curved light wood and neutral upholstery. The prints on the walls showed soothing brushstrokes too soft for Selene to find a grip on. One was splashed with red, so she sat as far from it as possible after speaking to the receptionist.

Felicia sat on one side of her, in the next chair in an attached row, too close for what Selene would have predicted human comfort to be. Tom sat on the other side, separated by an end table covered with magazines. He and Felicia eyed each other across Selene, he suspiciously and she balefully. Selene desperately wanted to leave them behind and pace, but she suspected that a patient pacing the waiting room was the kind of thing psychologists took note of.

She snatched up a magazine with enough violence to crinkle the back page and read about celebrities entering rehab or hiding possible pregnancies. Names, names, none of them that mattered. Those worked much better than the stupid art to concentrate on.

And then they called her. Selene sat for a moment, gathering herself. Normal. Be normal. Forget the blood, forget her brother, forget the one who'd killed her pack. She was Selene, a normal human whose boyfriend's daughter had played a nasty trick on her. She left the others and walked into the hallway to the individual offices.

"Welcome. Selene Powell? I'm Dr. Doyle." The psychologist came forward with his hand outstretched to shake as she entered his office. He was African American, but otherwise looked nothing like Boston, leaner faced and much more solemn. Still, something in the timbre of his voice reminded her of the Were. She clung to that. Talking to Boston was nothing to fear.

Dr. Doyle gestured for her to take a seat on a couch opposite a chair. It had several pillows, but they weren't placed with the precision decorative ones usually were. They looked slightly smushed and bowed in places, like people actually used them. Boxes of tissues stood on tables at both ends of the couch, their sheets pulled tall, crisp, and inviting. Selene glanced at the art, a couple of shore landscapes, and then away. She should keep her attention on the psychologist.

Better to hurry things along. She didn't want to lose the battle of endurance, if this became one. "I'm not crazy," she told him. "I know I was stressed out, and I have the stupid memory thing—" She wiggled her fingers near her temple. "But it's not really that bad. I knew what I was doing, I just didn't realize my boyfriend's daughter didn't know those people—"

The psychologist nodded, expression neutral. Selene imagined him smiling as Boston would have, but it didn't help. "Don't worry, that's what we'll figure out. Ms. Terrell shared some information with me, but can you tell me your side of the incident?"

Selene nodded. She was ready for this, at least. She'd thought over how to explain it. "My boyfriend's daughter—Felicia—is eighteen, and her father told her to get a job or go to school, we'd even help her with the cost. But he had to leave on a business trip to Alaska, no cell reception. It seemed like she was working on it, filling out job applications. But now there's some new boy she's chasing and suddenly she's disrespectful all the time. We fought, and she stomped out."

Dr. Doyle had a pad to take notes, but he was better than most actors portraying psychologists at minimizing its importance. He glanced down only often enough to keep his writing on the page, and he otherwise ignored it with his body language.

Selene sat forward. "So when she called and said she wanted to apologize, of course I tried to meet her halfway, even more than halfway. She's been telling everyone that she just told me a corner and I was the one who went into the house on my own, but that's not the whole story. She must have been walking on wet grass, because I recognized her shoeprints on the sidewalk when I got there. They went right up to the door. I think she did it on purpose, walked up there and then walked on the lawn so she didn't leave prints going back. I figured it was her friend's house, so when the door was unlocked and her footprints were right there, I knocked and let myself in. And then the owner came home."

Dr. Doyle nodded as if that was all perfectly comprehensible. Selene doubted it would be that easy, though. "Some believe that the roots of what we do in the present lie in our past, where we came from. Can you tell me about where you came from? Your childhood?"

Selene took a deep breath. Family. Stepping out onto that topic was like stepping out onto a floor that vibrated with the steps of what she didn't want to think about. Steps coming closer, so she'd best use her time well.

It had been a long time since she'd used these particular lies—or perhaps not lies, more of a translation of her life into human terms. "My father wasn't really in the picture much. My parents never married, and he moved on when I was maybe four or five. I remember his—" She almost said scent, but that would be strange in human terms. "Face. There was me and my older brother, Ares. Mom always liked Greek myths." She managed a smile.

Dr. Doyle exhaled in amusement before his bland neutrality returned. "How did not having a father figure affect you?"

The question caught Selene off guard, and she swallowed a dismissal that would have been too quick. She'd had a pack, but humans didn't have those. A missing parent should have left a hole in her life. "I had plenty of other adult role models. We lived with my uncle and aunt—Mom's brother."

Selene hesitated, wondering what the psychologist would make of her lack of a mother figure too. But to cover that would be too many lies by half. "When I was twelve, so Ares must have been seventeen, I guess, Mom died of cancer. I don't remember the type off the top of my head, but it was a nasty one. They found it late, so the end was pretty sudden." Her mother's real death by gunshot wasn't so uncommon among humans either, but it would raise troublesome questions about what she'd been doing at the time. Minding her own business, just running in wolf.

Dr. Doyle nodded in acknowledgment. "So you'd essentially lost both parents. How did you deal with that?"

Selene hesitated, trying to think while balanced over much more painful family memories. She'd dealt just fine, but was that too strange, too different from how a human would have coped? Again, she couldn't see a way to shade the truth without creating lies so complicated they tangled and tripped her without warning. "It wasn't great, but it wasn't as bad as it is for some people. We were already living with my aunt and uncle, so we stayed with them. Ares lived at home to save money when he went to college, and my cousin was around too. I'm still really close to him." Poor John. She supposed he couldn't get rid of her now that she and Andrew were his alphas, not that he seemed to want to.

"Are you still close to your brother now?"

Selene took a deep breath. She picked up one of the pillows because the fringe was tangled on the corner, and she ended up holding it tightly to her chest because she had nothing else to hang on to. Lady, if only Andrew were here. "About four years ago was the car crash. Ares, my sister-in-law, their children, all of them—" Blood, and silver stink. But this was a human translation, different from those memories. Keep going, she reminded herself. Just keep going. "I had head trauma, that's why my memory is screwed up now. And nerve damage in my arm." She set the pillow aside to lay her bad arm flat across her lap, palm up. Her sleeves were long today, hiding the scars from when Andrew had slit the welts to let the silver-tainted blood drain out. Those would certainly give the lie to her translation.

"So now it's me and my cousin left." Selene tucked her bad arm away against her stomach. She hated seeing it lying there like a dead fish. "He's married, and his wife is a wonderful woman, and their son is adorable. Four years old. Runs everywhere at full speed until he smashes into something. And I'm living with my boyfriend and his daughter, of course. Andrew's—" How would humans say it? "My anchor."

Dr. Doyle raised his eyebrows, inviting her to expand on that particular topic. "And his daughter is the one who precipitated the incident."

Selene agreed and repeated a briefer summary of the human

version of events, but her heart began to pick up its pace. She could guess that now would come the harder questions.

Dr. Doyle looked down at his pad. "Outside the house, you saw shadows?"

There it was. Selene had the lie ready, but her heart raced as fast as a rabbit's even so. "My memory blipped for a minute, so I couldn't remember why I'd gone into the house. That's why I ran. So I was already pretty upset when I ran into the policemen, and they looked so *tired*, you know? Hardened by their experiences. That's all I meant by shadows. I thought maybe they'd think the worst of me, but I couldn't find the words for it at that moment."

Selene smelled the psychologist's attention sharpening. Did he believe her? He'd have to believe her—what she'd said to the police officers about Death and shadows had been the most damning part. Everything else was easier to explain as confusion.

"Your memory problems—how long have they been going on? How often do they occur?" Dr. Doyle's attention did not ease.

Selene swallowed. She hadn't prepared that. She should have, should have expected they'd want details when she and Susan made it sound like a human mental illness. Stupid. But she couldn't sit here berating herself, she had to say something. "Since the car accident. I don't really . . . don't really know how often, because I don't always notice, until people point it out, I guess." No, that didn't sound right, so Selene tried to rescue it. "It happens in unusual situations. Like I only go to the airport a couple times a year, and sometimes I can't remember the word 'airport,' but I picture the place in my head. People coming and going. Traveling long distances." She was speaking too fast, she knew it.

"It sounds if your memory problems are frustrating to you? Perhaps even upsetting?"

"I'm used to them by now." Selene smiled to emphasize her nonchalance, but he didn't relax. What was it about her words that he didn't like? She caught a flick of his eyes to her hand, the way she clenched it on her knee. It came to her like cresting a hill and seeing everything laid out below: he was reading her. Not with scent, but in other human ways. She should have expected it, she'd certainly seen the way Susan could guess at people's moods with observation.

But if she treated Dr. Doyle as a Were who could smell her, wouldn't that also remove the signs he was reading? Selene concentrated on her breathing, setting her emotions at a distance, as she would when trying to keep them from her scent. They twisted and fought her, clinging to their grip on her heartbeat and the wavering fear at her core, but she kept at it. Calm. Just as if he was a Were.

Dr. Doyle nodded, apparently accepting her answer this time. "And do you think Felicia expected something like that might happen?"

Selene relaxed her hand with an effort. "I don't know. Even if I was sure, how could I tell my boyfriend that when he gets back? 'I think your daughter tried to get me arrested, maybe because that boy of hers talked her into it.' But she knows about my memory problems, she had to know I'd . . ."

She'd have thought talking about Felicia would be easy in comparison, but her attention was divided, some of it chasing a scent she didn't have the energy to capture at the moment. If that roamer was from Madrid, Andrew's enemies in Spain had to be involved.

"How do you feel about your boyfriend's relationship with his daughter?"

"I don't feel threatened, if that's what you mean!" Selene couldn't restrain the heat in that answer, for good or ill. "I'm *glad* they have a relationship. Her mother died when she was a toddler, and that side of the family got custody, and they didn't allow him contact until three years ago. He missed her whole childhood! She only came to live with Andrew because she was finally old enough to make her own choice."

"So did you meet your boyfriend before his daughter was in the picture, or after?"

Selene pulled the pillow to her chest again. What did any of this have to do with whether she was crazy? She'd thought they'd finished with family. "About a year before. But I told you, I was happy when she came to live with us." Selene could smell him react, probably to the ring of a lie about that, and she hurriedly corrected it. "Maybe I don't always know how to deal with her, but I was happy for *him*! Being part of his daughter's life made him whole again."

"You say you don't know how to deal with her; how do you feel about your own relationship with her? Do you see yourself as a mother figure?"

Selene gritted her teeth, then put the pillow aside. "I can't have children of my own, so I'd love to be a bigger part of Felicia's life. But the world doesn't always give us what we want."

"If she did mislead you into going into that house, why do you think she did it?"

Selene concentrated on her nose, but sorting out whether

he believed her would take familiarity with his base scent she didn't have. It didn't matter if he believed her or not, she supposed, as long as he considered it a reasonable conclusion from real events, not something she'd made up in her mind. Lady grant it wasn't something she'd made up in her mind. "To humiliate me after the fight, maybe? But she hasn't seemed that defiant. Even when she was arguing with her father about getting a job, she wasn't acting like she wanted to defy him, she was acting like she was terrified he was doing it as the first step on the road to kicking her out of the house. Which of course he'd never do."

Selene twitched the fingers on her bad hand. Think, she needed to think. "And then I felt like this was all to push us away, but that doesn't make any sense either, if she didn't want to move out yet. Do you think it might be that new boy she's chasing? Don't people do that sometimes, try to get their lovers to push away everyone but them?"

"That's one of the strategies abusers can use to isolate their victims, yes. How long did you say Felicia has known this boy?"

Selene had to count carefully, probably for longer than she should. She didn't usually keep close track of days, or even weeks. Months were the important part, for the Lady, and the seasons. "Only a week or two. I don't think they're serious, and I know she's a damn smart girl, the timing is just suspicious."

Of course, if Felicia was smart, she wouldn't have been trying to impress the roamer, or punish Tom, or anything like that. She wouldn't have been listening to Enrique at all, to allow him to influence her to push people away, even if they had known each other in Madrid. So if she wouldn't have let him influence her willingly, what about unwillingly? Had he threatened her?

"I obviously can't form any conclusions without speaking to the young woman directly." Dr. Doyle cleared his throat, signaling a shift of topic. "Tell me more about the circumstances of the fight with Felicia."

From there, it wound down, the last few questions overlapping things she'd already answered. It made it easier, having the human translation ready to hand, but she knew her control over her emotions was wearing very thin. Just a little longer, she had to keep herself calm.

And finally it ended, thank the Lady. Dr. Doyle set his pad and pen to the side. He rose and Selene followed his example. "Thank you for being patient with all the questions." He offered a hand to shake once more. "You need have no worries about my report. I'm not sure why you even needed one for something like trespassing, but you're healthy."

Selene shook the hand, thanked him, and held in a hysterical bubble of laughter. If only he knew. She couldn't release the memories yet, though, she had to get away from human eyes. She didn't want to take the chance of collapsing or losing her way. She made it successfully from the office to the reception area, where Tom and Felicia shoved to their feet. When she didn't stop to talk, Tom hurried to get ahead of her and Felicia fell in behind.

Few humans were around in the building's lobby. Her appointment had finished late enough the rush of people leaving at the usual quitting hours had trailed off. Selene allowed herself to relax enough to see the worry in Tom's drooping shoulders. "It went fine," she reassured him.

The door to the men's restroom was open ahead, and Selene caught a waft of cleaning chemicals and a slice of reflection from the mirror. As she passed, Enrique stepped out from behind the door and gripped her good arm. The smell of silver metal suddenly revealed under the chemicals resolved into the knife now jabbed into her ribs. "Why don't we take a walk?" he said, the intensity of a snarl in his low voice. "Discuss what a good evaluation I just heard you had."

The burst of anger from Felicia's scent turned into a growl behind them, but Selene held up her hand to stop her from doing anything stupid. Either to help, or to harm. Shouldn't she have smelled a little more surprised? Was this what Enrique had meant about something being arranged?

"You forget, boy. Silver doesn't hurt me." Selene mentally calculated who would hear and come running if she screamed. Making a scene as a victim in front of humans could be a good strategy, better than letting Felicia and Tom attack him where they could be seen. But that knife could still cut and she could still bleed, bleed worse than a normal werewolf. She could die from blood loss, same as a human.

Enrique must have had the same thought, because he jabbed the knife again. "Madrid told me all about you, don't worry." He leaned in close to hide the knife between their bodies. His grip on her arm tightened past ache to pain.

Ahead of them, Tom whined and settled his weight forward, ready to attack. Selene glared him down too. Not yet. "Let's all go down to the car, like friends," Enrique said, accent smearing his words together. "Talk things over." He pulled her around Tom, who whined once more but stayed where he was.

Enrique led the way to the elevator banks that would take them all the way down to the parking garage rather than just within the building. Selene didn't look back, but she heard scuffling, like Tom and Felicia were arguing through looks and Felicia had had to restrain him physically.

Selene felt a strange sort of clarity formed of relief. This attack, she could fight. Perhaps not on her own, muscle against muscle, but this young man stank of panic. He should be easy to trick, frighten, or otherwise escape from. She couldn't let go of the memories just yet, not while they were moving, and the flayed feeling of such prolonged exposure to them made her laugh inside.

Enrique had no idea who he was dealing with and what forces she'd defeated before. He was an upstart little rabbit trying to snarl.

The walls of the elevator weren't mirrored, but the metal was polished so they might as well have been. Selene watched the others in it as they rode down. Tom was practically vibrating with his inability to do anything. Felicia wasn't much better, probably with the effort of keeping Tom in check. They held each other's eyes in the reflection.

Selene watched Enrique's face in the reflection. If he was from Madrid, then she had been threatened by his alpha before. In comparison to that calculated maliciousness, this boy was only a boy, but with him pressed against her, his knife at her side, that didn't cheer Selene. Panic made the insecure lash out. At this moment, she felt in more danger from this boy than she would his alpha, because no logic would prevent him from reacting if startled.

She needed to stay Selene for now lest her transition startle him just when she was at her most vulnerable, but stress shredded her control worse than ever. Tom's phone rang as the doors opened onto the first parking level, now only dotted with cars here and there where it had been packed when they arrived. Selene tried to find the tune in her memories, ground herself that way. It sounded like an old-timey movie soundtrack, but nothing she recognized.

"Wait!" Enrique said, when Tom reached for it automatically. He wrenched Selene around so the two of them faced Tom. "Who is it?"

Tom snarled silently and turned the screen. ROANOKE stood out clearly.

Enrique hesitated, stink of panic congealing around him. Selene took a deep breath to calm her racing heart at the thought of speaking to Andrew. This was a possible danger, not a source of rescue. She had to handle Enrique carefully. "Let me talk to him," she said, low and calm. "I won't tell him anything. You'll be right here, you'll know. And then he won't get worried."

The phone began its song again in Enrique's silence. Finally the young man growled. "If you say anything I don't like, you'll bleed white long, long before he gets here," he said.

Selene nodded and accepted the phone from Tom. "Hello?"

Andrew breathed a deep sigh of relief. Just hearing him made Selene want to collapse. So close, so close, and yet not here. No help. "Oh, Silver. Tom's there listening too, I assume? We're at Sea-Tac, just heading for the car now. We'll be home soon, love. How did it go?"

His tone changed on the last part, because of course he didn't know that she'd understood the first part just as well as Tom at the moment, and he didn't need to translate.

"It was fine. No hurry, Andrew." Selene kept her voice absolutely steady. "I'll meet you at home. Love you."

Andrew didn't reply for a beat and Selene ended the call before he could comment on what was wrong with what she'd said.

Enrique yanked the phone away and threw it to smash against the nearest pillar. He used his off hand so he didn't have to change position and give her an opportunity to get away from the knife. Selene wasn't sure if she could even if the opportunity appeared. Holding on sapped her strength in a steady stream.

"And yours." Enrique pointed to Felicia, who dug out her phone slowly, jaw clenched. She tossed it lightly away, possible to retrieve later. Enrique started down the slight slope descending deeper into the garage, glaring at the cars. The tension stretched and stretched as they wound deeper, and Selene realized that Enrique must not be used to parking garages and hadn't thought of noting the floor when he rode up so he could take the elevator directly to it.

Other cars and the possibility of distractions so Felicia or Tom could jump Enrique decreased. Their footsteps echoed oddly off the concrete, surrounding silence emphasizing how alone they were. Even the human's cameras had thinned to one or two a level, easily avoided. Still they wound lower. Enrique seemed to have parked right at the very bottom.

Finally, she spotted a single car in the sea of empty spaces, down half a level. She assumed it was Enrique's, since there were no others within sight now. She had no idea how Enrique expected to get them all into the car and drive while still threatening her. His steps slowed like he'd just realized that himself.

Whether or not his panic had decayed enough for logic, Selene didn't have time to wait any longer before prodding him. "Now what?" she asked. "Now you have me, have us, what are you planning to do?"

Enrique looked pointedly to the side. "Felicia? This is your show. I'm sure Madrid would be grateful to you for helping me."

Selene didn't follow his gaze, but she could imagine from the choking noises that Felicia was probably flushed with rage. "He was blackmailing me. He has these forgeries, like I was feeding them information, but it's not true! I'm loyal." Her outburst sounded angled in Tom's direction.

Selene didn't quite follow that, but when Felicia held a knife on her, Selene would worry about her. Until then, she would accept the young woman's assertions of loyalty from before and worry about Enrique.

"Just look on my phone, you can see all her e-mails to us, giving us all the information we needed. But if you don't believe that, you have your own unquestionable proof that she's not loyal." Enrique smirked, panic ebbing in the face of his delight in this game, this . . . revenge? Another thing in Felicia's favor, if she had done something to make him want to seek it. "She lied about not knowing me. Of course Madrid sent me."

Tom growled, the sound twisted with desperate anger decaying into betrayal. "You must have threatened—"

"I didn't need to. This was her idea. All of it." Enrique glanced down at his knife and roughly jerked Selene into him as he switched sides. With his arm across her back, he used the pressure of the knife against her side to hold her close while he unlocked the car.

Now. Someone had to do something now or Selene would completely lose herself. She took her eyes off Enrique long enough to check the other two. Tom's expression roiled with betrayal and anger, Felicia's with desperation. Neither of them would do anything, because it would get her hurt, she was certain of it.

When Enrique leaned into the car to reach something, Selene lunged away.

The pain came out of order somehow—first she felt just a line of cold or pressure along her side. Then it hurt in a blaze of heat along the line and Selene put her palm to the cut as she stumbled out of the way.

Tom slammed into Enrique and Felicia screamed for Selene, with the wrong name, but what were names anyway? Not someone's essential qualities. Burn away everything else and you were left with more than someone without a name. Someone who knew herself.

Someone held her so she didn't fall, pressed at the blood too. Blood held no names either. It flowed out and Silver found her essential name there waiting for her, not carried away on that tide. Not a quick tide, but inexorable. But the ocean ebbed and returned. The ocean did not die. The Lady waned and returned.

"Are you going to gather clouds in your jaws forever or be useful?" Death snapped.

Silver concentrated until the important things around her slid from the mist. The roamer and her assistant snarled and snapped, the assistant's wild self already marked with ragged wounds, and her mate's daughter held her. Her wound hurt, but manageably. Already, the wet warmth against her hand was easing as the blood slowed. "Go," she snapped at the young woman, borrowing Death's tone. "Help him, not me. I am not dying."

20

Felicia almost stopped breathing when Silver lunged out of Enrique's hold, slicing the knife along her own side. Tom threw himself at Enrique and Felicia longed to help, wanted to pound Enrique into the concrete all on her own. But Silver was hurt, blood wicking through the whole side of her shirt. Felicia ran to her, caught her before she could stumble too badly, and pressed her hand down on top of Silver's. Lady, don't let her die from blood loss. Didn't humans manage to survive it all the time?

In her peripheral vision, Enrique twisted, bringing the knife up in a horizontal backhanded slash. The silver metal could definitely burn Tom, and he stumbled back, off-balance. Enrique pressed his advantage, body slamming him into the nearest pillar. While Tom was still shaking off the stunning effects of the crack of his head against concrete, Enrique backed up and traded hands, knife to left, and whip he'd picked up in the car to right.

Tom didn't stand a chance. Enrique gave him a precision whip slash across his eyes and Tom screamed. Felicia spat Spanish obscenities at Enrique. Even in a fight back in Madrid, that was a dirty tactic, usually disallowed. She'd never taken a blow right across the eyes herself, but she'd had them come close. Everyone knew it wasn't the pain that undid you, it was the sheer visceral terror of damaging something so vulnerable.

Enrique laid stripe after stripe across Tom's chest and up-raised arms as Tom clutched at his eyes and gasped with the pain. Felicia jerked toward him—she'd take that whip from him and flay every inch of skin from his body, the Lady her witness—and Silver swayed and she had to stop or drop the woman. She wavered, torn in two directions, while her mind could only scream *no* over and over.

Silver straightened and pulled away from her. Felicia wasn't sure whether to believe her when she said she didn't need help, but her feet decided for her, taking her away from Silver and into the path of Enrique's next stroke. Her skills were rustier than she'd realized because she took a solid slash across the shoulder and had to catch the whip on the next stroke. Enrique had sidestepped to try to get at Tom around her, but she sacrificed some skin on her arm and got a good grip when it wrapped.

"What, you want your turn?" Enrique grinned at her and raised his voice, as if Tom, panting where he'd propped himself up against the pillar, could fail to hear. "Felicia was always a little less precise than me, but much, much more thorough." He rolled the word, enjoying every syllable.

Felicia didn't let herself turn to see Tom's reaction, though she almost couldn't bear not to see it. Later. She could explain to him later. "I want my turn to beat you bloody, Enrique. I won't let you hurt them any more. Don't be stupider than you already are. My father's going to get home soon and come looking for Silver when she's not there. What are you going to do then? What are you planning to do *now*?" She jerked at the whip to pull it from Enrique's hands, but he knew the techniques as well as she did, and braced.

Tom stumbled forward, clearly meaning to rejoin the fight, and his movement behind Felicia provided the distraction Enrique needed. Enrique yanked her to the side using her grip on the whip. She let go too late. He moved his grip down the handle, reversing it, and smashed Tom's temple with the weighted end. This time, when Tom's head cracked against the pillar, he slumped slowly down and didn't get up.

Felicia wanted to sob, but satisfaction made Enrique's grip looser and she darted in and yanked the whip away. They wrestled over it and he almost got her with the knife, but his aim was poor with his off hand. She smashed the whip's weighted end into his jaw. He stumbled back far enough for her to coil up the rest of the whip. It was entirely in her power now. She slashed at Enrique before he could gather himself.

Enrique took the score across his forearm and pressed forward, slashing his knife almost at random. Felicia had to back up to keep him within the correct range for the whip. Another two blows in quick succession halted his forward movement. Dimly, Felicia remembered she should make sure Silver wasn't in the line of any of her backstrokes, but she didn't hear any cries of pain, so she trusted the woman to stay out of the way.

Enrique got close enough that she had to block his knife stroke with the whip handle. She smacked into a pillar with her back, sidestepped quickly to give herself more space, and dealt him a blow that opened his cheek. The blood gushed rather than seeped this time. She kept her following strokes light, kissing his skin, the whip there and gone before he could catch it. It would take longer to wear him down, but that was all right. She started to count each as it landed, balancing them against the ones Tom had received. She didn't know the conversion between those heavy strokes and these light ones, but she'd make sure Enrique got plenty.

Ten. Eleven. Blood spattered the gray concrete of walls and pillars, blended into the dark dirt on the floor. Small splatters, bigger splashes here and there, and Felicia was gaining ground. Twenty. As long as she stayed far enough from Enrique, she could bleed him cut by cut until he had no healing left and started to stumble. Thirty. She had a few lines of blood along her own skin from miscalculated strokes, but they were small enough to heal almost immediately.

Enrique began to gasp as Tom had and Felicia reveled in the sound. Yes. It was right he should suffer too. A wild satisfaction washed into her and swept away the anger and the memory of the betrayal in Tom's voice. The air was thick with Enrique's blood; she could practically taste it in each breath. Yes.

Enrique's heel caught in a depression in the uneven pavement and he fell back onto his ass. Felicia let her whip hand drop and strode up to him. She grabbed a chunk of his collar, but his shirt was in tatters and the fabric tore. He flopped onto his back. Felicia dropped down and straddled his chest.

She placed the base of the whip against his throat and leaned. He choked and bucked with what little strength he had left as she cut off his air.

Yes. She could see his face as he died, and he could see who was killing him. He would remember why. He was unworthy. He'd hurt her pack. Hurt her family. "Lady-fucking shotgun hunter," she hissed under her breath.

Someone's hand closed on her shoulder. Felicia leaned harder. She had to hurry.

"Felicia!" Silver's voice. Felicia had thought the woman too injured to be interfering. Surprise made her let up enough for Enrique to wheeze a single breath before she pressed down again. Silver's feet came around to Enrique's shoulder. When Felicia didn't look up, Silver crouched and lifted her chin. "Look at me, puppy. This is not a path to walk unconsidered. I have seen its mark on your father. I know he would not wish it for you."

Silver's shirt stuck to her side with a large red stain, and her hand on Felicia's chin was sticky, but no more blood seemed to be flowing. Felicia met Silver's gaze and drew a great sobbing breath, feeling like she'd just remembered she needed to breathe herself. "Silver, I'm sorry . . . he . . ."

Silver slid a hand under the whip's base beside hers and gently lifted. "I know. You think he deserves to be killed, but you deserve to be someone who hasn't killed."

Felicia finally saw Enrique properly. He looked worse than Tom had, because they'd been fighting longer. Gashes criss-crossed his body and blood caked his black hair. One of his eyes was swollen shut, and a flap of skin over his cheek hung down sickeningly. She'd done that. Enrique had done it to Tom, and she'd done it to him.

And that made her the same as Enrique.

Her stomach contracted, ready to retch, but Felicia told it sternly to behave and got unsteadily to her feet. Silver watched her with an expression so gentle, so forgiving, that it was all Felicia could do to not fling herself at her and hold tight like a child. But Silver and Tom were hurt and she was the only one left, so she needed to . . . what? Felicia pushed herself to keep going and not fall apart. She needed to tie up Enrique and clean up before any humans arrived.

The pack car, up several levels, had towels in the trunk for when you got muddy out hunting. And Felicia thought she remembered seeing zip ties in the in-case-of-breakdown tool-box. And her phone. Her phone was up there too. She could call the pack and . . . explain all this. Somehow.

No one could get here immediately, anyway. Felicia guided Silver's hand back to her side and curled her fingers down. Even if the blood wasn't flowing now, better safe than sorry. "Stay here, I'll go and get . . ." She gestured up the ramp.

"All right." Silver's lips quirked and she removed her hand from her side. She crossed to where the knife had tumbled from Enrique's hand, picked it up, and stood over him. Felicia gave a ragged laugh and started running upstairs.

She was almost to the car when she heard voices. She pressed herself behind a pillar, cheek against the dirty concrete, and tried not to pant harshly. She couldn't let herself be seen like this, covered with splatters of Enrique's blood.

"You check the office, I'll see if their car's still here." Her father's voice.

"Papa?" Felicia's knees tried to collapse, but she needed them to work, needed them to run up the last ramp to where he and John had stopped by their car in surprise.

She threw herself against her father and clung to his solidity as she sobbed. *"Papa, I did everything wrong . . ."* She pressed her cheek against his chest. John's footsteps receded as he ran down the ramp, following her trail.

Her father smoothed her hair, movement hitched every so often when he hit a sticky spot of flung blood. "All right, puppy. We're here now. We'll figure it out."

Felicia drew in a shuddering breath and a few thoughts drifted back in. "How did you get here so fast . . . ?" It hardly seemed real, now Felicia thought about it. There hadn't been enough time for them to have driven home to find Silver gone before coming here.

"Silver doesn't call me Andrew. Only Selene does. And I knew if she was hiding it, something was wrong. We got the address from Susan and came straight here."

Felicia nodded and tried to use the heel of her hand to wipe away some of the mess blood and tears and snot had made of her face. "He's—Enrique's out right now, but we should still go tie him up soon."

Her father exhaled in a low laugh and helped her wipe with the side of his thumb. "Enrique? Were you the one to take him down? Good job."

The praise made Felicia feel even worse. She wouldn't have had to do a good job fighting Enrique if she hadn't screwed up in the first place. She shook her head wildly. Her father cut off whatever he'd been going to say and pulled her into another hug. Felicia pressed her face into his chest again, like maybe the world would go away for a while and leave her alone. She knew it would all be there, angry and betrayed, when she got back, but for now she wanted to let her father hold her and pretend otherwise.

21

Silver wished she could do more to help her cousin, and then Dare when he returned with his daughter, but she couldn't *see* anything properly. Mist caressed the surrounding world with clammy tendrils, like it wanted her to be jealous that it could touch those things and she could not. At least the people stood out: Felicia bright, hard to look at with the draining flush of her anger; Dare warm and familiar and so comforting if she had let herself run to him; and the young roamer, a twisted mess of pain and the arrogance that had led him to make threats, to hurt Tom.

She didn't run to Dare, because Felicia needed her father more than she did at the moment. So angry, too angry, and wobbling at the edge of incorporating that into her core and her voice for good. That was not a way to live. "I wonder if Dare sees his reflection in her," she murmured, low, to Death, who had only recently returned from prowling around and around the young man as Felicia hurt him. Was that how Dare had once been? Had his anger burned so bright?

Death yawned, and his intent focus on the roamer vanished as if it had never been. His teeth still looked wickedly sharp, however. "I don't see how he can fail to. If he's smart." He whuffed, like he rather doubted that last part. "He's ignoring you."

"I'm standing, Tom isn't, and there's more than enough blood to go around. I'm not surprised he hasn't noticed, and I'm not going to tell him until later." Silver ruffled Death's ears, because that seemed like a normal gesture and she was fast running out of things to focus on. She felt rather close to tears herself.

"Silver?" Her cousin left Tom after helping him sit up gingerly and joined her. He ran a hand along her back until he had the length of her shoulders encompassed under his steady arm. She shivered and leaned against him. "Are you all right?" She flinched when he resettled his hand at her side, and his scent flared with sharp worry. "That's your blood, isn't it?"

"It was never deep, and it's not flowing any longer." Silver bunched her good hand in his shirt when he would have left to tell Dare, held him there beside her. "His daughter needs him. One thing at a time."

Her cousin growled his protest but stayed where he was. "What happened?"

"The roamer." The name escaped her and Silver couldn't muster the energy to begin to chase it. "He said he was from somewhere else, so I gave him permission to pass through. I could tell something had happened between him and Felicia, but then Portland and everyone and their omega were questioning my authority, and I didn't pay as much attention as I should. Then Felicia was wearing tortured flowers and being disrespectful, and the cat . . ."

Her cousin's silence was resounding for a moment before he laughed. "Explanations later." He ushered her over to sit, frustrating the mist by barging right through it. It drew back in disgust and let Silver see a little again. Normally, she would have shrugged her cousin off by now, but this time she needed his touch. He stepped away only reluctantly. "Not enough room for all of us. Dare can take the three of you home, and I'll stay and deal with the boy."

Silver sat while her cousin went to get Tom. He could walk with help, that was good, at least. He moved painfully, however. Death settled on her bad side where they sat, which frustrated her, because she would have liked to bury a hand in his fur, but she saw why soon enough. When her cousin coaxed Tom in beside her, she put her hand on the young man's knee. Her turn to give comfort, instead of being comforted.

"I'm fine." His voice had the whine of a young one putting on a brave front who still hurt on the inside. "No thanks to *her.*" He pushed Silver's hand away, so she tangled her fingers with his instead. He grumbled but allowed it.

"I think the circumstances were more complicated than that." Silver hesitated.

"He won't hear you," Death said mockingly.

"She would have killed him for what he did to us. Especially to you," Silver said anyway. True, he wouldn't hear now, but maybe he'd remember the words later. When he was ready to hear them.

Tom turned away and drew deep into himself as Dare and

Felicia joined them. Silver held herself tightly contained, and she and Dare could only share a look before they started home and he was distracted again. Lady, she would be grateful when they had a little time to themselves.

Felicia wished she could have stayed with John and whoever came to help him clean. Then again, Enrique remained at the parking garage too, trussed up with the zip ties and probably out cold for some time yet. Since she didn't stay, in the car she had to listen to Tom's labored breathing and imagine how he was glaring at her. Silver remained as calm and apparently forgiving as she had been at first, which was something, Felicia supposed, though she didn't understand it. She'd hurt Silver the worst emotionally, even if Tom had taken the physical brunt.

They got home eventually. It was drizzling, which did nothing for the blood that remained speckled on Felicia's clothes. She hung back, suddenly remembering that technically she was kicked out, but Silver jerked her head to the house as she passed Felicia. "That carcass is buried. Go inside," she said, tone weary but kind. She disappeared inside herself before Felicia could figure out how to phrase her thanks.

Inside, she dropped Tom's keys in the bowl with those of the other pack vehicles to tell everyone else she was officially back. Her father guided Tom to the kitchen, hand on his shoulder, but Felicia slipped away upstairs. She needed to shower more than she needed to eat right now, and she needed to avoid Tom more than both.

She took a long time in the shower, until no hint of red remained even in the droplets around the bottom of the tub. She left her clothes in a pile on the floor—she knew all the tricks for washing out blood, but they were torn in places and she didn't know if she'd ever want to wear them again even clean—and went to her room to rummage for new ones.

When she arrived downstairs, she could smell that Enrique must be down in the basement. John was back and discussing something in low tones with her father in the kitchen. Felicia slipped past to the big platter of hot wings on the stove. Once those were gone, someone would start another batch of some high-protein finger food.

John looked over at her and lifted his hand to indicate the phone he was holding. Enrique's, she realized after a beat. "Those e-mails Tom said he was talking about, they're clearly fake, don't worry. It's all there in the headers, if you look."

Felicia looked down at her plate and fought off an impulse to renewed tears. She hadn't even thought of that. John worked with software, so of course he'd have some secret way to tell an e-mail was faked. She nodded her gratitude and retreated with her food.

"—better call Raul now," her father said as he passed her in the hall, probably heading for the basement.

Felicia dropped the bones from her current wing on the side of the plate and ducked into the dining room to slide it onto the table. "Wait." She hurried to catch up with her father, ignoring the way her voice tightened. It didn't matter if she didn't want to do this, if she wanted to go hide in bed with the covers over her head. She needed to help clean up the mess she'd made. "Madrid already knows if he tangles with you, he loses. That's why he waited to get me alone. I need to call, so he knows he can't get to me either."

Her father stopped and frowned. "One could argue that this is a matter between alphas. One of his people attacked one of mine."

Felicia's words tumbled over each other as she hurried to get them out. She knew that phrase. "One could argue" meant that her father was still open to hearing other options, if presented logically enough. Maybe he'd even thought of the same thing that had just occurred to her.

"But that's big. Big, nasty political shit. I could talk to him . . ." Felicia had to scrabble to find a way to say it that wouldn't hurt her father. "Because he used to be my alpha." Because he'd helped raise her. "And then it wouldn't be political, just a personal insult."

Her father cupped the corner of her jaw so he could examine her face better. "Only if you're up to it."

"I have to be." Felicia pulled away and headed down to the basement before he could object to her less than enthusiastic tone, but her father smelled like approval when he caught up to her. It helped her feel more balanced. Slightly.

She'd hoped it might be better, seeing Enrique once he was healed, but she remembered what he'd looked like before, and her mind filled it in. They'd zip-tied him to a kitchen chair from the basement's collection of mismatched and worn-out furniture. There was a chain used for troublemakers set in the wall, but Felicia supposed they didn't plan to keep him that long.

He dozed now. His skin was unbroken, but his color was bad, meaning he'd eaten, but healing was still underway. His hair and clothes were damp from when they'd sluiced off the worst of the blood. He'd set himself braced and ready for action, but his head lolled forward. He probably hadn't meant to sleep, but his body had ambushed him regardless.

Her father handed her Enrique's phone, then stood close, probably so she could lean against him if she wanted. She placed herself squarely in front of Enrique, alone, and dialed Madrid. She could do this. She needed to do this.

"What's gone wrong now?"

Hearing her former alpha's voice again after three years made Felicia's voice weaken, made her hesitate. She gritted her teeth. *"Madrid. I wondered which piece of Enrique you wanted back."*

Madrid was silent for several breaths. She wondered what it was like for him hearing *her* voice after so long. She continued while her courage lasted. *"I'm earning my own money now, and shipping a whole body is Lady-damned expensive. He did bring me Blanca, I appreciate that, so I figure that should at least be worth a finger for you to remember him by."*

"Felicia. You didn't really kill him." Madrid's voice grew coaxing. He was good at that, sounding kind and reasonable when he wanted to.

Felicia swallowed and closed her eyes. *"I would have, if Silver hadn't stopped me. If Papa was the Butcher of Barcelona, I'm the Butcher's Daughter. I didn't mean to, but . . ."* She swallowed. *"Think about that before you push me again."* She supposed that sounded like grandstanding, but every word was true, and Madrid must have heard that in her voice. His silence this time was resounding.

Felicia handed the phone off to her father and went back

upstairs, arms hugged tightly across her belly. No more. She needed to hide from it again. She heard her father speaking as she jogged up the stairs, but she didn't turn around.

"*Raul. The only direct flight in the next twenty-four hours is into Barcelona, and I'm not going to do that to the boy, with Death's toothmarks in his voice. Who are you on speaking terms with in Europe for him to connect through? Is there anyone at the moment?*"

Felicia shut the basement door and went to collect her plate of wings to eat in the privacy of her room. That way, she wouldn't run into Tom or have to see the way everyone looked at her.

22

Silver ate, washed, let her scratch be fussed over, and found that Dare was still dealing with the roamer. She would have gone to their room to wait for him, but Death seemed to be expecting something else to happen. He planted himself by the entrance to the den and waited pointedly. Silver sighed, took the hint, and joined him in waiting there instead.

That's where Tom found them. He was leaving with a load, much of which smelled like food. On seeing her, he hesitated, but his expression hardened into deeper resolve. "I can't . . . deal with this right now. I have a couple of friends over in the Billings pack, I might stay with them, or my parents in the Boston pack if I have to."

"Boston would be happy to have you visit, I am sure." Silver smiled, very small, at Tom's confusion. In the plan of the hunt he'd laid out in his mind, clearly this was the time for her to protest, to forbid him to go. But better he not be around to have truths said to him so often that by the time he was ready to listen, they had lost all power. He could go now and later find his own way to the truths, so they'd reach his core. Then hopefully he'd return, for Felicia's sake.

Silver hugged him, and some of his confusion melted away into mock exasperation, hiding gratitude for the gesture. "Talk to Dare. At a distance, I mean," she told him. "When you're ready. I think he can help. Or me." Not that she thought her particular perspective would be of much use to the young man, but you never knew.

Tom kissed her cheek. "You hate talking at a distance," he reminded her. He squeezed her in a last hug and then slipped out of the den.

His departure was not quite so easy, however. A few moments later, Tom reappeared and dumped a load of cat-scented things and the cat itself in its container inside the den. "Forgot her Lady-abandoned animal." Then he was gone for good.

The box rocked and yowled. Silver bent and opened it before she thought too hard and forgot the trick of it. A purple-gray head popped up and a purple-gray body followed it in a great bound.

"You sure about that?" Silver said, eyebrows raised. She stayed crouched where she was to avoid sending the cat skittering off farther into the den. "Felicia's not in much shape to be championing you at the moment, little Morsel."

Death extended his nose in a casual sniff of the beast. "Half morsel, more like."

The cat puffed itself up all over, tail transformed into one long bristle. It swiped a paw at Death's nose. Death jerked his head back in shock and growled on a low note that seemed to loosen one's voice. The cat shrieked and jumped almost straight sideways. Then it seemed to notice the twitching tip of its own tail, and jumped just as violently away from that. It streaked off into the den.

Silver laughed. She laughed until tears came into her eyes and Death glared with eyes that seemed to be facing straight onto the void. "I like you, Morsel." Silver followed its trail and found the cat cowered under a seat. She pulled it out and held it close. It was very warm, with silkier fur than most wild selves.

"Disrespectful," Death said, chilly, from by her feet.

"A cat can look at an alpha," Silver quoted, and then grinned at Death. "Provided it can run fast enough afterward." The cat rumbled a tentative little purr, and the noise strengthened when she ruffled its ears.

She took it up to their bedroom and let it dart under the bed. Death took himself off, so she waited for Dare alone.

When Dare entered, Morsel streaked back out again, past his feet. He followed its path with his gaze and then looked back at Silver. "A cat."

"Felicia's cat. Its name is Morsel." Silver smoothed the bedding. "I rather fancy keeping it. It sassed Death, I think."

"Did it?" Now Dare's eyebrows went up. He flopped down beside her. Silver had meant to ask him about the child in Alaska, ask him about where he'd sent the roamer, about how Felicia was, but his scent insinuated itself under and around those things until it filled her up and she forgot them for the moment.

She leaned over and kissed him like she could steal all his heat for herself. He kissed back, fingers lacing into her hair, lulling her until the moment he rolled away, laughing. They tumbled until she caught him again, ground her hips against his. He slid his arms over her lower back and held her tight against him, too tight to arch as she wanted. He grinned as she groaned in frustration and nipped at the side of her neck. She allowed it, lulling him in turn, and then writhed so the sensation she created made him loosen his grip, distracted. She grinned and claimed another kiss.

He'd mentioned plenty of plans the last time they'd talked, but none of them got used this time, when she was injured and their intensity was better matched by simplicity. Afterward, Silver pressed close to him and felt relaxed for the first time since Portland had arrived. Things were far from settled, but at least she could see their destination now, if not the exact route to it.

First, she told him everything that had happened since they last spoke. Knowing what she did now threw the underlying logic behind Felicia's behavior into sharper relief. Dare growled in agreement when she mentioned her conclusions about the roamer.

"Felicia told me she lied about knowing him at first because she thought she could convince him to break with Madrid and stay in North America. I'd never thought about it, but of course she'd want to save the others if she got a chance. I could have told her it would never work. She encountered direct evidence contradicting the lies Madrid told her. That kind of evidence doesn't exist for those Enrique's been fed." Dare blew out a frustrated breath.

"But how could you know that it would come up?" Silver petted her mate's hair, smoothing the white lock at the temple she could reach. "If we predicted every problem, Death would have nothing left to be smug about."

Death growled. Silver looked up, because she hadn't heard him come back in. He still looked greatly put out by the cat. "And the child, in Alaska?" she asked.

"I did some calling, and I found a splinter couple in Maine who were willing to move out. Having a little privacy suited them, and they can always run with the Alaskans if they get lonely." Dare pulled a face, and Silver gathered he was still getting over his experience with the Alaskans. "It's not forever, anyway. Just until the child would normally move away from home, and then he can visit his biological mother as much or as little as he wants."

"Good." Silver brought up his hand and kissed his knuckles. "We're not done yet, down here. Portland's beta and sister are still hanging around, and there's Felicia and Tom to worry about, now Tom's run off to stay with friends or family."

"Has he?" Dare's scent clouded with concern. "I suppose it's for the best. He sounded like his voice had been pretty thoroughly ground into the dirt. He probably feels that even if Felicia lied to everyone else, she could have confided in him."

"Stop whining. He'll be back," Death said, sighed, and went to sleep.

"And what about you?" Dare pushed himself sitting and traced the lines of her face, smoothed her hair. "Are you all right, Silver? More than physically." He touched her side, fingers light over the bandage there. Their exercise had given it only the faintest ghost of a brown line.

Silver drew in a slightly hitched breath. "I've been better." She sat up too and tucked her toes under Dare's wild self to keep them warm. "Felicia was not particularly kind to me, either, except that I'm too mature to sulk about it." Now she allowed herself to think about it, frustration knotted up her voice.

"I'm sorry." Dare pulled her against his chest, and Silver took the words the way his tone suggested: sympathy, not responsibility. "I can talk to them about the trespassing, see if I can persuade them to drop it. And if you sulk to me, I promise not to tell anyone."

Silver exhaled on a note of weak laughter. "I think we can safely say she's learned her lesson. Just promise me I don't have to call up the memories again anytime soon." That, Silver still shied away from thinking too hard about. "It hurt."

"Promise." Dare pressed a kiss to her forehead to seal the promise. He lay back down again, and Silver curled up beside him. They drifted off together.

23

Felicia glowered at the bushes outside the kitchen window as the impersonal voice of Tom's voice mailbox told her to leave a message after the tone. Why wouldn't he pick up? It had been four days, and he hadn't answered a single one of her calls. She'd left him a couple messages already, so he had to know she was calling to apologize.

The tone sounded. "Hi, Tom, I don't really know what to say, but I'm so sorry—"

Her father jerked the phone out of her hand as he passed and thumbed End Call . "If you don't stop that, I'm going to confiscate this."

Felicia stared at him. What in the Lady's name was that about? "What?"

Her father offered her phone back. "Leave him *alone,* Felicia. That's an order from your Roanoke, not a suggestion."

Sheer frustration started tears in Felicia's eyes, but she didn't let them fall. She jerked the phone out of his hand. Lady, she hated when her father meddled sometimes. "I need to *apologize*."

"First of all, he'll be more likely to listen to you if you let him cool down for a while—maybe even a good long while. And second—and more important—are you really trying to apologize, or are you trying to make yourself feel better?"

"Of course I'm not—" Felicia's father cut her off with a gesture, and she glowered at the linoleum.

"Because if you really want to make *him* feel better, you won't talk to him again until he's good and ready to talk to you."

Because he was her father, and Lady-damned right far too often, he didn't press his point, just got a National Park mug covered in evergreens and poured himself his morning coffee from the pack's large pot. Felicia considered smashing her phone, or bursting into tears, or wailing at her father about how she hated herself for what she'd done to Tom and why couldn't he see that?

She didn't do any of those things, however. "You can't confiscate it, anyway. This number's on my résumé. People might be calling me for interviews." It came out sounding sulkier than she'd wanted, but she supposed that still beat tears.

Her father paused midsip and raised his eyebrows. "Good for you. Had any yet?"

Felicia glared at the floor. "Not yet. But I put in a ton of applications. Seriously, a ton. Ask Susan. Or Silver—she kept grilling me about it all the time."

Her father swallowed a mouthful in silence, and Felicia wondered whether he was thinking of saying she could set the job search aside awhile. That made her angry for some inexplicable reason, and she hurried to cut him off. "And Susan says there's an opening for a teller at her bank branch, and I'm really hopeful about that one, because she can give my résumé directly to HR." So there. She relaxed a little while her father merely nodded. She needed at least *one* arena to prove herself in right now, Felicia realized. That's where her anger had come from when she thought her father was going to take it away from her.

"So long as you're not going to run off roaming . . ." Her father squeezed her shoulder and trailed off meaningfully.

Felicia couldn't figure out what his meaning was, though. His dry tone suggested he was making some kind of joke, but . . . "What's that supposed to mean?" She crossed her arms.

"To find Tom, I mean—" Her father winced and cut himself off, probably at seeing her expression.

"I'm not that stupid!" Felicia shouted it, even as something at the back of her mind noted that if she'd had that idea herself a minute ago, she'd have thought it was a pretty good one. "Lady, Dad!" Frustration surged up, bringing misery back with it, and she jerked into pacing steps. "I mean, he deserves an apology in person, if he was here, I'd do that, I'm not a coward, but all this, I can't—" She felt tears starting up and growled.

"Sometimes, having all the pack return from the hunt, no matter the state they return in, needs to be counted as a win." Her father would have touched her comfortingly again, but Felicia dodged. He looked so sympathetic, she didn't *want* that right now. She wanted someone to punish her, be outwardly angry with her, so she could atone for her mistakes, instead of imagining the resentment he or Silver or the others might be hiding.

"Shut up." Felicia put her hands over ears and headed out of the kitchen for the stairs. She didn't want to deal with him right now. Time to hide in her room again.

Silver drifted over to look at Felicia's closed door a few moments after the resounding slam. While overhearing the young woman's conversation with Dare, she'd decided her presence wouldn't help the situation, but now she wondered if anything could have changed this inevitable result.

"The young are so talented at moping," Death commented.

"What she broke can most likely be fixed," Silver said. "It'll just take time. And time stretches long for the young."

"A mother would go and comfort her." Death said it much too sweetly, and in his own voice. The voice of Silver's mother came into her mind, dropped by an errant tendril of mist. Not the words, just the tone.

"She's had comfort. A friend would go and comfort her. By now, a mother would go tell her to pull herself together." Silver remembered that in her mother's tone, much as it had frustrated her at the time.

"Your choice, Silver." Death spoke in her mother's voice now, exactly as she remembered, though of course her mother wouldn't have used that name. "No one will fault you, whichever you choose."

Silver went up to Felicia's room and knocked instead of making the decision. She didn't know what she should choose, wasn't even sure now what she wanted to choose, faced with it. She'd talk to Felicia, anyway.

"What?" Felicia's voice was subdued.

Silver took that for assent and entered. Felicia was cocooned in her bed, wild self and a plush puppy in her lap, white on top of black. Morsel was curled up high, out of reach. Her fur looked disarranged, like Felicia had tried to cuddle her and the cat had disagreed.

"Do you want to come on the hunt tonight?" A weak beginning, but a beginning, at least.

Felicia hunched farther over her puppy. "I can't, Silver. All I can think of is everyone looking at me, knowing what I did. How can they ever forgive me? How can I ask them to?"

"I'd like to tell you a story, if you'll listen." Silver picked up a brush and held it up as an additional invitation. Felicia eyed her for several moments, then shrugged with exaggerated unconcern, set her toy aside, and pulled off her clothes. Silver looked away as she switched tame self for wild in a few moments of effort.

Silver brushed her ruff first, smoothing it so it puffed up evenly, pretty. "In the time after the Lady had left Her children, a beta led the hunt one night. He was proud, because it was his first hunt as leader. He was determined to show he was worthy of being beta. He thought strength lay in never asking for help, instead of being confident enough to know that everyone needs help."

Silver did Felicia's flank next, leaning into the strokes. The young woman's ears were slightly flat, which was probably a good sign that she was listening. Otherwise, she wouldn't have spotted the parallels to her own situation.

"And since he didn't ask, he didn't know about the danger. He led them right into a band of human hunters and could not escape before one of his pack mates was dead. He led his remaining pack mates home, prostrated himself before his alpha with his apologies, and left that night, to be a lone.

"The pack grieved, and cursed the beta for a fool, but life held more than grief and curses for them. They lived and loved and grieved, and the beta settled into their memories. Only the mate of the one who had been killed began each day reciting the wrongs the beta had done her. He had gotten her mate killed. He had killed her mate."

Felicia's ears slowly lifted as her attention sharpened. Silver lengthened a stroke down to the tip of her tail. "Over time, as the rest of the pack grew frustrated with the mate, her list of complaints grew. He killed her mate. He turned the pack against her. He ruined her life. He made her an object of pity.

"Her pack told her she needed to forgive him, but she said what he had done was unforgivable. She hugged her grievances closer and closer to herself, until she walked hunched over around their weight. Her wild self grew hunched and small too."

Silver let her strokes slow, but Felicia didn't seem to notice. Her attention was tight on Silver's face. Perhaps she was surprised the story hadn't followed the beta.

"Then the beta returned. He was older, wiser, and did not ask to be forgiven. But they forgave him anyway, because he was family and pack, and because life had moved on for all of them. All except for the mate. She burst into the den where they had offered the beta a share of the kill, stood as tall as she could anymore, and ranted at him, every grievance in the long list she had hugged to herself until it had become part of her very voice.

"The beta looked at her sadly. 'Do not forgive me, then,' he said. 'I don't deserve it. Forgiveness would be for me. But let your grievances go, for you. Holding them so close is hurting you.'"

Silver gently rubbed her fingers behind Felicia's ears, where the fur was softest. "But she couldn't hear. She shifted form to tear him to pieces with her teeth, but her wild self was so twisted and stunted, she could only slither along the ground. She shook her tail, where all of the grievances had solidified, and they rattled together. So she slithered away as a rattlesnake, poisonous and alone, able only to rattle her grievances to the world for the rest of her life."

Silver leaned her cheek against the top of Felicia's head. "Forgiveness can't be earned. It can't even truly be asked for. It can only be given, as a gift. If our pack is smart, they'll let their grievances go, for themselves. But if they do more, if they offer you forgiveness, don't ask how you can deserve it. Accept their gift and remember, for some later time when you might find a chance to give it, undeserved, in return."

Felicia's ear flicked against Silver's hair, in thought. She pulled away and went to the edge of her bed and changed back. Her face showed confusion still. "Easy for you to say," she said, but it lacked a note of the earlier whining.

Here was Silver's choice, she realized. To comfort, or push. Lady watch over her on this path, but she knew which, now. She took Felicia's wrist and tugged her up. "Easier for you to do if you at least try." She sharpened her tone. "Stop hiding in here, Felicia. Come on the hunt tonight. Tom will come back or he won't. You have to pull yourself together."

"But . . ." Felicia frowned at the ground.

As an alpha, she could order Felicia to come on the hunt. Instead she raised her eyebrows and waited until Felicia looked up and absorbed the expression. Silver wasn't going to order her, but that's what she thought Felicia should do. Would she?

Silver dropped Felicia's wrist and left the room to leave her to make her decision in privacy. Lady grant her efforts had helped the young woman.

24

Felicia threw her pillow at the door as Silver closed it behind her. Why did Silver have to be so . . . so infuriatingly *right*, the way her father always was?

Or was that, "the way her mother would have been?"

Felicia's stomach rumbled, reminding her that what with stomping out on her father, she hadn't actually gotten any breakfast. She already knew she didn't have anything left stashed up here, but she looked around the room anyway. It was kind of a disgusting pit at the moment. She'd spent a lot of time here the past few days, so several dirty plates were stacked on the dresser, and she'd dropped clothes all over the floor. Much longer and the smell would change from a more concentrated form of her own scent to a stink. She pulled on her clothes and picked the rest up. By the Lady, she would show Silver. She'd pull herself together in record time.

When she took the plates downstairs, the kitchen was mostly deserted, the breakfast rush finished. Odds and ends of food hadn't been put in the fridge yet, and though she detected her father's meddling, Felicia collected them onto a new plate. The sausages left in the pan were all burned on one side, but Felicia took them anyway. She could cut off the charred bits and save them for Morsel.

Someone knocked on the front door. Curiosity flaring weakly to life, Felicia paused with her food to listen for who it was.

"Is Roanoke Dare available? I'd like to speak to him." A voice Felicia didn't recognize, followed quickly by one she did.

"Eliza, shut up. We're saying good-bye, nothing more. I'm sorry, Roanoke." Portland's voice sounded like she was speaking from between gritted teeth.

"I'll see if he's available," Silver said frostily and crossed into the kitchen. Her father stepped in from the dining room, coffee still in hand. They exchanged an exasperated look packed with meaning Felicia didn't quite catch, then her father exhaled on a note of amusement. He stepped over to Silver and pressed a kiss to her head.

"I'm far too busy to meet with them at the moment," he said very low against her hair. He stepped back and lifted his coffee mug to toast her with an air of wishing her luck. He squeezed Felicia's shoulder as he took his coffee through the dining room deeper into the house. Silver braced her shoulders and headed back to the entryway.

Felicia remembered she was standing in the middle of the kitchen with a plate of food that was not getting any warmer, so she slipped into the dining room to eat just as Silver showed in Portland, her beta, and the new woman. Seen and smelled closer, she reminded Felicia of Portland, so she presumed she was the sister, here about Portland's pregnancy and her beta's petition. When the pack had filled her in on the gossip, Felicia had been shocked at how much she'd missed while dealing with her own problems.

Felicia sat down at one end of the long table—they left all the leaves in, so the whole pack could eat dinner at the same time, if schedules worked out that way—and the sister and Craig sat down at the other. She kept her head down over her plate. This didn't concern her, but no one had kicked her out yet. Besides, eavesdropping was a welcome distraction from crafting another apology to Tom in her head.

Silver and Portland chatted in the doorway and eventually drifted deeper into the house, leaving the sister and Craig to pointed boredom. Craig took it better than she did. He slumped down into the stance of someone who could wait forever, lost in his own thoughts. The sister fidgeted.

"I suppose the two of them are in there plotting their strategy," the sister burst out at length.

Craig hauled himself upright. "Eliza. For the love of the Lady, tell me you're not planning to take that tack with Roanoke Dare against his mate."

Felicia started eating slower, so she wouldn't end up with an empty plate and attract notice for sitting there with it.

Eliza pressed her hand flat to the table, as if to help her keep control. She and Craig seemed so focused on each on other and their mission here, Felicia suspected she didn't need to worry about notice. "And you're not here to hear his ruling separate from hers, then?" Eliza's sarcasm was not particularly under control.

Craig made a fist of his hand on the table. "I don't think

Roanoke Silver is unbiased about the dangers to our child given Michelle's . . . history, yes. But . . ." He trailed off, apparently frustrated with his inability to find the right words.

"And they're in there getting more biased right now." Eliza smoothed the dark waves of her hair back behind her ear and crossed her arms. "I don't think it's right for Shelly to model herself on Roanoke Silver. Leaving aside whether she can have a family or not, Roanoke Silver could never have a normal life the way Shelly can. She might willing to dedicate her life to being a leader, but I don't think Shelly understands what she's doing."

Craig slammed his fist on the table and Eliza jumped. She'd apparently been so caught up in her own rhetoric that she hadn't been watching his expression grow darker. "Michelle is an alpha whether you like it or not. That's not what's at issue here. If only you'd stayed home, everyone would be a lot happier."

Eliza silently snarled at Craig. "You began this! It's your petition to have her stand down as alpha that I'm trying to support."

"Yes, I made that petition, for while she's pregnant. To protect the child from a shift from the stress, nothing more. All this shit about being an alpha being a phase is your prey-stupidity, not mine."

Felicia could hardly believe what she was hearing. Her plate was empty, and she'd even eaten the charred sausage she'd meant to save for Morsel. Any minute she was going to burst out and call them prey-stupid herself, so she got up as quietly as she could. If they noticed her and got annoyed, there was nothing for it.

They both seemed locked in their argument, though. They continued as she dumped her plate in the dishwasher and went to find Silver. She and Portland were in the living room, Portland down on the floor helping Edmond zoom his cars around.

Felicia slipped up beside Silver. "Seriously? Portland's sister hopes you'd ever support her on *that*?" How could anyone think to go up against Silver on an issue of a woman leading and hope to win?

Silver burst into a startled laugh. "I think I've let them stew long enough before I go enforce my ruling once more—with teeth, this time." Silver's smile had an edge, but buried underneath Felicia thought she seemed tired. "And I could use your help, alpha's daughter."

Well, she certainly deserved to look a little tired. It was a weird feeling, but Felicia realized that she did want to help her. Not that she really saw how, but she figured Silver must have some kind of plan. She shrugged. "Okay."

Portland looked up, her expression suggesting similar confusion about where Silver was going with this. Levering herself up without stepping on any of Edmond's cars delayed her slightly, putting her behind Silver and Felicia as they entered the dining room. Craig and Eliza had fallen into sullen silence.

Silver waited for Felicia to come level with her, then put her arm across Felicia's shoulders before addressing the two Were. Her smile held the full force of her creepiness, no tiredness visible. "I have been thinking. I could simply dismiss you both and borrow my mate's strength to force you to go. Or I could turn my thoughts to appropriate punishments for questioning your alpha. For some reason, my store of patience has been drained of late." Silver smiled wider, and Craig ducked his head, shoulders hunching defensively. Even Eliza, who had struck Felicia as awfully dense in the conversation she'd overheard, looked worried. It sounded like Portland was fidgeting behind them, but Felicia didn't spare much attention for her.

"But." Silver squeezed her hand on Felicia's opposite shoulder. "Since this is all for the child, let us consider the *child*. Felicia?" She turned her head to Felicia. "Tell us. Has being the alpha's daughter scarred you?"

Felicia snorted. That one was easy. Might as well have a little fun with this. "Not particularly. I'm sure parents are designed by the Lady to be unbearable no matter their rank."

Eliza drew herself up. "But Roanoke Dare—"

"Is a man?" Silver gave the words a mocking twist. "But your argument is that Portland is not suited by her particular personality to maintain the position of authority while raising a child, is it not? You are not saying that all women are so unsuited?"

Eliza flushed slightly. "Didn't raise her, was what I was going to say."

Felicia crossed her arms in annoyance. She knew that was common knowledge, but it still felt too private for someone else to use as ammunition. "Well, he raised me since I was fifteen. So once Portland's kid hits his or her Lady ceremony, she can do whatever she wants without affecting the kid?" She flicked a glance to Silver, hoping she didn't mind Felicia snapping back an answer like that, but she smelled decidedly pleased.

"Well, no . . ." Eliza floundered for a few moments longer before Silver stepped in.

"And if your father was forced by circumstances outside himself to step down from being alpha, how do you think he would react?"

Felicia winced. It didn't bear thinking about. "Are you kidding? He'd go Lady-fu—" She coughed. "Lady-darned insane in, like, a day. He'd turn it inward and get all"—she curled both sets of fingertips into her palms—"silent and always hurting."

Silver dipped her head in agreement with the assessment. "And if you knew *you* were the reason?"

Even though Felicia knew this was all imaginary, all aimed at Eliza, visceral fear tore at her voice even thinking about it. Everything else she was struggling with was too close to the surface, and the question brought it surging up. She'd made mistakes enough in her life, mistakes that had hurt many people, but to have put her father through that . . . She couldn't find the words right away, but that didn't seem to matter. Everyone in the room seemed to have smelled or read her reaction on her face. Portland made a small noise of shock.

"My sister would never blame her child for such a thing," Eliza said, defensiveness sharpening her voice.

Felicia looked at Silver first this time. She nodded. "Kids aren't *stupid*!" Felicia's volume crept higher than she'd intended, but she didn't bother moderating it. "No one needs to blame them for them to know they were part of whatever bad thing happened. They know. They especially know if everyone's trying to hide it from them. You know they tried to tell me my father had 'gone away for a while'? Later, they fed me lies when they claimed to be explaining it, but in the beginning they tried to hide it. I was four, five, but I *knew*. Knew my mother hadn't 'just died accidentally' and my father hadn't 'gone away.'"

Silver moved her hand to rub Felicia's back once, and Felicia realized she was panting. She'd been annoyed by private matters being brought up before, and now she'd brought them up herself. A deep need to make Eliza *understand* had taken hold of her, though. She suspected Silver felt something similar.

"Would you like to be the one who consigns a child to hurting so much, because his or her parent hurts so deeply in turn?" In contrast to Felicia's volume, Silver's voice was low and smooth.

"Shut up." Craig dropped a big hand on Eliza's shoulder when she would have spoken again. "Lose with some Lady-damned dignity." He removed his hand and dropped to one knee in front of Silver. Felicia edged quickly to the side, back to watching rather than participating.

"I never meant for this to extend beyond the child's birth, but it's clear the issue is much deeper than that. I withdraw my petition. My apologies, Roanoke." Craig dropped his head.

Portland released a ragged breath of relief. Craig looked hopefully up at her, but she shook her head. "It's not that easy. Even if all of this hadn't happened, Silver's right, you can't properly be my beta anymore, not when the rest of our relationship is so complicated. It's your child too, but we need to"—she caught her lower lip in her teeth—"figure out how it's going to work." She came forward and offered Craig a hand up. He accepted, though it was clear he didn't rest any of his weight on the contact.

Eliza smelled like stewing anger, but she didn't say anything else. The other two ignored her completely as Silver ushered them all to the door, offering wishes for safe travels home.

Felicia slipped away, searching for her father. As she'd suspected, she didn't have far to go. She found him in the living room, well within eavesdropping distance. She felt weird, having said all those things about being his daughter, and maybe he did too, because he didn't say anything right away.

The awkward pause gave his appearance time to finally register. He was wearing a sport coat, hair combed so that the white locks stood out at either temple. He looked polished, the charming alpha who would set you completely at ease so you gave concessions before you even realized. "Are you going somewhere?" Felicia asked him.

He drained his coffee and headed to the kitchen. "The owners of the house you lured Silver to. They've agreed to talk to me. The Caballeros. I'm meeting him and his wife at his office."

Felicia winced at his choice of "lured," but she couldn't really object. She followed him after a slight delay. "I should come."

No answer, and the dishwasher door slammed. Her father must be pretending that he hadn't heard her in the distraction of putting his mug away. Felicia caught up with him and gathered herself. Confidence. She could show them all how confident she could be, and help fix things too. "Please? It's my fault, and I can help explain." Felicia suddenly remembered what he'd said about apologies earlier. Maybe that was why he didn't want to her to come. "This isn't just to make myself feel better. I want to do something that actually helps."

Her father sighed. "I appreciate that, but status was already difficult even when I talked to him on the phone. I'm going to have to play it delicately, and you're of very low rank in human terms."

"Wouldn't that swing the balance in your favor, though? Having a follower along who stands silently and looks contrite? I can look contrite. And I won't say anything unless you prompt me to, promise." Felicia dropped her head to demonstrate how low ranked she could look. Her father took her shoulder and nudged her around to face out of the kitchen.

"I'm leaving in fifteen minutes. If you can make yourself look presentable that fast, you can come."

Felicia bolted for the stairs. It took her sixteen minutes, all told. She changed into one of Susan's fitted jackets over a camisole. Susan wouldn't mind her borrowing it. Hopefully. She had more bust than Susan did, so she left the jacket unbuttoned. Her hair took the longest, getting it braided back without curls escaping everywhere. Her father was just climbing into his car when she hit the front door. She paused on the doorstep to tug on the hem of her jacket then hurried over to climb in with him.

Rather than a high-rise downtown, they pulled into an office park with shorter buildings and trees liberally planted among the parking lots. Except for the big logo over the entrance, Mr. Caballero's office building could have held any company. Felicia thought she recognized the name of the man's company as something to do with insurance.

They checked in with reception and were directed up a floor to the man's office. Felicia practiced looking apologetic as they

walked down the hall. Her father seemed surprisingly comfortable in this kind of environment. He nodded in pleasant
greeting to passing workers, and they smiled back and made
room for him like he was high ranked in their hierarchy and
not a stranger. Felicia felt vaguely like she should be taking
notes for when she got a job.

The man who met them in the office doorway wore his
power much more ostentatiously than her father did. He held
himself very straight, and his suit was immaculate. The room
wasn't full of antiques, but the complex multilevels of expensive wood desk covered with the latest in electronic equipment
spoke of wealth in another way.

The men shook hands and Mr. Caballero introduced his wife,
a woman who matched her husband in projecting ostenta-
tious power, including a very masculine cut to her suit and
graying hair in a tight twist at the back of her head. Susan
always seemed to manage to look authoritative without anything so stark.

Felicia didn't take part in the handshaking. Her father introduced her a bit dismissively, like a naughty child dragged
along to rub her nose in what she'd done, and she did her best
to play along, making her body language droop.

Her father sat in a chair in front of the flat table wing of the
desk monstrosity, and the wife sat with her husband inside its
curve. Felicia listened more to her father's tone than to his
words. He was being coaxing, as she'd expected from how
he'd dressed. The charm wasn't working, though. Mr. Caballero apparently valued his territory quite highly.

It struck Felicia that he looked much more like a person,

not a ranked position, in the photos on the walls. There were plenty of them: Mr. Caballero out fishing, smiling with his wife in vacation destinations, and posed with different combinations of what she presumed were his three children, though they were all teens or adults themselves.

But none with both wife and children, she noticed. She subtly turned and found none with both on any of the office's other walls.

Mr. Caballero cleared his throat. "You say your daughter has admitted to tracking footprints off the path to lead your girlfriend there as a joke, but I don't understand the point of this joke."

"Because she's practically my stepmother." The words burst out before Felicia could stop them. So much for her promise to keep quiet. Better see it through now that she'd spoken. She stepped forward. "If Dad would just get around to asking her." Her father sputtered, and Felicia smiled when she saw a flash of amusement in the wife's eyes.

She caught the woman's eyes, appealing to her. "That's been getting clearer lately, and I didn't know what to think about it. I mean, my mother died so young I can hardly remember her. So Dad's away on his business trip, and I end up fighting with S—" Felicia remembered at the last second, Silver's old name would be on the court documents. "Selene over something incredibly stupid, and I stomped out, and I could only sort of . . ." She rubbed at her cheeks as if to scrub away the flush they should hopefully read as embarrassment over her behavior in front of Silver. Really, it was more from worrying about her father's reaction now. At least he wasn't interrupting, just watching with his go-on-keep-digging-we'll-see-if-you-come-out-the-other-side-or-end-up-crying-in-a-hole-you-can't-climb-out-of expression.

"I could only think of showing her how angry I was. When I walked up to your house so she'd follow me, I thought she'd be embarrassed, you know? Give someone a surprise and they'd yell at her for being stupid and getting the wrong house." Mr. Caballero's expression was unmoved, but his wife looked exasperated, as if she recognized the sentiment exactly. Recognition didn't mean she was willing to let Felicia off the hook for it, though.

Felicia took a deep breath. All right, here was her last possible lunge after retreating prey. "Selene shouldn't be the one paying for this, I should. I wish I hadn't done it, but I was mad, and sometimes you just . . . do things, you know? Without knowing quite why. But it was wrong, and it's my responsibility. I don't want her punished for me being stupid."

"The stepparent role is difficult." The wife caught Mr. Caballero's eye. "And it wasn't like Ms. Powell damaged anything inside the house. The way Ramon describes her behavior matches someone who had been misled that way."

Mr. Caballero's brows drew down, but Felicia's father spoke before he could. "My daughter will be punished. I'm cutting off her allowance completely. If she can't find a job, there are plenty of community-service opportunities to keep her out of Selene's hair and out of further trouble."

Mr. Caballero shared another look with his wife and then stood. "Fair enough." He offered a hand across the desk to shake on it. "We'll speak to the prosecutor's office to ask them not to pursue the case, since it was a . . . misunderstanding." His expression went very dry.

Felicia held herself together until the car, where she bent over her knees and pressed the heels of her hands to her temples. Lady, if that hadn't worked . . .

"Where did that come from?" her father said as he started the car.

"The pictures. I think he has kids from a previous marriage." Felicia lifted her head to draw a deep breath. No anger from her father.

"Good." Her father concentrated on the road as they approached a stop sign and his scent gained an undertone of confusion. "Has Silver ever mentioned marriage to you?"

Felicia couldn't help herself. She laughed, a little longer than she should have because the release of tension was so great. "No, don't worry. Anyway, you should ask Susan. She'd be the one to know."

Her father sank into deeply thoughtful silence, and Felicia waited with a little glee to find out what he'd say next. "I didn't think all the human trappings, the ring and all that, would mean much to her."

"You were married to Mama. I assume that means something to Silver." Felicia picked at a piece of lint on the hem of Susan's jacket. That had sounded too serious. She wanted to tease her father, not make him feel guilty. There was enough guilt sloshing around lately. "If you don't know what she'd think of a ring, you could show her one and ask her."

Her father reached over and shoved her shoulder without looking. "You think you're a helpful one, don't you?" But she could hear the resigned laughter in his tone.

25

The idea of a larger house must have been percolating in Silver or her father's mind in the three months since Portland and everyone were tromping through the pack house, because Felicia came home from work one day to find the dining room table spread with fliers for home-construction firms.

She'd carpooled with Susan—silly not to when they worked at the same branch—but Susan was already deep in conversation with her husband at the table when Felicia returned from her shower upstairs. A customer's perfume had lingered annoyingly in her hair today.

Felicia stepped around Edmond, who was loading plastic pigs and chickens into his mother's kicked-off high heels, and snagged one of the fliers. It pictured in vivid color a backwoods cabin clearly made for someone who never planned to step outside its comfort into the actual woods. One might as well hang photographs instead of having windows, as far as Felicia could see.

"We probably are going to have to custom build, if we want this many bedrooms as well as decent common-living spaces," John said, tapping a booklet full of floor plans. "If we try to remodel a hotel or something, it's going to still feel like a hotel when we're done."

"If we can find adjoining properties, we could do something like a main house and a guesthouse," Susan offered. "That's what's driving this, isn't it? We're fine here until people come petitioning the Roanokes and want to stay the night. They can walk across the yard to go to bed."

Felicia slid into a chair down at the end with Silver. She didn't appear to be listening to the others as she pored over one of the glossiest of the booklets. Felicia swapped for a different one and paged through. Ugh, gold-plated faucets. She scrubbed at her eyes. Lady, being pleasant to people made her tired. Susan had showed her the trick of it, but it still wore her out.

She took out her phone and brought up Tom's entry in the address book and stared at it for a while. She'd followed her father's orders and hadn't even e-mailed him for three months. She liked to imagine what she'd say to him every so often, though. Well. Frequently. No more than once a day.

"Felicia!" Her father's tone told her that wasn't the first time he'd called her name. While she'd been lost in her thoughts, they'd cleared away all the other fliers, and people were getting up. Her father leaned back in his chair, encompassing everyone in werewolf earshot with his next comment. "I had an idea for something a little different instead of hunting tonight. A surprise, if Felicia's willing."

That sounded ominous. Felicia frowned deeply at her father, but he just winked and held up his hand for her to wait a moment. "Go ahead, everyone. We'll catch up to you out there."

Felicia had to sit on her curiosity as all Were past their Lady ceremonies got themselves organized, deciding who would ride in which car and who would watch the children—Susan as usual, since she couldn't shift anyway. It seemed to take a Lady-damned long time before she and her father were alone downstairs.

"You kept Enrique's whip, didn't you?" Her father seemed completely nonchalant about the question, but Felicia's heart picked up speed. He knew she had. She hadn't done anything wrong. They'd relieved Enrique of all his weapons before shoving him on the plane, of course, and Felicia couldn't bear to see such a well-crafted, expensive weapon go in the trash. It was stuffed as far back under her dresser as she could shove it.

"Calm down." Her father stood up and came to set his hand against the back of her neck. "I was thinking. I doubt this will be the last time we tangle with Madrid or his people. This pack should learn how to defend themselves against those kind of tactics. You learned defensive techniques, right?"

Felicia licked her lips. Her immediate reaction was that her father should leave well enough alone and let people forget what she could do with a whip. She opened her mouth to say that, but then her mind started to actually work it through. If people worked with whips a little, maybe the weapon wouldn't seem so scary. "The unarmed defensive techniques mostly revolve around getting the other person's whip and using it. But yes."

Her father gave a low chuckle. "True." He squeezed her neck. "Consider it a project. Getting everyone willing up to Spanish defensive standards."

Felicia twisted around. "What do I need a project for? I have a job!" Parents were infuriating.

"And you're moping. You need a challenge to keep you occupied." Her father kissed the top of her head and retreated immediately out of smacking range. "C'mon. Get the whip, they'll be waiting for us."

Felicia only realized the big weakness of her father's idea when they got to the pack's hunting lands. "If I'm demonstrating how to defend, someone needs to attack me with the whip," she called after her father, who was striding off up the vehicle track to the gathering in the cleared space behind the gate where people usually parked. Her father had had everyone pull off along the driveway this time. The ground was moist, but it hadn't been raining hard enough in the past week to make everything into a mud puddle. The sunlight was fading fast, but the light pollution was confined to the horizon, so werewolf eyes could adjust properly.

"I'm rusty, but I'm sure I can manage. I reached the level of not embarrassing myself, when I was there." Her father planted himself and held out his hand for the whip. Felicia had been keeping it minimized, coiled tightly down by her hip, almost behind her back. The pack fidgeted and a few whispers started at sight of it out in the open, but her father ignored their reactions, and she tried to do the same as she handed it over.

"Okay." Felicia blew out a breath and stepped away from her father. "As a werewolf, the basic strategy to counter someone with a whip is to sacrifice a little arm skin to get a grip on the weapon. It'll heal fast enough, after all. Then you either pull it away, or use it as a handle to pull your opponent closer." She had no idea how she was supposed to teach people who were nearly all older than her, but she tried to channel her father's tone when he was instructing people. It seemed to at least mostly work. Several of the pack members stopped glowering off in random directions like they were imagining their escape and started watching her.

Her father took a few practice flicks well to either side of her, and then nodded. She watched him, and as the lash fell, she held up her arm so the tip wrapped around several times. She hissed with the pain. She was badly out of practice, if that little graze threw her off.

She hadn't lost her skills entirely yet, though. She clamped over the whip's tip with her free hand and yanked. A little blood oozed up, but not enough to even threaten her grip. Her father let the whip go without much resistance, probably to help her better demonstrate the principle. "See? Simple."

Felicia would have never admitted it to him, but the physicality of the task did help her in a way the endless talking to humans at the bank hadn't. She began to feel a more satisfying fatigue as she either swung the whip for others to catch, or caught it to sneak in a few pointers for how to swing once they'd gotten the whip away.

The routine of it came back to her, the rhythm, and Felicia let her world narrow to her target. She needed to aim her strokes so that even if her current opponent, Pierce, didn't catch it right, he wouldn't be badly hurt.

Then the wind changed and brought her Tom's scent. She started, sure she was imagining it, but there he was: lanky, light hair more shaggy than ever, and his expression wavering on the edge of an easy, good-natured smile. That was the Tom she remembered from before, perpetually smiling or ready to smile.

Surprise made her screw up the next stroke, though fortunately Pierce had already stepped back, knowing when to fade into the background. On the backstroke, the whip kissed her cheek. The scratch healed as easily as any of the others, and she scrubbed away the blood with the heel of her hand. It seemed almost fair that Tom should cause her to take a few extra licks or get in a few of his own. She offered out the whip. "Did you want to practice too?"

"Felicia, no." Tom flinched from the whip and only took it to toss it aside. His smile disappeared, but he smelled concerned, and maybe frustrated, not angry. Not betrayed. Felicia groped after all the words she'd planned over the past few months, but she couldn't find a single one. "I don't want to risk hurting you."

"I hurt *you*," Felicia said, soft.

Tom pressed his lips together and looked out into the trees, though they'd been making enough racket no animals or birds were hanging around to be seen in them. "You made me very angry. I'm not an angry person, and I don't want to become one, and I've sort of . . . found my way back to that, these past few months."

Felicia nodded, completely at a loss. That was true. Another thing to blame herself for. But how would an apology for that be better than any of her others?

Tom licked his thumb and swiped the rest of the blood off her cheek. "We can't—I don't want us to have that kind of accounting. You hurt me, I hurt you. It's unhealthy. You have to do everything in your power not to hurt each other, and figure it'll happen anyway sometimes, no matter what you do."

Tom ran out of steam and looked down at his hands before starting again somewhere else. "I've actually been in town for a little while, but I didn't want to ambush you at work or at the house, and you haven't gone anywhere else." He laughed awkwardly. "Roanoke Silver told me she thought your father had something planned that would bring you out here, though." He took a deep breath. "I talked to the Roanokes about other stuff too. They told me why you did what you did." He eyed her from under his bangs. "That was prey-stupid, you know."

Felicia laughed, hysteria threading through it. "I know." Tom slipped his arms around her, and she held tight, tight as she could. "You said 'we.' And 'us.' What about my father's orders?"

"There's a time to fight the tide and a time to swim with the current." Felicia's father wandered up, and she flushed, suddenly acutely aware of the pack around them. No one was looking, but not-looking was its own kind of pressure. "Don't be any more stupid than you can possibly avoid. Either of you." His tone was firm, but humor lurked somewhere underneath. He walked off before Felicia could pin it down.

"So we can. If you want to try fresh." Tom pulled back far enough to look at her but didn't let go. "No accounting."

"I swear on the Lady." Felicia freed a hand to press her thumb to her forehead.

Tom laced his fingers with hers and tugged them toward the trees, away from the bulk of the gathered pack. "We could go run, or something." His grin at her was vintage Tom, but the assurance with which he pulled her along was something new. "Personally, I'm in favor of 'or something.'" He waggled his eyebrows.

Felicia followed before he could change his mind. Silver was right: she didn't deserve this second chance, but it was a gift she wasn't going to refuse. A laugh bubbled up. "Sounds good to me."